O9-BUC-852

Hating
Olivia

Also by Mark SaFranko

Hating Olivia

a

love

story

Mark SaFranko

HARPER ● PERENNIAL

NEW YORK ● LONDON ● TORONTO ● SYDNEY ● NEW DELHI ● AUCKLAND

HARPER ● PERENNIAL

This book is a work of fiction. The characters, incidents, and dialogue are drawn from the author's imagination and are not to be construed as real. Any resemblance to actual events or persons, living or dead, is entirely coincidental.

P.S.™ is a registered trademark of HarperCollins Publishers.

HATING OLIVIA. Copyright © 2010 by Mark SaFranko. All rights reserved. Printed in the United States of America. No part of this book may be used or reproduced in any manner whatsoever without written permission except in the case of brief quotations embodied in critical articles and reviews. For information, address HarperCollins Publishers, 10 East 53rd Street, New York, NY 10022.

HarperCollins books may be purchased for educational, business, or sales promotional use. For information, please write: Special Markets Department, HarperCollins Publishers, 10 East 53rd Street, New York, NY 10022.

FIRST EDITION

Library of Congress Cataloging-in-Publication data is available upon request.

ISBN 978-0-06-197919-4

10 11 12 13 14   OV/RRD   10 9 8 7 6 5 4 3 2 1

To P.G., for staying the course

Introduction

I am a fan of marathon runners and soccer players and guys who can go ten rounds with the champ and still manage to finish on their feet. I'm also a great admirer of Mark SaFranko's work and have been for years.

As a writer he's the most tenacious son of a bitch I know. Because we share the same occupation and many of the same emotions I can tell you that there are days when I'd rather chew lightbulb glass than strap myself to a computer keyboard. Not SaFranko. Compared to Mark SaFranko, I'm Tiny Tim. A novice and a flyweight.

Listen to these statistics: A hundred short stories, fifty of them already in print. A box full of poetry and essays. And ten complete novels, eight of them yet to hit the bookshelves. A dozen plays, some produced in New York and others staged in Ireland. SaFranko writes songs too, a hundred and fifty so far.

I know why I write. I write because I must. I cannot stop. I'm driven by rage and insanity and crushing ambition. Mark SaFranko scares people like me. I believe the guy would rather write than breathe. I envy his talent and commitment.

Now comes *Hating Olivia*, my favorite piece of work by the author. It is a story of love and human addiction. Here the scenes between Max and his lady love are open heart surgery done with an ax. If you're a Henry Miller or Bukowski fan then *Hating Olivia* is fresh meat, a gift tied together with a bloodstained bow. This is the kind of book—the kind of memoir—that must have been lived first. Survived. So strap yourself in. It's time for a real treat.

DAN FANTE

I suffered like the most foolish of fools.

—PHILIPPE DJIAN, *37,2° le matin*

In the end, one experiences only one's self.

—NIETZSCHE

Hating
Olivia

1.

The war was over. I'd managed to avoid it, but it didn't mean a thing. Since that time—when I wasn't on the dole or living off food stamps—I'd worked every job under the sun: factory hand, chauffeur, reporter, bank clerk. I hadn't done any whack-ward time, but members of my immediate and extended family had. Major depression. Bizarre phobias. Alcoholism. Shock treatments. Suicide. All of which worried me—genetics are everything. For months at a clip I wandered all over the country. The parade of forgettable days that made up the long, hazy years always seemed to be a matter of struggling to keep my head above water, and a roof over it. It was nothing much of a life.

After the sixties the world had gone to sleep again. The blue-collar suburbs were a drag, but unless you were a millionaire or willing to shack up with three or four other people you couldn't stand or would come to hate in a short time, Manhattan was out of the question. I was neither. That left me out in Jersey, holed up in the attic of a boardinghouse on sedate Park Street in the city of Montfleur at a rent of fifteen bucks per week, excluding telephone charges.

My room was a two-by-four number with a slanting roof that collided with my head a dozen times a day. In the jake were half a refrigerator and a bathtub—not even a shower. There was something else—cockroaches. Lots of them. The black dude next door, a short-order cook by the name of Benny, shared the facilities with me, including the cockroaches. Benny was quiet and not there most of the time, which was okay by me. My window overlooked the train station. It seemed that every other week there was a suicide on the tracks that transported the commuters into the city. I often wondered if or when I would be next.

The landlords were an elderly couple by the name of Trowbridge. Lou, a bag of bones with glasses, happened to be a painter of uncommon talent. His nudes and landscapes decorated every square inch of the faded yellow walls. It looked to me as if he'd set out to become some kind of Sisley, or Francis Bacon even, but for whatever mysterious reason he'd fallen short of the mark, like most of us do. Lately he'd taken to carving fantastic totem poles of all styles and dimensions, an idea he'd picked up while visiting his son, an army officer stationed in Alaska. But whether from lack of business sense or sheer bad luck, the poor guy never sold a thing. A regular sad sack, he wore his defeat on his sleeve. Whenever I bumped into Lou in the hallways I could hardly coax two words out of him. He never even talked back when his wife chewed him out for one of his numerous peccadilloes. "How many times have I told you to keep the back door shut so the *cat* doesn't get out? Lou—how could you be so *stupid*! Now who's going to chase that beast all over the neighborhood? Well—what's your excuse? Nothing? Cat got your *tongue*? Oh, for heaven's sake! What was I thinking when I married such a simp?" It was brutal to witness.

Myself, I didn't mind Caroline Trowbridge. Despite my gig on the loading platform, I was forever in arrears with the rent and she never said a word about it. Since she was a gimp and had trouble getting around, she sat in the parlor all day long with her ear pinned to the antique radio. Aside from the problem of her husband, she seemed content with her Puccini and Mahler and Mozart. Whenever I passed en route to my cell, she had a joke for me.

"Max, you wouldn't *believe* what that idiot husband of mine did today . . . !"

As I climbed the stairs listening to her tirade, I'd catch the man of the house cowering in the shadows. We'd nod at each other, both of us a little embarrassed.

I couldn't say that I knew which end was up, either. One day I pulled the number of an astrologer off the announcement board at a secondhand bookstore in Chelsea. I dialed it that evening and set an appointment for the following week. Before she could cast my horoscope, she needed the date, time, and place of my birth.

"December 23, 1950, at seven eighteen P.M., Trenton, New Jersey. . . ." I remembered the information from the official hospital record, which my mother had passed on to me years before.

No matter what, I figured, things couldn't get much worse. I was smarting over the bloody breakup of an affair I'd been carrying on with the wife of an up-and-coming young attorney in the county prosecutor's office. Months later, I still couldn't get her out of my mind. Our dates had consisted of furtive meetings in a practice room in the music department at the college where she taught American literature. While trying to make do on the piano bench, Lynn swore to me that she was going to leave her husband. But beyond fucking her, I didn't quite know what I'd do with her if that actually happened, since I didn't have two nickels to rub together and she was used to some of the finer things. Once she came up to my garret and had a good look at the sagging mattress and rotting carpet, she backed off. She could see the invisible writing on those flaking walls, all right. A part-time musician. An aspiring writer. A truck-loading bum who liked to read books and listen to obscure records—thanks, but no thanks.

Still and all, Lynn haunted my dreams even months later. What made the loss unbearable was her beauty. I'd always had an eye for beauty—fool that I was, I believed that it counted for something. Like a beggar who covets the palace of the kingdom, I wanted what I couldn't have. But I was tired of coveting the unattainable.

Most of the time when I wasn't stuffing the ass-end of a semi I lay around and read—Conrad . . . Tolstoy . . . Hamsun . . . Henry Miller . . . Sartre . . . Camus . . . Hesse . . . the Zen masters . . . Nietzsche . . . Céline . . . whoever and whatever I could get my hands on, so long as they held a certain appeal for the outcast. I smoked cigarettes by the carton. I masturbated compulsively over the glossy centerfolds in *Playboy* and *Penthouse* and *Club International*. I wrote songs on the guitar. When I had a few bucks to spare I hit the bars and nightclubs.

The day of my celestial appointment arrived. I rode a bus into the Port Authority and jumped the empty A train to Brooklyn Heights. After wandering around in circles for a half hour, I finally located Mrs. London's brownstone.

"You're late," she announced. It sounded like an accusation.

She was full and curvy and bleached blonde and at one time she must have been attractive. But she was beyond that stage now.

I apologized for keeping her waiting. She showed me into the parlor, an airy space decorated with birdcages and stuffed furniture and expensive-looking collectibles and souvenirs, all suffused with that singular, muted Brooklyn light. It struck me that Mrs. London had some change to spare.

We sat at a large, circular oak table. She pulled my hand-drawn chart out of a folder and positioned it in front of herself. Catching a glimpse of the abstruse squiggles, I was all set to hear how my life was about to take a turn for the better, maybe even a spectacular leap forward that would result in fulfillment, prosperity, fame, and maybe even a little money, though I never gave a damn about that; at the very least a few beautiful, adoring women who wouldn't put me through the trials of Job.

I lit a cigarette and waited while Mrs. London gathered her thoughts. I glanced at her fingertips, which had been painted with scarlet nail polish, then at her tits, which bulged against her crepe sundress. My cock stirred in my jeans.

"Ah. *Now* I see the problem. You're under a curse for the next five years, Mister Max."

"What?"

"I don't mean to alarm you, but you're about to enter the most difficult period of the thirty-year cycle of Saturn. Some call it the 'obscure' period. The ringed planet—harbinger of fate and destiny—is about to cross into your tropical ascendant."

Bull flop. "You must have gotten something wrong," I protested.

She pointed at the southeastern quadrant of the circle.

"Right here. You will undergo many severe trials. It won't be easy. At times you'll think you might not make it. You're going to have to come to grips with yourself. You'll have to sink all the way down to the bottom before finding your way out of the black hole. Prepare yourself for the long, dark night of the soul."

I had no interest in sinking to the bottom of anything. Shit—wasn't I already there?

I was speechless. I didn't believe a word of it—this stuff was all mumbo jumbo. What made me think it was anything different?

I lit another smoke. "Any chance you're wrong?"

"It's possible. Anything is possible. But it's not likely. Only the masters have the power to overcome the influence of the planets. Think of Paramahansa Yogananda, or Krishnamurti. And even they had their share of troubles."

A telephone rang somewhere. Mrs. London got up from the table.

"Be right back."

I could make out her ass jiggling beneath the crepe as she walked toward the back of the apartment. It was a very nice ass. It disappeared into another room.

If she was a *Mrs.*, where was her husband? The phone stopped ringing. "Oh, hello, Donald. . . . I'm with someone now, but let me see if I can give you a few minutes. . . ."

Palm over the mouthpiece, Mrs. London popped her head out.

"I have to take this. You don't mind waiting?"

I shook my head. Where the hell did I have to be? She slid the door half shut, but I could still see part of her as she sat at her desk back there. Her bare leg was sticking out from her bunched-up dress, and the line of her panties was visible beneath the flimsy material. I could still hear her voice, too. She went on about where Mars was in the heavens today, and how Uranus was afflicting Donald's Mercury and that was causing whatever problems he was having.

It had been months since I'd gotten laid. Between that ugly fact and the heat, I was a crazed jackal. I would have made a move on Mrs. London, but she was the all-business type, no hint of flirtation there at all. Besides, she showed no personal interest in me whatsoever.

But as usual, my dick was like a billy club just from seeing a woman's naked flesh. The damned thing was straining like a caged beast to get free. I reached down and undid my fly. It popped right out from the leg of my underwear. Since Mrs. London was easing into her phone-counseling session, I figured why not. . . . It was one of those days when I only needed a hard stroke or two to get there. I beat it in time to the slap of Mrs. London's sandal against her pedicured foot. When she started in on Pluto's ingress into Donald's eighth house, which happens to govern the sex drive, I was riding her like a dog, and she didn't even know it.

My trunk arched. I was a silent rocket launcher. . . .

Boom. Boom. Boom. Boom. Boom.

The first missile landed on the rim of the table. The following volleys drifted through the air squiggling like baby snakes and fell to the carpet with a soft plop. I immediately tucked my organ back into my jeans and reached into my pocket for my handkerchief. I wiped the table clean, then moved my sneaker onto the jizm on the carpet and ground it in. Then I sat back and waited. Mrs. London never knew what hit her.

When she got back, she proceeded to analyze my personality, and then say a few things about my past. But I'd already tuned out. The Sibyl's dire warnings hung now like an ominous cloud above my head. The expectant mood I'd carried in was gone— she'd annihilated it. Suddenly I felt like Ishmael. Or a leper.

At precisely one hour her egg timer went off. She slid the chart across the table to me.

"That'll be twenty-five dollars."

By now I was thoroughly deflated. "I meant to tell you up front. . . . I'm a little short on cash. Would you mind if I sent it to you in a week or so, when my next paycheck comes in?"

Mrs. London's green cat's eyes narrowed with suspicion. "All right. Next Thursday at the latest. Make sure you leave me your telephone number."

I wrote it down. She saw me to the door. The street was as quiet as a morgue. As lots of people said, Brooklyn was a place for nonbelievers. And, as someone once wrote, it was only known by the dead.

It was August. It was very hot. I was due at work in a few hours.

2.

That night it must have been 150 degrees Fahrenheit inside the trailer I'd been assigned to. The truck had rolled up from Arkansas or Mississippi or some other godforsaken place like that, and was filled to the rafters with the fattest, heaviest packages I'd ever set eyes on. My job was to haul the cargo to the conveyor belt at the rear of the vehicle. When I was finished with this baby, there was another waiting, where I would reverse the process. Nothing but lugging boxes back and forth until six in the morning.

I'd started at the depot a few months back after running out of jack for the thousandth time. Kleingrosse, the floor boss, had taken one look at all six feet, 175 pounds of me and gave me the nastiest jobs. Since he was management, he wore a shirt and tie and jacket and never got his hands dirty. Needless to say, he wasn't my favorite fellow.

At three that morning I took my fifteen for a smoke and a cold Coke. In the harsh light of the lunchroom I noticed my hands. They were glazed with a sticky orange substance. Within seconds they were on fire. One of the packages must have been leaking a contraband substance, acid or astringent.

I went running to the medic's station and stuck out my paws for the guy on duty.

"Wash with soap and water," he shrugged without taking his eyes off his Superman comic book. "That should do the trick."

I hurried to the john and followed his instructions, but the burning sensation continued. Even under the cascade of cold water, it felt like the vile stuff was about to sear the flesh off my bones.

I marched over to the central dispatch desk and asked Kleingrosse to let me go for the night.

"Occupational hazard," he sniffed. "I can't let you go. I'm short two guys tonight as it is. You walk out of here, you forfeit your pay."

I looked at his clean fingernails, his neatly combed hair. That was all I could do. Whenever they have you by the balls, that's all you *can* do.

You fucking asshole. You big fucking asshole.

I was fuming. But I returned to my truck anyway, cursing all the way. That's life—when you gotta have the money, you gotta have the money. All five bucks an hour.

Somehow I managed to make it through to the end of my shift. I was too exhausted to go someplace for a beer, so I jumped into my wreck and drove back to Park Street, where I sucked down gallon after gallon of water like a camel. I was sweat-drenched from head to toe. Even my work boots were saturated— they squished when I walked back and forth to the sink for refills.

As usual, I watched the sun come up through the porthole. Already a few commuters were gathered on the station platform below, waiting with their *Wall Street Journal*s and Styrofoam cups for the six thirty-eight train. Sure, I was glad I wasn't one of them—but where the hell was I?

Somehow I've got to get out of this, I told myself. But how? I didn't have the money for Paris, and besides, nobody went there anymore. And I damned sure didn't have the savings to take an early retirement.

I stripped naked, dunked myself in the bathtub, then stretched out on the narrow mattress. Outside the window the sky was painted robin's-egg blue. Summer had made it so stifling up here on the fifth floor I could hardly breathe. I was sweating all over again and it was only seven thirty. My hands were as crimson as boiled lobsters and still faintly burning. I leaned over and switched on my ancient, dust-coated, portable electric fan. Then I closed my eyes and tried to find a dream.

3.

Between trucks I'd occasionally pick up a gig playing acoustic guitar and singing. What with the rise of disco, it was a dying art. If the joint had a piano, I'd bang on that, too. There were a few holes in the wall in the Village and one or two in Jersey where I could make up to forty smackers a night, not bad change at all, and it sure beat humping tractor-trailers for UPS.

I was delivering a lugubrious, Leonard Cohen–like rendition of "Greensleeves" at a popular Montfleur coffeehouse called the Purple Turtle when I looked up from the catgut strings and saw her.

She was all by herself at a table near the entrance, a cup in front of her, a dreamy half smile on her face. Right off I could tell she was really something. Rich ebony hair gathered into a ponytail by a gold-and-scarlet silk bandeau. Features that were strong and broad, just the way I liked them. Was she Creole? Gypsy? Puerto Rican? A caramel-skinned African queen? Her eyes were like a pair of glowing black coals, her lips thick and luscious.

She glanced at me, and then away. Quickly. In that single instant I forgot all about my DA's wife.

When it was time for a break, I made a beeline for the door.

"Hey," I said to her, slowing down as I passed. "My name's Max. I hope you're enjoying yourself."

She seemed startled at being spoken to, even suspicious. Her mouth was full of large, even white teeth.

"Oh. I guess I am. . . ."

The preoccupied, lukewarm response was disappointing. But no matter—her smile was enough to encourage me, at least a little.

I ducked out and fired up a Marlboro. All sorts of questions flashed through my mind: Who is she? Where'd she come from? And, as always: *Where's the guy?*

On my way back to the stage, I stopped at her table again.

"Been here before?"

"No. . . ."

Her "no" had the inflection of a question, which didn't put me any more at ease. It was like she was thinking, *What the fuck do* you *want?*

"What's your name?" That's what I wanted, for starters.

"Olivia."

"A lovely name."

And that was all. She refused to rise to the bait. I felt the blood rush into my face. Women could always force me into making a fool of myself.

Like a crooning sleepwalker I strummed and picked my way through another rambling set. "Magdalena," one of the finely cut gems of the uncelebrated Danny O'Keefe. "To Ramona," Dylan. "Winter Lady," Cohen. *"Traveling lady, stay a while / Until the night is over. . . ."* Then one of my own ballads. Every one was directed at her.

A few seconds into the last piece, Olivia wasn't alone anymore. Her companion was a blond, heavily muscled, scowling young buck in a polo shirt and jeans who stared out the long picture window rather than at me. Once in a while he and Olivia exchanged a word or two. After another tune, he got up and stormed out. She followed moments later, wearing a pair of over-sized sunglasses, even though it was night.

Just my luck.

At the next break, I made for the door again, slowly this time. One of the waitresses handed me a slip of paper.

"Here, this is for you."

Call me, it read. *226–9164.*

4.

I decided to wait it out. The one thing you never want to show a beautiful woman is desperation. Instead of jumping for the telephone the very next day, I planted myself on the floor and interrogated the *I Ching*.

> *Six in the second place means:*
> *The woman loses the curtain of her carriage.*
> *Do not run after it;*
> *On the seventh day you will get it.*

Ambiguous, as usual. But tantalizing. Even promising, if you bought into that sort of thing.

I'd been dozing on the carpet when I heard Mrs. Trowbridge's bleat. "Max! *Maaaaaaax!*" I jumped up and peered five flights down through the railing curves.

"Lou needs some help! Would you mind coming down?"

What the fuck is this all about? My landlady never summoned me for anything besides phone calls. I pulled on a T-shirt and a pair of shorts and headed downstairs.

"Sorry to bother you, Max."

Since I hadn't made good on my bills in at least a couple of weeks, I figured a charitable gesture wouldn't hurt.

Lou was outside on the front lawn, skinny arms folded over his chest, waiting for me in the brilliant sunshine.

"Thanks for coming down, Max." He seemed more agitated than usual.

"No problem," I lied.

"Elkins next door is about to die. Incurable cancer of the pancreas. The hospital let him come home for the final days. But the poor son of a gun keeps rolling off his bed. His wife can't handle him at all."

Well, here was something to feel good about—I wasn't as bad off as Elkins. I'd never been inside the house next door. We traipsed across the driveway and climbed the steps. Inside the parlor it was shadowy and cool, the rays of the sun broken down by the heavy drapery.

In the dank atmosphere was the stench of rotting meat. Elkins, a flour-white cadaver, was rolling back and forth like an inverted tortoise on the Persian rug, moaning and groaning. It was hard to imagine that one day I'd be in the same boat. But I had an inkling of the future at that moment, and it made me shudder.

"All right now, Max, the objective is to get him back up there."

"Up there" was a hospital pallet complete with stainless-steel handrails and an electronic control for adjusting the position of the torso. It was a long way down to the floor, and for a man without padding on his carcass, the impact must have hurt like kissing the pavement after a leap from the roof of a ten-story building.

Elkins's elderly wife was standing by, wringing her hands.

"It's the drugs," she fretted. "Those damned painkillers are so strong that my poor Howard lapses into a delirium and doesn't even know where he is! Next thing, he's on the floor! I can't very well sit here every minute and watch over him. I hope you can do something, Lou. . . ."

Lou ignored her like he ignored his own wife.

"Max, why don't you step over there and hoist him up under the armpits. I'll take him by the legs."

Wanting nothing but to get the infernal task over with as quickly as possible, I did as ordered. It seemed incongruous for a man to kick the bucket on a spectacular summer day, but death, as we all know, spares no favorites, respects no specific time or place.

The touch of Elkins's sallow, desiccated skin gave me the creeps. His cheeks, which were decorated with a nexus of broken blood vessels and a patchwork of blue and green bruises, had collapsed into his mouth. The only hair left on his head was scattered in a few unsightly white tufts. His lids were stretched tightly over bulging eyeballs.

In a matter of seconds—he was as light as a feather—we had him tucked safely in his crib.

Lou leaned over the railing with a goofy smile on his lips. "Now try and stay in there, Howard, will you?"

It was supposed to be funny, but nobody laughed.

The ugly specter of Death was enough to spook me back to life. The next evening, after a supper of soggy canned beans and franks that I whipped up on the hot plate in the basement, my fantasies got the best of me. I decided to call Olivia. After the seventh or eighth ring, she picked up.

"It's Max, from the Purple Turtle. Thought I'd take you up on your offer."

I could picture her clearly in my mind's eye—sultry and remote and delicious.

"I enjoyed your music," she said.

"Thanks. I do the best I can."

"Somebody I know—*knew*—is a classical musician."

The fair-haired guy she'd been sitting with? He didn't look the type.

"No kidding."

Her laughter tinkled like wind chimes.

"No kidding. I adore all kinds of music. But Basil" (pronounced *Ba-zeel*) "says that the only music Americans know is 'Light My Fire.' "

"What's his instrument?"

"His instrument?" She gave a suggestive little giggle. All right. So whoever Basil was had screwed her. And I was turned on.

"Yeah. What does he play?"

"The violin, in chamber groups mostly. He specializes in Prokofiev and Bach. On occasion he'll brave Shostakovich."

Was I supposed to be impressed? Intimidated? Okay, but no way I was about to let on.

"I see. The guy at your table, by any chance?"

A few long seconds ticked away.

"No."

If Olivia wanted to come off as a riddle, she was scoring a great success.

"Actually, *I* start at the Purple Turtle next week."

"Really. . . . What doing?"

"Waitress. I'm working on an advanced degree in literature. A few nights a week at the Turtle will help with the bills. . . . How about you? Can you make a living playing the Purple Turtle?"

"I do whatever I can to make ends meet. These days I'm on the graveyard shift. Whenever I can squeeze it in, I play the coffeehouses. I write music. Someday I want to write books, novels. That's my great ambition."

"Mine, too."

My ears pricked up. "We're talking the same language then."

"I have to go," she said suddenly. "It was nice talking to you."

Why did she have to go? *Where* did she have to go? Was somebody with her? On his way? The blond guy again? The back of my neck began to burn.

"Nice talking to *you*," I said. "We'll have to do it again sometime."

There it was—smooth and casual and self-assured.

"Maybe we will."

Before I had the chance to ask when, she'd hung up.

5.

That little conversation with Olivia kept me guessing for days on end. I told myself I didn't give a damn, but somewhere down deep I did.

One night when I had off from the loading dock I was roused from my sleep by a bloodcurdling scream. It was like someone's throat was being torn out. Since my dreams tended toward the violent and frightening, my first guess was that the sound had come from some uncharted region inside my own skull.

My eyes shot open. The ceiling of my cage was a black slate. Outside the porthole the sky was colorless. As usual, I was sweating like a pig.

Another scream ripped out of the darkness. There was no doubt about it now: somebody was being murdered beneath the very roof of the boardinghouse. I leaped off the mattress, toppling the reading lamp in the process. When I succeeded in finding and switching it on, I saw by the alarm clock that it was three thirty.

Where the hell were my cigarettes? I fumbled around for the pack, lighted one, and cracked the door. What I heard out there was the gibbering of a wild animal, followed by a burst of hysterical laughter. It wasn't murder after all—somebody was losing his mind.

Somewhere below a light flared. Mrs. Trowbridge, in her flea-bitten nightgown, stood on the second-floor landing outside her bedroom and squinted up at me.

"What's going *on* up there, Max?"

Just as I was about to tell her that her guess was as good as mine, there was another yelp.

This time I figured out where the commotion was coming from. I took three steps down the hall and knocked on Benny's door.

"You okay in there? Benny—you all right?"

"Ugh . . . agh . . . EEEEEEEEEEEEEEEEEEEE. . . ."

I turned the handle and pushed the door open. Benny was thrashing around in his sheets, his spindly black legs spastically pumping the pedals of an invisible bicycle.

"Christ! What's wrong, man?"

"MY EAR!" he shouted into the pillow he clutched with two fists.

"Your ear? What's wrong with your ear?"

"IT'S IN MY EAR! ONE OF THEM GODDAMN COCKER-ROACHES CRAWLED INTO MY EAR AND I CAN'T GET THE MOTHERFUCKER OUT!"

I ran to the bed and yanked him by his arms into a sitting position. Then I forced his hand away from his ear.

"THE SON OF A BITCH BURROWED IN THERE WHILE I WAS SLEEPIN'! THIS PLACE IS A FUCKIN' OUT-HOUSE! THEY SHOULD BE ASHAMED TO CHARGE RENT! THEY SHOULD PAY *US* TO LIVE HERE!"

Before he lost it all over again, I twisted his head and peered inside the canal. Sure enough, there were the creature's bent hind legs.

"GET IT OUT! GET IT THE FUCK OUT, MAX, BE-FORE IT CLIMBS INTO MY BRAIN!"

"It can't climb into your brain, Benny, it's not anatomically possible!" I assured him, though I wasn't at all certain.

"PLEASE, MAX! BEFORE IT DRIVES ME FUCKIN' CRAZY!"

I made a grab for the insect with my thumb and forefinger, but no dice. The harder I tried, the farther in the beast scurried, until it disappeared entirely.

By now there was a crowd huddled in Benny's door, including Lou and his wife and the drowsy, shell-shocked tenants from the lower floors.

"Anybody got some tweezers?"

"Tweezers!"

"I think I got some in my room. . . ."

"DO SOMETHIN', MAX!"

"Just hold on a minute, Benny, hold on, help is on the way . . . !"

Heavy footsteps banged down the stairs.

"MAX! *PLEASE!"*

"Oh, my *Lord*," warbled Mrs. Trowbridge.

"Try turning him over on his side," Lou suggested feebly.

"What good will that do?"

An argument broke out. Heavy footfalls up the stairs.

I pulled the tweezers out of Jimmy McNulty's paw and gently inserted the tongs into Benny's auricle. But it was too late. The cockroach had forged onward into the jungle of the inner ear.

"YOU GOT HIM, MAX?"

I removed the tweezers. "Benny, I hate to have to tell you this, but there's nothing I can do. You're going to have to get out of bed and make a trip to the emergency room."

That prompted a vessel-bursting bellow from the poor bugger. He tore at his hair.

"I'll call an ambulance!" offered McNulty.

"Forget it. I'll drive him over myself," I said.

The gathering slowly dispersed while McNulty and I dressed the trembling Benny in his Bermuda shorts and T-shirt. Since his equilibrium was destroyed, I draped his arm around my neck and carried him down the staircase.

"I'm gonna sue you, you slumlord!" Benny shouted over his shoulder at Mrs. Trowbridge. "I'm gonna take you for everything you're worth! You got no business runnin' a lodging for human beings! THERE'S A GODDAMN COCKROACH IN MY EAR! YOU'RE TRYIN' TO KILL ME HERE!"

"Relax, Benny. . . ."

I hauled him across the lawn to my decrepit Chevy Impala and laid him across the back seat. Caroline and Lou watched with sleepy horror from the porch.

Benny was still cursing them for bastards as we pulled away from the curb into the steamy New Jersey night.

6.

Benny didn't follow through on his threat to sue, but the next day after being discharged from the hospital he packed up his stuff and moved out. The incident was one more that made me question what I was doing with my life, drifting from one cockroach palace to another, nursing puerile fantasies about writing great novels but never actually trying, barely scraping by on survival jobs while most normal people my age were embarking on real careers and starting families and all the rest of it, American-style. The problem was, Norman Rockwell was rotten to the core, and I knew it. When I contemplated what a man had to endure in order to get by in this world, it turned my stomach. Nevertheless, an undefined sense of guilt dogged me. Why was it I detested all things conventional and bourgeois? My head was in the clouds, for sure. Or up my ass, as my blue-collar old man liked to say. My best friend, Bernie Monahan, always accused me of "Too many books! Too much Dostoyevsky! Too much Henry Miller! Too much of that ridiculous Shithead Shinsky!" (his bizarre moniker for Nietzsche—or any other intellectual for that matter).

Maybe all that was true—it *was* true, in fact—but there was something more that accounted for my restlessness and disaffection. I was also out of step with the world in some fatal, cement-solid way. Yours truly always had to be different. Whatever everybody else loved, I hated. My tastes in music and literature and film and theater ran to the esoteric, and the more obscure, the better. Give me Arthur Machen over Stephen King any day! Marguerite Duras over Erica Jong! Bowles and Bukowski over any bestseller on the list! I was most decidedly a lone wolf, a *contrarian*, and a foot soldier to my own private drummer. Moreover, I wanted to *accomplish* something unique—a calamitous urge, especially when connected with the so-called "creative" or "artistic" temperament.

Worst of all—*absolute worst of all*—I never listened to anyone's advice.

One morning, after a brutal eight-hour stretch of lifting, with another scheduled for that night, I dialed the loading dock.

"Message for Kleingrosse, the guy in charge of bay C."

"Okay. What's the message?"

"I quit."

Clean. Simple. Decisive. There was a pause on the line.

"And your name?"

I spelled it out for the operator. I thought I could hear her scribbling something down.

"Don't forget to send my last check," I reminded her before hanging up.

As usual, I did not fully consider the consequences of my actions. Monahan had warned me beforehand to think it over, but I refused. All I knew was that I had enough cash to buy food for the next couple of weeks, as well as scrape by on the rent. Surely something would happen between now and the day when the coffer ran dry? It always had in the past. I was still here, wasn't I?

A few minutes later Mrs. Trowbridge called up the stairs that the telephone was for me. I went for the hall extension.

"Candace London here. Your horoscope, remember? I'm still waiting for payment. When can I expect it?"

"Damn—I thought I sent that out. You'll have it in a few days, I promise. I'll get it out to you no later than tomorrow. . . ."

"Just make sure you do."

Mrs. London did not sound pleased. Some streak of perversity in me wanted to make her wait as long as possible for her twenty-five bucks. Why should I compensate the messenger for a baleful message? Not to mention that I didn't have it to spare.

Now that I had some free time on my hands, I was going to write. Do what I'd read that real artists did: rise at the crack of dawn, plant themselves at their workbenches in the holy quietude of first light, and wait to be struck by the lightning of inspiration. If it worked for them, why shouldn't it work for me?

The very next morning I dragged myself out of bed at five—*five*, when not even the birds were awake!—boiled water in the aluminum pot for instant coffee, gobbled down two chocolate-coated donuts, and sat with my pens and pencils and blank pad of paper at the tiny, scarred desk facing the porthole.

The setting was perfect. There I was—the impoverished, budding genius in his garret, armed with weapons to conquer the world of ideas, to set his name forever upon the world's tablet. . . .

The problem was nothing—not a single word—would come. Like an impotent lover or outclassed prizefighter, I couldn't get a thing off: not a bolt of sperm, not a single stiff jab. Morning after morning I hunched for hours over that cramped student's desk, mulling, brooding, cogitating. I sweated and strained. I puffed cigarette after cigarette. I compiled mountains of notes about nothing. I contemplated unanswerable quandaries, such as: *How does a writer discover his own voice? Isn't the unalloyed inner flow transformed into something else altogether—something contam-*

inated—immediately upon contact with open air—or paper? What's more, every human being has a million voices coursing through his being! Which is the real thing? The exhortation to "Find your own voice!" was absurd, really, even after two seconds' worth of thought! The veneer of authenticity could be a falsehood, and the appearance of uncertainty and dubiousness much closer to truth and honesty. I would call up examples of each, then reverse the process, until I was thoroughly confused. Finally, out of complete paralysis and frustration, I'd turn to the latest girlie magazine and begin to fantasize in another direction altogether.

Once in a while I'd succeed in starting a novel, or a story, or a play, in a blast of self-assured afflatus, but for one reason or another—usually that I was mysteriously without the wherewithal to follow through—each project was aborted in the early stages of pregnancy. Ten or fifteen incandescent pages, then a perplexing meltdown. I tried to muddle through the problem, but eventually got entangled like a fish in the net of my own ponderings.

Those early mornings never amounted to much of anything. Well, fuck it all anyway—maybe I just wasn't cut out to be a writer. . . .

7.

Within a few short weeks I was staring straight into the black bottom of my meager bank account. There were no gigs, musical or otherwise, on the horizon. I figured I'd better do something, and fast, before even Mrs. Trowbridge lost her patience and evicted me. To add to the pressure, the sorcerer had called for her money again. Welching on that chit wasn't going to be as easy as I thought.

But as always I struck pay dirt in the classifieds. Mister V. Kishan Rao was in need of coaching in the English language if he had any hope of passing his examinations to become certified as a medical doctor in this country, and he was paying eight bucks an hour and willing to visit the roach palace for it. The Pentel Corporation of North America likewise wanted someone to come out to its facilities in a Fairfield industrial park and converse with a recently arrived employee from Japan, in order to prime him for life in the United States. Within twenty-four hours, I'd nailed down both positions. It was one rare day.

With a little jingle in my pocket again, I could breathe easier.

The balmy evenings of late summer passed like a lilac-scented dream. Before I noticed, autumn had tossed its longer nights over the world like a soft blanket. Olivia was still on my mind, but I wasn't banking on anything. A couple weeks after talking to her, I cruised over to the Purple Turtle around closing time to try and snag myself a booking. I peeked into the window. There weren't any patrons left in the place, and the waitstaff was turning chairs upside down onto the empty tables. I rapped on the glass. Olivia, who was wiping down the table on the other side, opened up.

"The boss around?"

"She took off about an hour ago. You're just a little too late."

"The story of my life." Before she had the chance to get away, I said: "How about a drink?"

Five minutes later we were in my wreck en route to a beer-and-burger joint in Paterson. We took a table in a quiet corner. Olivia was wearing that peculiar half smile I'd noticed the night we met, as if she knew something that I didn't. All the same, it was the first time I had the feeling that something was sealed between us. It turned out we were both taken with many of the same writers, though she didn't share my passion for Henry Miller, and I argued against the precious Virginia Woolf, whom she admired. When it came to anything personal, a veil descended. Afterward, when I drove her back to her car, she seemed nervous and preoccupied, but she let me kiss her a few times. The brightly lit parking lot behind the Turtle wasn't a good place to do much else.

"My boyfriend's the jealous type," she revealed, apropos of nothing.

And who might he be?

The guy with the blond hair. She suspected that he may have followed us tonight, and that he might just be spying on us from the shadows at this very moment.

Not to worry, she assured me. Lately Edward was getting to be too much. She'd been trying to set him straight: She was a free woman and wouldn't be tied down.

I said nothing. Better never to betray what you were thinking when it came to rivals.

We kissed again.

A few days later Olivia phoned and invited me over to her place for dinner. It was the least she could do for me since I treated her the last time. The address was in a decent neighborhood of Caldwell and featured a view of the noisy thoroughfare below. All around there were similar characterless, garden-variety apartment buildings. She'd moved in just recently, she said, while giving me the tour. The place had been freshly painted. Light and airy, it was a brilliant and startling contrast to my shithole. The predominant notes were white and cerulean. It was sparsely and tastefully furnished, with lots of wicker everywhere. A swag lamp with a basketball-sized frosty dome dangled from the ceiling in the breakfast nook, and a big peacock chair sat majestically in a corner of the small living room. There were framed reproductions of Impressionist paintings on the walls, including a large poster of *The Kiss* by Gustav Klimt. Fluffy throw rugs and miniature straw mats were strewn across the hardwood floors; the total effect was a pleasant admixture of the Oriental and the American Southwest.

I wondered vaguely how she could afford such relatively upscale digs, but it was none of my business so I didn't ask.

She popped open a flask of Italian red and offered me a glass.

"So—did you get in trouble with Edward on account of me?"

No, it was okay, she thought she'd managed to straighten everything out. With drink in hand I watched while she deftly whipped up a heap of pasta, garlic bread, and sweet bay scallops. Then she ignited a pair of long brand-new tapers and we ate by candlelight. Very romantic. It was the best meal I'd had in months. I was beginning to feel like one of the living again.

My cock revived, too. Livy—which was what she preferred to

be called—had legs straight out of a Vargas illustration. In sheer black stockings they were nothing short of magnificent. Her preference for dark clothing, rather than creating an impression of mournfulness, lent itself to a steely bohemian sexuality. I didn't know what was hidden beneath her dress, but I could venture a good guess. My mouth watered at the thought.

Livy pushed the dishes aside when we were through eating, and we went on working the red. Words flowed as easily as the booze, but we were still only feeling each other out. Beneath the sounds we made was an unstated question that held fast in the deep current like a big, powerful fish: How far were we willing to take this thing? Were we ready to throw in our lot with each other no matter what?

I peeled open a second bottle. In a pleasant haze we moved to the small couch in the living room. She produced a joint from somewhere and I fired it up. I was drunk and ready for anything, ready to go anywhere the night took us. Even as it was happening, I realized it was one of life's nonpareil moments—a man and a woman with a few drinks and good food in their bellies, locked away from the world, talking about the most important things under the sun. After dimming the light, I launched into a disquisition on literature, philosophy, religion, music, film, even love itself (as if I knew what I was talking about) . . . the entire gamut. For a twenty-three-year-old, she chipped in more than enough, too, but she also possessed the extraordinary ability of allowing me to fill the atmosphere with the din of my own ludicrous grandiloquence. That's a great facility women have—they understand how important it is for a guy to hear himself blab.

"Let me tell you about a very rare experience of pure revelation, Livy. Now don't laugh, okay . . . ? It was just a few years ago. . . . At the time I was working the assembly line of a brewery in a coal-mining town outside of Pittsburgh. I'd recently discovered Dostoyevsky, and at night after my shift I plowed straight through *Crime and Punishment* and *The Brothers Karamazov*, and I was maybe halfway through *Demons*. . . . Now on my day off I happened to be walking beneath the Gothic arches of an old Benedictine monastery in the hills nearby, where I sometimes went for peace and quiet from the infernal racket of bottles and cans dropping into cases, when all of a sudden—*kaboom!* Here! Now! This was it! The *moment of moments!* It comes to me in a bolt of lightning—I'm a *genius!* And all this time I hadn't a *clue!* I hadn't *realized!* It took this twenty-four-hour-a-day living with the Verkhovenskys, Smerdyakovs, and Stavrogins to bring it to the surface. *A fucking genius!* Don't ask me *how* I knew—it was an alchemical thing—I just *knew*. . . ."

What bullshit. . . . I was a little embarrassed. I had to laugh at myself. But Livy didn't. She seemed to be taking me seriously. Of course I hadn't the slightest morsel of evidence, aside from a few pages of a play and half a notebook full of songs untested outside the coffeehouses and bars, that would bear out my preposterously grandiose claim. And I didn't mention the prodigious quantities of hash I'd been smoking at the time of the great revelation, or the mescaline trips I'd been fond of taking on the weekends. Nevertheless, it made me feel good—*validated* me almost—to be listened to by a beautiful female without derision. That's something else women are good at.

"You're going to be famous, I can feel it," Livy nodded. "I have a sixth sense about these things."

A chill shot up my spine. *Yes!* I knew it all along! I'd only needed somebody else to say it out loud in order to believe it myself. Or at least half believe it.

"Come over here."

I wrapped her in my arms and plunged my tongue into her mouth. She gave back as good as she got until we were both huffing and puffing like long-distance runners. I began to strip off her clothes, piece by exquisite piece. I was in no hurry to get where I was going. Then she yanked on the flap of my belt. . . .

We were both naked. I swept her up and carried her through the open bedroom door. In the soft blue shadows cast by the streetlamps I laid her on the bed and stood over her, my erect prong hovering like a hummingbird in the air between us. She reached up and wrapped her long fingers around the shaft. I let her pull me down on top of her, then gripped her flanks for support. Then I pushed into the wetness inside and drove upward.

I'd had a few women in my life, but I was to learn something new about sex from Olivia Aphrodite (her true middle name). We were to take the plunge together into the subsoil of raw concupiscence, from which both ecstasy and madness spring, and forgo the dusty, worthless upper strata of passionless habit and duty that most humans know. I would come to live for fucking Livy. For the first time I knew what it was to truly *bang* a woman, to ram like a battery, to bury my body, obliterate my *self*, in the mysterious folds of a cunt. Like a devoted master of the Kama Sutra, I discovered the rude pleasure of enjoying the female in an infinite number of contortions, to forge onward when there was no juice left, to bludgeon myself into insensibility from the sheer act of fornication. We would finish our sessions in a state of complete and utter exhaustion—in a delirium, really—oblivious altogether to the outside world. . . .

And could Livy *scream*. . . . It was a giddy delight, knowing I could coax such a welter of howls and caterwauls out of a bitch. With every yelp, a strange thrill traveled up from the tip of my cock and into the depths of my brain. . . .

That first time we fucked it was a haunted night in early November. Some time after midnight we stopped for a bite to eat. I was famished, and so was she. All that exercise had built up a ravenous appetite. In the living room the television was murmuring. I couldn't remember how or when it had gotten switched on. Puppets in suits and evening gowns clasped their hands jubilantly above their heads. A man with a Southern accent delivered an impassioned speech from a podium. Numbers—vast, incomprehensible totals in the millions—flashed across the screen. They meant nothing to me or to Livy. Standing there nude with chunks of leftover Italian bread in our mouths, my red-and-purple cock bobbing, we learned that Jimmy Carter had just been elected president of the United States. . . .

8.

Life got to be what it's supposed to be at least some little part of our time here on earth: perfect. When you first invade a woman's body, you stumble into the realm of the dream—the dream of nirvana. You move through the days like a contented sleepwalker. The more depleted you are, the better: the senses are heightened, the boundary between illusion and reality pleasantly blurred. And that's the way you want to live—inside a beautiful dream.

It was like I'd been granted a new lease on the whole deal—my ship, as they say, had come in. Every evening I found myself climbing the steps to Livy's spare but recherché apartment on Roseland Avenue. When she opened up to my knock, we'd go right at each other, fucking before we even said hello. She wanted me there with her all the time. What was the point of being any-where else? We were on the same page from the get-go.

Suddenly it seemed as if nothing else was quite so important as Olivia Aphrodite. We spent all our free time at her flat, fuck-ing, talking, reading. We put on our clothes and went out only when we had to—usually to a hole-in-the-wall Chinese restau-rant up on Bloomfield Avenue. There wasn't ever more than a few inches between us.

Since I felt myself to be pretty much a failure in real life, winning this knockout's attention was a singular achievement when not much else was going great guns. I *liked* to think that I was a somebody, but I could never be sure. Maybe, I figured, Livy could help. She was always telling me "You're handsome," and "You're talented"; it made me feel good just to be around her.

And the one thing we couldn't resist doing when we were around each other was fuck. Everywhere. In the peacock chair . . . on the couch . . . the floor . . . the kitchen table . . . the shower . . . the bathroom sink, and anywhere else we could manage.

The instant of orgasm was often agonizing in its extremity of pleasure, punctuated as always by one of Livy's delirious raves. The quantity of fluid expended by each of us was immense—a fucking flood. Wherever I moved there was semen and cunt juice: her belly and ass, me, all over the sheets.

In those first days it struck me sometimes that I had no idea who Livy *was*. Here we were, living like a pair of monkeys in a jungle tree, and she was a stranger to me. Mysterious moods like swift-moving clouds passed across her onyx eyes; she never betrayed what they were. You can get inside a woman's body, but you can never get inside the head. Not really.

Once in a while the telephone would ring. Mostly Livy would let it go on ringing, but when its persistence broke through our insular contentment, she'd have no choice but to climb out of bed and pick it up.

Some of the calls were peculiar. After saying hello, she'd hold the receiver to her ear and listen for a long time—five, ten, fifteen minutes. Now and then she might answer "Yes" or "Maybe"; invariably the one-sided conversation would terminate with *"No!"* or *"Please don't do that!"*

After she hung up I interrogated her delicately about the calls, but she was evasive, as she was about so many other things. She seemed preoccupied, on the verge of flat-out panic. I didn't press her. What did it matter, after all? She was here with me, and that was the important thing.

One night she let slip that it was Edward who'd been phoning. Yes, *that* Edward, the fair-haired Nazi she wasn't seeing anymore since she'd taken up with me. Edward, the luxury automobile mechanic who was thoroughly unappreciative of her intellectual aspirations and artistic talent and only wanted to own her like a car. And to think she'd nearly *married* somebody like him.

"What does he want?"

Silence.

"Come on, Livy, what does he want? He keeps you on the line for long enough."

"Nothing you have to know."

"Why not? We sleep together, don't we? If this guy wants to see you again, that's a natural enough thing. He used to sleep with you, too, I presume."

My attempt at generosity of spirit. More silence.

"Come on. You can tell me."

"Well, okay . . . if you really have to know."

"Well, all right then."

She took a deep breath.

"He's got a gun. And he's threatening to come over here and blow us both away. Me for betraying him, you for coming between us."

Oh. Nice.

"Do you think he'd actually *do* it?"

"I hope not. But you never know. Edward can be pretty violent."

"How violent?"

"At my other place he busted down the front door in the middle of the night to make sure I wasn't cheating on him. And he threw a fit once that was loud enough to make the neighbors call the cops. And he took a swing at me that missed and shattered all the crystal in the cupboard. And—well, things like that."

"Things like that . . . I see."

Recent odd occurrences in my life suddenly began to make sense. Such as that a certain car with a tinted windshield—a Mercedes or some similar expensive model—had tailed me out of the parking lot of the Purple Turtle once or twice. That on the rare occasions when I checked in at the roach palace I got telephone calls from someone who refused to speak but would only listen while breathing hard at the other end. And the typewritten anonymous letter that arrived in the mail and warned me to "mind my own business or *suffer the consequences. . . .*"

Later, when I showed it to Livy, she admitted that it might have come from Edward but not to worry. She suspected that eventually the storm would blow over. In the meantime, we'd just have to wait it out.

"You love me, don't you?"

"Hell, yes. And I won't let anything happen to you, either."

"I didn't think so."

"He comes over here, I'll deal with him."

"Thanks, Max . . . I need somebody to look out for me."

She dissolved into tears. But I had to admit that some part of me felt sorry for Edward. Here I was screwing the daylights out of his girlfriend—ex-girlfriend—while he sat at home and stewed about it, pictured the sordid details in his mind's eye. No wonder he was teetering on the brink of committing mayhem. There was nothing worse than being on the outside looking in. I knew the feeling well.

If Livy could do it to him, did it mean she could do it to me someday, too?

No. Because I was different. Sure, I was a whole different ball game from everybody else, anybody she ever had before me. Me, I was special. Nobody had what I had. She didn't really love Edward. It was me she loved.

Why, all I had to do was think of how she fucked me . . . right?

I braced myself for the worst, but Edward never showed up to kill either one of us. The threatening calls stopped, too, and I didn't receive any more ominous letters in the mail. The boy had come to his senses, just like Livy predicted. Still, I thought it was rather strange that he'd given up the ship after all that bluster and bravado. But hey—I wasn't complaining. When things go your way, there's no point in trying to figure out why. This was a gift horse, and I wasn't about to look in its mouth.

9.

Tutoring the foreigners sure beat hell out of breaking my ass on the loading platform. I didn't have to jackass a thing, never got dirty, and the hourly rate was a lot more respectable. All I had to do with the aliens was sit and talk. I was good at talking. Maybe I was better at talking than anything else. The downside was instead of packages, now I was dealing with people. You never knew what people were going to do next.

For instance, Mister V. Kishan Rao failed to show up at the appointed time for his eighth session. He never called to give me a reason why, and since he'd refused to divulge *his* number, I couldn't call him. A piddling fifty-six tax-free dollars and it was over. I never heard from the man again. . . .

As far as the Japs were concerned, something similar happened not long afterward. Again I was blindsided, because things got off to a fine and dandy start with them, more or less. We were all smiles and bows at first, a regular lovefest in the making. After greeting me with "You—caw-hee [his best attempt at the word 'coffee'] now," Hizimitsu Takahashi and I would take our cups, seal ourselves in one of the conference rooms, and go to it. He was competent enough in the "Herro, how are you," "Good morning," and "Thank you velly much" phase, but at each new tongue-bending English word he would cock his head like a bewildered parrot. It was going to be tough, I learned early on, to bridge the cavernous linguistic gap between Occident and Orient. For weeks the salesman never progressed further in conversation than "My company bling me here" and "Tonight I go to Mah-hah-ta [Manhattan]." Damned near every utterance was prefixed with "my company." It was my company this, my company that, until I reached the conclusion that my student did indeed regard his employer as a sort of supreme being or all-powerful deity—which was the Japanese way. The poor fellow needed some loosening up, I figured. So I did some research and came in one afternoon with a few choice items calculated to melt the ice between East and West.

"Ah, my *kintama*"—testicles—"are itchy as hell today!"

No reaction. Had I pronounced the word correctly?

"I had a damned good *asa mara*"—morning erection—"you?"

Nothing. And: "What do you think of American *omanko*?"—cunt.

No response, only a half grin and a nervous push of the horn-rimmed spectacles back up the bridge of his nose.

The very next day, Mister Kimitake, my charge's boss, phoned to inform me that my services were no longer needed and thank you very much.

"But I thought you were going to use me through the end of the fiscal ye—" A click and a buzz. Another sinecure down the drain. No doubt the Japanese sense of propriety had been offended by my choice of terms for translation. Of course it was all supposed to be a lighthearted joke, but they weren't getting it. Or maybe they thought I was coming on to the guy. Or maybe it was the fact that I'd not responded with sufficient enthusiasm to the seaweed crackers proffered as a snack whenever I came to work.

They were a damned curious lot, those Nipponese pen hucksters. Tight and formal and inscrutable, they never betrayed a scintilla of what was going on inside their skulls.

The upshot was that I was about to be as poor as a church mouse all over again. I didn't worry much about it, though—I had Livy. Having Livy was like having an ace up my sleeve. I had a hunch she was going to save me.

Just before Christmas I hopped the train to Philly to visit my brother. When I got back a few days later and rapped on Livy's door, it swung open with a vengeance.

"I missed you," she said, her eyes flashing with something like rage.

"Yeah. I missed you, too."

"I don't want us to spend any more time apart."

"That's what I want, too."

"Are you going to stay?"

"If you want me to."

"I only want you to if you really want me. . . ."

I grabbed her hand and guided it to my crotch. "What does this tell you?"

And it was true. I'd done nothing but think about her from the minute I left town.

"This is the way it has to be. Just me and you."

"Yeah. This is how it's going to be."

Within seconds, we were tearing each other's clothes off. Next day I moved the rest of my stuff in.

Late at night Livy and I spun out elaborate plans for the future. We were going to be together. We were going to travel. The main thing was we were going to write. From the beginning it was a given, a fundamental presumption—though neither of us was writing. Maybe when all was said and done we'd pack up and move to a sunny foreign country—Spain or Italy or Portugal (the climate for artists was sure to be more conducive)—but since neither of us had been abroad we were at a complete loss where to go. We avoided talking about money, but I couldn't help noting Livy's champagne tastes in couture and dining. But I figured that if she was covered, then so was I. Everything I have is yours, she said.

Winter was the coldest on record. The Arctic winds that blew in were vicious and bitter. Day after day shrouds of snow fell over the world, blotting out the sky. The stuff accumulated in huge, swirling mounds that choked the boulevards and backstreets. A crusty frost adhered to everything in creation, from the sidewalks to the telephone wires to the windows of homes and shops. Going out of doors at all became an excruciatingly painful chore—like trudging through Siberia. Livy and I spent more time than ever holed up and between the sheets. We were slowly drifting, like twin feathers in a vacuum, into some separate existence all our own, where we only needed each other for sustenance. Of course, neither of us recognized, or cared, that it was happening. That's what a certain kind of love can do. . . .

Coincidentally, circumstances conspired to facilitate our metamorphosis. Livy complained that she was growing bored with her classes and was thinking about dropping out of her program altogether. Weren't all the great ones autodidacts anyway? Hemingway, Steinbeck, Faulkner, Miller, Kerouac—they'd all gone running from the halls of academia! The worst fate would be to end up a Joyce Carol Oates, ensconced in a cushy ivory tower, scribbling page after page full of desiccated words that had no relation whatsoever to anything organic, anything *living*. So more and more often Livy cut her classes. She called in sick to the

Purple Turtle whenever the whim ambushed her. As for me, I lay around doing nothing but waiting for her. . . .

All the dead time on our hands meant even more fucking. When a man has nothing constructive to do, he immerses himself in sex; Livy and I went on inventing endless variations on the theme. The boudoir filled with lotions, perfumes, jellies, aphrodisiacs—it became a veritable harlot's chamber. One day she came home with a floor-to-ceiling mirror so that we could watch ourselves in the act. I became hypnotized with the sensual poses we struck, many of which recalled the mythological statuary of the Hindus. My favorite was Livy astride the bed, heels high on the stems of her Candies, while I scuttled from behind. . . .

Late one January afternoon. . . . Everybody else in the world except for us was at his job. The building was so still we could hear the merciless wind soughing at the window sealings. Livy happened to be on all fours on the mattress at the time, like a dog, with me slamming into her from behind—another favorite position. She was screaming with ecstasy when a soft tap sounded at the door.

That knock stopped us dead, since whoever it was could no doubt hear *us*. We held our breath, thinking that maybe we were mistaken, that we'd only been jostling the bed frame against the wall.

Then we heard it again.

Livy slipped off the bed and tiptoed to the door. I followed, and watched as she put her eye to the peephole.

She jerked back, like she'd been punched in the face. "It's my *father*."

She laid her forefinger over her lips. We turned and retraced our steps, lifting our naked legs high, like people slogging through quicksand.

We sat on the bed and waited. "Jesus *Christ*," I whispered after the slow, heavy footsteps died away down the stairs to the street.

It wasn't that I was ashamed or embarrassed over what the guy had just heard. It was just so goddamned creepy to realize that somebody had been eavesdropping on your intimate grunts. You had to wonder how the porn actors did it.

We tried to go back to screwing, but the mood was broken. I pushed a cigarette between my lips, leaned against the pillows, and stroked Livy's still-wet pussy.

"Your old man ever pull a stunt like that before?"

She was oddly detached. She shrugged. The steel curtain had descended with a crash.

I let it go. In a matter of minutes Livy was back to herself. It was like nothing at all had happened. Good—I wasn't finished with her.

"Hey, d'you think he really heard us?" I laughed after shooting my wad. "If he did, he sure got an earful."

She giggled. She didn't seem to give a damn one way or the other now, and that pleased me.

"There's my baby. . . ."

That night I dreamed that Livy's old man broke into the apartment and ransacked it, ripping underwear out of the dresser in a rage, skulking from room to room searching for some trace of me, while I cowered in fear, hiding behind the hollow door of Livy's closet. . . .

10.

It's extraordinary how time disappears when you're doing nothing. Blink once and the days have vanished into history. . . . How did I spend those early days with Livy? Who knows. . . . Sometimes we pretended to write. While our schedules were completely haphazard—there really was no timetable to speak of for any aspect of our lives—Livy would manage to sit for stretches at her black mahogany desk in the bedroom while I commandeered the kitchen table. We never showed so much as a word to each other. One afternoon when she'd run out to replenish her supply of birth control pills, my curiosity got the best of me. In the bottom drawer of her desk I discovered a few words written in her beautiful hand on the top sheet of a legal pad:

Life's colors are indistinct, like the chiaroscuro painted on the early night sky.

One sentence, that was all. Yesterday's date was printed in the top right-hand corner. She'd spent half the day working on that single sentence. I riffled through the rest of the pages—nothing. That fragment of prose was all she'd produced in weeks. I wasn't doing much better. The situation was absurd, and more than a little pitiful. We were so young and naive.

Which was how we reassured each other after another wasted day: "We're young. We have time."

Maybe I was lazy. Maybe life with Livy was too damned easy. If you're lucky enough to shag a gorgeous piece of tail, you're bound to lose your ambitions—it's an immutable law of nature. After all, once you've reached the Promised Land, there's no use wandering in the desert.

In time I reached the point where I no longer even *pretended* to put words to paper. Instead of crawling out of bed at noon or thereabouts and reaching for pad and pen, I lifted whatever book I was reading from the nightstand and picked up where I'd left off at four A.M. Along with my insatiable desire for Livy's cunt, I'd developed a new hunger for words, words, and more words—so long as they weren't mine. Roaming through the public library one day I happened upon the complete, unabridged *Memoirs* of Giacomo Casanova. After checking out number one, my course was fixed. As the days passed, I devoured volume after volume. Through the words of the aged, invalid narrator, writing by this time from the private library of a nobleman's castle in Bohemia, I was able to vicariously live the young roué's countless debaucheries and swindles;, his wild escapades, flights and travels, his incestuous fornications and orgies, to participate in the world's upheavals, to witness unique moments in history. I figured that if I wasn't likely to live such an adventurous existence myself, then Casanova was the next best thing.

Not long afterward I discovered *My Secret Life*, that sprawling, salacious diary of a Victorian man of leisure. As with Casanova, I followed the anonymous hero of quenchless sexual appetite around the world, from Mediterranean spa to English country estate to French village as he pursued every last one of his whims, obsessions, and fetishes, fucking, sucking, masturbating, "minet-ting," "gamahuching," and raping his way through an army of females, from the prepubescent to the middle-aged, without once suffering even a pang of conscience or guilt. Pleasure for its own sake—that's what I was after, too. When Livy appeared, I'd im-mediately entice her into some new sex game I'd picked up from those pages, and the day would be complete.

When I ran low on classic erotic literature, I dug out the works of Henry Miller again, a man whose apprehension and sensibility of the world was almost exactly my own. Here once and for all was a rationalization for why I felt so out of place in the Western Hemisphere, why I was so loath to stick with a humdrum job, why I was devoid of conventional ambition, why I was addicted to women's bodies, why I nursed the sentiments of an anarchist. Once and for all I'd found justification for the way I was, and, like Henry himself, if I didn't find my way out of America before I got too old, then I was going to pop my cork.

But I went nowhere. All those books, of course, were nothing but a big, fat excuse for not coming to grips with my own self. The fact is I had no idea who I really was, had no clue whether I possessed talent—or even value—of any kind, hadn't the faintest idea what I was supposed to do with myself in this life. Whatever happened, it was always easier to let Livy show the way, to bury myself inside her, to black myself out in the folds of her fragrant snatch. To drift like a leaf down the ol' Mississippi. . . .

Hey—who could blame me?

11.

Spring was threatening to show. It takes a long time for anything resembling fine weather to arrive in this part of the country, and that year the interminable winter, snow and all, dragged on into the middle of April. It was okay, I didn't really mind—the cold had served Livy and me all too well. Besides, the .44 Caliber Killer had begun his rampage, and everybody in the entire area around the city of New York was on edge and holing up—nobody knew where the maniac was going to strike next.

Sunday morning. . . . We were lying in bed waiting to do nothing but crawl on top of each other again.

"Let's take a ride." It was her suggestion.

"Sure, why not? I suppose we have to get out of here sometime." Saturday had been a late night at the Turtle for Livy.

After coffee, toast, and eggs, we slipped into our coats. Sunday morning is always the best time to drive. The roads are deserted. The civilized world is in church or at the in-laws for lunch or at home with the Sunday edition. Unlike me, they were all resting up for work on Monday.

We jumped into Livy's new, unpaid-for Chevy Nova and cruised for twenty minutes. As always, I was behind the wheel. She navigated me south, then east. For two or three miles there were strolling Orthodox Jews everywhere we looked. This was the suburb of West Orange.

"Turn here!" she cried suddenly, pointing to a narrow fissure in the woods.

"Here?" I couldn't even see a footpath, much less a road.

"Just do it!"

The spoor was in a thatch of trees, well hidden from the fast-food restaurants, convenience stores, and service stations along Northfield Avenue. I yanked the wheel and steered over soft gravel past scraggly bushes and stripped maples and horse chest-nut trees, down a rough decline and around a bend into a clearing the size of a football field. On a wooden fence post a sign pro-claimed NO TRESPASSING in forbidding black letters.

"Stop here!" Livy's black eyes scanned the plain.

"Wow. . . . From the main road it's hard to believe there could be so much land back here," I said like an idiot.

"We owned it all," Livy whispered solemnly.

I checked her face. She wasn't putting me on.

"See that house over there? That's where I spent the first sev-enteen years of my life."

It was a rambling three-story pseudo-Victorian with boarded-up windows.

She nodded to my left. "And over there?" A mansion-sized colonial perched on top of a rolling hill.

"That's where my grandparents lived. Destroyed by fire, a mysterious fire. . . ."

Black scars rose in jagged tufts from the upper-story windows. I understood now where Livy's expensive tastes had their origin. Whoever had owned this spread must have been a millionaire a few times over.

"I haven't been back here in so long. . . ." The mask had

cracked. Her eyes were glassy with tears. I reached out to touch her, but she pushed me away. The entire scene was depressing, forlorn. At that moment for some reason, I thought of her old man creeping around outside our door when we were making it.

"Want to get out and walk around?"

For a long time Livy was quiet. Then she shook her head violently, as if trying to clear it or throw off some horrific recollection.

"No. Let's get out of here."

"Whatever you say."

I swung the car around. Livy's eyes changed from water to stone. When we were back on the main road, she wrapped her fingers around my prick.

"Let's go home, Max."

"Sure," I agreed. "Let's go home."

I ran my hand up under her skirt to the oven-warm crotch of her tights. It wasn't a good time to ask questions about the old homestead.

I stepped on it.

Despite Livy's weird emotional reaction, our little excursion turned into a ritual. Once every two or three weeks we had to climb into the car and drive out to the family "estate." Then we'd sit there in the hard glare of the spring sun and stare at the abandoned buildings; it was as if we were waiting for someone to arrive or emerge from one of the houses, or maybe for something to *happen*. Always in silence, and in Livy's eyes there was always that melancholic haze. I had no idea what the fuck it was all about.

From time to time she would drop disconnected hints about her past out there—not that they amounted to an epiphany. In fact, most often they merely surprised me because they were something I hadn't surmised or wouldn't have expected.

"My father was a carpenter. . . ."

"A carpenter? No shit. Now I wouldn't have guessed that."

"Yes, he married into my mother's money. He has a nose for a certain kind of woman."

Interesting. Or so I supposed.

"And bet you didn't know I have two sisters. Sherry lives in the city—she works on the sixty-fifth floor of the Empire State Building. Mary-Jo is somewhere in California. I haven't talked to her in years."

"Really. . . ."

"My mother hated my father with a passion. . . ."

"Hmm. . . ."

"My grandfather who owned this place was called Gaetano. When I was in school everyone made fun of his name. He came to this country from Palermo. Once upon a time he was one of the biggest slumlords in Newark."

All news to me. And still, I wasn't making a lick of sense out of what she was *really* saying, or trying to say, to me. She was dropping the pieces of a jigsaw puzzle into my lap without a guide to the big picture.

But I went along with it. What could it hurt, right? When you're in love, you go soft. You do things she wants you to do, even if what she wants you to do is a little wacky.

Sitting in the middle of a field staring at two gutted houses wasn't all so bad. In my time I'd done a lot worse.

12.

"Well, I did it!"

Livy flounced into the apartment and began stripping off her clothes. I rested my guitar against the arm of the sofa.

"What?"

"Dropped out of my classes!"

"Why? It's just a matter of weeks before your finals."

"So what? I'm not interested in a degree anyway. I mean, I'm just withering on the vine in that place. A bunch of old windbags blowing hot air around, that's all they are!"

"You'll get no argument from me on that score. It's just that. . . . well, you came this far, it seems like maybe you should have just seen it through until the end of the semester at least. I mean, you *did* do some of the work, right?"

"Are you kidding me, Max? I haven't done an *ounce* of work! Have you seen me pick up Keats or Wharton any time in the past four months?"

"Maybe you'd have used the degree some day. Like to get a job or something, if it came to that."

"You mean like you?"

"Me, I'm different. A completely different case. Leave me out of it."

"Since when are you so concerned with my professional career? I thought you and I were going to live. Travel. *Write.* I thought we weren't going to get caught like all the rest of them."

What she was saying was true—there was no denying it. Like I said, I could certainly talk a great game. It was just that I was of the mind that when you started a project—and were so close to finishing at least some portion of it—you should push through to the end. On occasions like this my working-class values still had the habit of rearing their ugly heads.

"Yes, but . . . why not at least finish the semester out and decide what to do later? That way you don't waste what you've already done. Not many people are lucky enough to win fellowships."

Livy shrugged. "You're not afraid, are you, Max?"

"Afraid of what? Hell, no, I'm not afraid. 'Course I'm not afraid."

"Because you can't be afraid to take chances in life."

"I just told you—"

"Look—we're going to be artists, and that's *that.* Those who can, do. Those who can't, attend a graduate program."

"Right."

I shut my trap, grabbed her around the waist, and pulled her toward me. Then I helped her out of more of her clothes. In her black brassiere and panties, she was a model out of the lingerie advertisements in the *New York Times Magazine.*

I forced my tongue deep into her mouth. I wanted her to shut up, too, and there was no better way to make her stop talking. There was always plenty of time for talking later.

A few days pass. One morning when I shake myself out of a deep coma I find myself alone. I feel the mattress beside me—cold. I shuffle out to the breakfast nook and rummage for a note. Nothing. I pull on my clothes and head out for the morning newspaper and a pack of smokes. When I get back, still no Livy. . . .

I went about my business, which on that day, as usual, did not include anything of particular importance. I killed time in all the usual ways. Late in the afternoon there was a thump on the door.

Here she is, finally, her arms laden with boxes and shopping bags.

"Jesus Christ, Liv, where the hell have you been? I was actually starting to worry," I said, helping her in with her stuff. "Looks like you've been shopping."

Shopping, nothing. It was more like she'd looted a few stores, and all the best at that: Bloomingdale's, Lord & Taylor, Neiman Marcus, Macy's.

"Want to see what I bought?"

"Sure, why not. . . ."

She disappeared into the bedroom. A long half hour later she reappeared in a revealing but elegant Givenchy evening gown and shiny new black heels. She was ravishing, with her luxuriant Asian hair pinned up in back, her bronze shoulders bare, and the flesh of her luscious melons bulging delicately.

"What do you think?"

"What do I think? Come over here, I'll show you what I think. Let me get my hands on you. . . ."

"No, no, no. You have to wait until the show is finished."

I grabbed a beer and resumed my seat on the sofa. For the next hour or so I was treated to a catwalk of sweaters and skirts, dresses, slacks and jeans, more gowns and evening dresses, shoes and frilly underwear, including garter belts and fishnet stockings.

"So *now* what do you think?" she asked after stripping nude and planting herself in front of me, hands on hips, in nothing but a pair of stiletto heels.

"I'm speechless."

"Which did you like best?"

"The getup you're in right now."

"No, I'm serious, you jerk!"

"Listen, they all look incredible on you."

"You seem less than overwhelmed or something."

"No, I am, really. I'm totally overwhelmed. . . . I'm just a little amazed you bought so *much*."

Her eyes sparked with irritation.

"You don't understand anything. You don't understand *me*."

"Come on, Liv. You know that's not true. And it ain't fair, either."

"I love clothes. Clothes make me feel good. Do I ever stop you from buying whatever you want?"

"No, but I never said you did. And besides, I never buy anything."

"I needed a new wardrobe. My things are falling apart."

"I hadn't noticed. You look fucking terrific in everything."

"You don't get women at all, do you, Max?"

"How did you pay for everything?"

"I charged it, how do you think?"

"*Charged* it . . . ?"

"Visa? Ever heard of it?"

"I'm just asking, is all."

"Don't worry about it. It'll get taken care of. Anyway, it's not your money."

"I didn't say it was. Baby, don't be upset with me. I'm just interested in what you're up to."

"Besides, I have ways of getting my money back."

"How's that?"

"Oh, never mind. You don't understand how things work."

The discussion ended the way every one of our discussions ended. Within seconds I had her on top of me, her tight, classical ass bobbing up and down on my rock-hard prong, her excited brown missile of a nipple between my teeth, my fingers holding on to the daggers of her high heels.

"Let's not argue, okay?"

"Okay. . . ."

"I mean, we shouldn't argue with each other, ever."

"Okay. . . ."

"We need each other. We're all we've got. It's you and me against the world."

"Right. . . . Still love me?"

"Feel that?"

"Okay, then."

And in this way the issue was settled—at least for the time being.

I never understood why Livy needed to dress in such finery to wait tables at the Purple Turtle, but two or three weeks later she decided that most of the stuff she'd bought on that binge had to go back.

"Didn't you already wear that thing to work?" I asked as I watched her tossing a silky violet pullover into its packaging.

"It's not right on me," she snapped. As if I was a complete dolt not to have noticed.

"I don't know—I thought it looked pretty damned sexy myself."

On that point she ignored me. "Are you coming with me or not?"

From the no-nonsense set of her jaw, I could see that my beauty was in an unusually determined frame of mind that Saturday morning. The mall parking lot was swarming with vehicles cruising for empty spots. Mall-crawling is the great suburban diversion, and you can't blame people—what else is there to do in the wasteland? Finally we landed something along the outer rim, which meant we'd have to lug our load damned near a quarter mile to the entrance.

The queue at Macy's was long; all bored housewives and tired career girls taking their sweet old time on the weekend. Every fucking transaction took forever. When we finally reached the register, Livy's resolve had given way to a brittle, unexplained disdain for the surroundings.

The twenty-something model wannabe with the nameplate identifying her as Giselle seemed bored and weary.

"I'd like a refund for this dress," Livy declared, pulling a diaphanous gown out of a bag.

With the tip of her tongue Giselle discreetly shifted the wad of chewing gum from the inside of her right cheek to her left.

"What's the problem?"

Giselle's voice was slightly nasal, annoying. Livy flipped the garment upside down.

"It's torn. Right here. You can see."

She pointed to a tear in the inseam at least three inches long.

"Was it this way when you bought it?"

Livy snorted. "Would I bring it back if it *wasn't*?"

Giselle looked from Livy's face to mine. Some uniquely feminine misgiving had appeared in her moss-green eyes. She pushed back a bang of pomaded hair and blew a stream of air through thin, lavender-coated lips.

"This hasn't been *worn*, has it?"

Livy glared.

"Because store policy states that if a garment has been worn even once—"

"I don't give a damn about store policy! I demand to see the manager!" Livy huffed.

"Look, there's really no need to—"

"I demand to see the manager *now*! *This minute!* Can't you understand English?"

Giselle glanced at me again. She was really quite attractive in her languid, indifferent, skinny fashion, a look that had never particularly appealed to me. Her expression was filled with a new skepticism, even fear of a confrontation. Maybe, too, she hoped that I would step in and intervene, slipping her off the hook of this embarrassing situation. After all, I was a man, wasn't I?

Moans and groans in the line behind us. "Make up your minds already!" someone muttered. I turned around. The queue had grown to a dozen customers. There were rolling eyes and nasty frowns. "Oh, for God's sake! This is the last time I ever come here on Saturday!" bitched another. "And only one cashier!" a third chimed in.

Giselle hoisted a telephone receiver from beneath the counter.

"Seven-one-one to women's wear. Seven-one-one to women's wear, please." The cashier was broadcasting our problem in code all over the store via the loudspeaker.

More griping behind us. The lousiest place in the civilized world to kick up a stink is in a long customer line in a ladies' wear department. Giselle leaned on her elbow and waited. Livy glowered, refusing to give an inch. When I tried to touch her, she flinched. Some of the customers behind us fell out of line and scattered. One middle-aged patron dumped her garments—pants suit and hosiery—into a bin brimming with brassieres on special sale and stormed off with a curse.

Seven-one-one appeared. She was a carbon copy of Giselle but forty years older. Her glasses sat primly on the tip of her nose and were attached to her neck by a black cord. She stared at Livy and me over the tortoiseshell frames.

"What seems to be the problem here?"

"This dress was flawed and I didn't notice until I got it home," fumed Livy.

Seven-one-one handled the dress with an adroitness born of years of experience.

"Mm-hmm, mm-hmm. Let me just have a look—"

"There's no need to look, lady," Livy shot back. "I just want my money back!"

Amazing. I never realized clothes could cause such a vile disturbance.

Seven-one-one ignored her. Evidently she'd heard it all before.

"The tags have been cut. . . ."

"Oh, for Christ's sake! I cut them because I thought the dress was in one fucking piece!"

Seven-one-one froze, then pointed. "This garment is stained. It's obviously been worn. This store would never sell a worn garment!"

Giselle's eyeballs twitched toward me again. Livy slammed the counter with her palm. "Are you accusing me of *lying*?"

"I'm not accusing you of anything, miss. I'm only saying that it appears this dress has been worn, and our policy is not to refund or exchange worn garments under any circumstance."

Livy's cheeks flushed a deeper shade of crimson.

"I demand to see your superior!"

"Liv, come on," I said, grabbing her arm. "Why don't we just forget it—"

"*Forget* it! And let them get away with this! No way! This is highway robbery! I want satisfaction, and I'll get it!"

It was bizarre. I'd never seen Livy like this before. I couldn't understand what had gotten into her. Worse, I hadn't noticed that tear in the dress during the modeling session, and if my memory served me well, I'd seen her walk out of the apartment wearing it one night for her shift at the Turtle.

Seven-one-one was immovable. A faint smile had begun to pull at Giselle's cheap purple lips. I felt like smashing her with a straight right, then crawling underneath one of the clothing racks.

"I'm sorry, Miss Tanga," said the manager.

"Oh, give it up already!" called a voice in the line behind us.

"Let's beat it, Liv," I tried again. "Who gives a fuck about their dress? I'll buy you a new one."

She turned on me like a cornered animal. *"Aren't you going to defend me?"*

"But Liv, I—"

"MAX!"

Motherfucker. I didn't give a damn for these salesgirls, either, but on the other hand, Livy *was* trying to sell them the Brooklyn Bridge—even I could see that. But the last thing I wanted to admit to myself was that Livy had put me in a bind.

I began to nudge her away from the counter. "Why don't we just chalk it up to experience. . . ."

"Because I don't *want* to chalk it up to experience! I want my goddamn money back! Or I'll never shop in this trash heap again!"

"Liv, it's not worth it! Let's just take your dress and get the hell out of here. . . ."

Giselle and Seven-one-one watched triumphantly as I swung Livy, spitting and smoldering, away from the counter.

"Can you believe some people!" sniffed the biddy next in line.

"Choke on it, bitch," I told her.

"Oh, go to hell, you too!" Livy barked as a parting shot.

I don't know how I managed to force her out of that place, but I did. Like a tornado she whirled through the mall and parking lot, dropping merchandise in her wake, and by the time I caught up with her she was already in the car.

I got in and drove. For a long time she refused to look at me or talk. No way I dared bring up her attempt to swindle the department store. Didn't I owe her the benefit of the doubt? Besides, even if she'd tried to take Macy's for a ride, who was I to judge? Mrs. London's phone calls to me had gone unanswered, hadn't they? What made me any better than Livy?

"You're supposed to be on my side, no matter what, Max," she hissed as we neared Roseland Avenue.

"I *am* on your side, Livy. . . ."

"Then why didn't you stand up for me—why?"

"Well, I—"

"If you love somebody, you're supposed to believe in them!"

"I do, baby, you have to see that I do—"

"But you didn't say a fucking word! You just stood there and let them humiliate me, Max!"

"I didn't! I mean, I didn't *mean* to—"

"Do you love me, Max?"

"Of course! God, yes! You know I do!"

"Then you have to promise you're with me forever, no matter what! You have to *promise*!"

"I'm with you!"

"Promise?"

"Promise!"

"Oh, Max. . . ."

It was a plaintive wail, like the cry of a wounded bird, and it came from a place much darker and deeper and sadder than the urge to fraud or kleptomania.

"Yes, Liv?"

She didn't finish what she was about to say. I pulled her over to me, hard. I grabbed her hand and guided it to my cock. Her fingers coiled like snakes around my stick. I slid my hand up her skirt and inside the band of her bikini panties.

She was wet in there. Very, very wet.

13.

The Macy's debacle was the only black cloud that passed over our idyll. It was a momentary aberration, nothing more. But as with any storm, there was fallout. Sometimes, lying naked on the bedroom floor, Livy would snare me in a debate of extravagant speculations.

"If I were asleep on the twentieth floor of a burning building, would you rush in and save me, even if you'd probably die in the process?"

"Jesus, Livy, that's insane."

"Would you, Max? I have to know!"

I'd tell her "Of course I would," just to soothe her peculiar anxieties.

"Are you sure? Do you swear?"

"I swear!"

"Now . . . what if you came upon me as I was being raped by a gang of six thugs, and you didn't have a weapon, and it probably meant your getting seriously injured trying to help me—what would you do then?"

"Whew, sweetheart, you sure can dream them up. . . ."

"I have to know, Max!"

"I'd do whatever it took to free you."

"Do you swear, Max?"

"Yes, I swear."

"That's the right answer."

"Well, I'm glad. . . . Why are we going through all this, anyway?"

"Because I have to *know*. It means everything to me."

Pause.

"Why didn't you defend me that day in Macy's, Max?"

"Oh, shit, Liv. How many times have I explained it to you? That was completely different! You weren't under attack. I was just trying to save you the trouble of fighting a battle you obviously weren't going to win."

"I could have won it if I stayed there and battled it out."

"Whatever. But if you saw it my way, you'd understand that I was actually defending you, Liv. . . ."

You can't really ever win an argument with a woman, but most of the time I could at least half convince Olivia Aphrodite of my intentions. Other times it wasn't so easy, and the row would drag on into the wee hours, until I'd find myself crawling off to bed well after Carson and Tom Snyder put the lid on another day of disappointment for America, wondering about the point of it all. . . .

Meanwhile, as the balmy days coasted by in a slow train of circus balloons, I had the eerie sensation of tumbling headlong into a sort of cotton-headed limbo. I'd wake up to the lazy symphony of the birds and the tranquil spectacle of the sun's golden rays pouring through the window, and I had to question where in the world I was headed. . . . Livy, too. Because I knew we couldn't go on like this—completely without direction—forever. Since I had little to do during the days but read my books and newspapers and magazines, it couldn't escape me that people younger than myself had already achieved worldwide recognition for their achievements. That the illustrious careers of some were already long over by the time they reached my age. That such towering figures as Mozart and Alexander the Great had already brought the world—or at least some portion of it—to its knees in homage. What had I done, by contrast? Nothing. Not the crappiest little thing. Dreams and plans and resolutions added up to less than zero. Worse, I had no idea *what* to do, or even what I was *capable* of doing—*if* I was capable of doing anything at all. Where in the world had I come by the idea that I possessed some sort of illustrious future as an artist in the first place—me, a product of the ethnic ghetto, the offspring of blue-collar drones who'd had to struggle for their daily bread from the cradle straight on through to the grave? What gall! What stupid audacity! What ludicrous castles built in the air! The fact was that I *had* no discernible talent. Through all the years of school and shit jobs, no one had ever given me the slightest encouragement of my abilities, let alone genius, except for a handful of club owners who needed cheap background music for their patrons and bosses who took on Neanderthals to stuff their trucks. . . .

Then I'd look at Livy, asleep there beside me, and I'd slowly drag my fingers over her perfect tits to the heavy black down between her legs, and all my anguish seemed completely ridiculous.

After all, what were a few million words more or less on this earth? Why fret over posterity when the sun, as I'd read somewhere, is certain to run out of hydrogen and commence dying in one billion, one hundred million years? On that day, who was going to remember the purveyors of measly words?

In life, you can't ask for the moon and the planets. It's definitely best to learn to be content with the small things, if you can. Only a few lucky ones—the Rockefellers and Gettys and Mellons—hold winning lottery tickets.

No, none of it was worth taking too seriously. Hadn't I realized the deep uselessness of existence a long time ago? Most definitely I had, when I was just a little kid and first took notice of what was going on all around me. I decided to live with that essential truth in mind.

Until the next attachment Livy decided to jettison—her job at the Purple Turtle.

That night she came home in a high snit. *What happened?* I wanted to know.

"I'm not going into it! I just decided I've had enough. I don't want to spend my life waiting tables for jerks and fools. Anything wrong with that?"

"Not a thing. I'm the last one to blame you for wanting your freedom. So what are we going to do now?"

"I don't know—maybe you can think of something."

What it added up to was that now we were without a source of income unless I came up with a gig. For the past several weeks, I'd been living off Livy's largesse.

"Well, I guess I could try Manpower again, or—"

"Don't sweat it, Max. Something will come up."

Sure, I thought, *something will come up. But it'll be my dick— which can't sign checks.*

talked Livy into hitting the road for a while. Why not? We had no obligations and nothing to hang around for. We locked the apartment, packed up my old Impala, and started driving, without a destination. I loved that old dinosaur; it had been with me for years through thick and thin, even surviving a ramrod front-fender shot from a pickup truck on a foggy highway outside Toronto shortly after I bought her. In those days everybody drove V–8s, it was nothing to be ashamed of. . . .

Whenever I set out I thought of all the great ones before me who'd taken to the road: Rimbaud . . . Miller . . . Hamsun . . . Dylan. (Never Kerouac and that bunch. I never did get what that Beat shit was all about.) When in doubt, I always headed west. It was a stunning morning and our spirits were high. The asphalt in front of us was like the promise of an unfurling destiny—which was nothing but romantic bullshit, but I had to believe that we were traveling for a reason. For the first few hours the open highway was great, until Livy began to get the fidgets from sitting on her ass too long. We decided to spend the night in a rustic cabin in some godforsaken western Pennsylvania forest. The accommodations were less than first class, but for twenty-five bucks we weren't about to get the Hilton.

I was outside gazing at Venus and Jupiter with a smoke and a beer when Livy came up behind me.

I want to go back home tomorrow morning.

Why?

No real reason. I'm just not in the mood for this roughing it crap.

I knew what that meant. Women have this thing about bathrooms with all the amenities. The Whispering Pines didn't even feature hot water as an attraction.

Come on, I said. You haven't given yourself much of a chance. How about we try one more day. Maybe you'll change your mind.

If you don't drive back to New Jersey first thing tomorrow morning, I'm going by myself.

There was nothing more to say.

14.

Sometimes without explanation Livy would disappear for long clips of the day, leaving me to wonder where the hell she'd gotten to. She'd show up finally toward evening laden with new stuff for the apartment—a loveseat we just had to have, an expensive Persian rug she couldn't resist, a wok we'd be sure to get tons of use out of. More often than not, there'd be a bag full of new duds, too.

Knowing that she'd used her credit cards for the binges, I'd try to sneak in a question about how she planned to pay for the items when the invoices arrived at the end of the month—especially with both of us being out of work and the last bill having gone unattended.

"How many times do I have to tell you? Shopping makes me feel better. And stop fretting, Max—it'll get taken care of one way or another."

She had reserves I wasn't privy to—that had to be it. No way Livy would purposely plunge herself into a slough of debt she couldn't extricate herself from—she was far too intelligent for something like that.

But I had my doubts. Not enough, though, to go out and scare up a job.

———

By now I was exasperated and bored with the melancholy that resulted from our weekend pilgrimages out to the old family "estate." No doubt Livy's dejection had to do with the fact that her parents had split up. But I had to cop to a nagging curiosity, too.

"If you miss your family so much, why don't we just go visit one of them?"

"You don't get it. It's not that easy."

"Okay, I'm sure it's not. But why not just face whatever it is that bothers you? That's always the best way—face up to it. Besides, I'll be there. That has to count for something, right?"

To that she had nothing to say. But when her old man phoned not long afterward, she agreed to go over to his newest digs, and she was bringing me along. She hadn't seen the guy in over two years.

"I just hope I did the right thing," she sighed after hanging up.

"You did, no question. And I'll be there, don't forget. What could possibly go wrong?"

Now we're getting somewhere, I thought.

Livy's father was holed up in a second-floor flat in the old North Ward of Newark. It was a quiet neighborhood—as in funeral-parlor quiet. We squeezed the Nova into a tight spot and walked around to the back of the orange baked-brick two-family house.

Livy was jittery. She tripped more than once in her platform heels.

"Just relax," I encouraged her, tossing my smoldering cigarette butt into a hedge. "If it's too much to handle, we'll just split, got it?"

We climbed the wooden staircase that gave out on a view of

two-by-four backyards, some with plots full of the tangled vines of tomato and pepper plants. Enrico Tanga made us wait before he opened up. Was he having his revenge on us for freezing him out that afternoon when he'd surprised us in the act? You can always count on people to be weird that way.

Livy's papa was handsome—I could see right off where she'd inherited her swarthiness and lush head of hair. His clothes— plaid shirt and khaki trousers—were neatly pressed. Despite his lack of ostentation, there was something of the delicate dandy about him. Latin dudes from the old school—they all think they're Valentino or Sinatra.

"Come on in," he said, letting us into the sun-splashed kitchen. I took note that he and his daughter did not touch. Odd— especially for dagos.

Livy introduced me. We shook hands. There was nothing much in the place—a ficus tree with sagging leaves in one corner; a few sticks of plain, functional furniture; a stove with an old-fashioned stainless-steel pot; a three-quarter-sized refrigerator. The sum of its parts suggested a man who was not planning on staying very long—or who wasn't really living there at all.

We sat around the small table. Enrico broke out a jug of Chi-anti and poured three glasses.

"So—what is it you do, Max?" he said without looking at me.

"Musician . . . I'm, uh, trying to write, too."

He didn't press for details, which was lucky for me. He was much more interested in his daughter. There was some unspoken tension between them that I couldn't put a finger on. I wrote it off as the typical family antagonism.

He asked a few perfunctory questions about the circumstances of her life—nothing about her screams of passion that afternoon we'd been going at it—before getting on to the crux of the issue.

"Talked to your sisters?"

"No."

"Mm-hmm. . . . Heard from your mother?"

"No. . . ."

"Doesn't surprise me. . . . You thought of getting in touch with her?"

Livy shrugged.

"I'm sure she's conquering the world with her precious career and all that. Well, I just hope she's happy with her life now—after what she did to the rest of us."

I kept watch on Livy. She shifted uneasily in her chair.

"Right, Liv? Wouldn't you agree with me on that?"

That's when she bridled. "I don't want to get into all that again! It's none of my business! That's between you and her!"

"Hey—all I'm saying is that your mother was the cause of all the—"

"It was you, too!" Livy cried, catapulting out of her seat like a surface-to-air missile. "Don't forget that! Don't you forget it for a second!"

She grabbed her purse and turned to me. "I'm getting out of here! Are you coming with me or not?"

She bolted for the door. Enrico jumped up and tried to block her way.

"Olivia! All I wanted was to talk to you! Don't go getting all bent out of shape here!"

But his daughter evaded his grasp. A pained grimace creased his face as he watched her stomp down the stairs.

"Nice meeting you, Mister Tanga," I mumbled, passing him.

"Take it easy, kid." I had the feeling he was about to add something—like "keep banging the piss out of her" or something of that sort—but maybe I was just being paranoid.

I followed Livy down to the street. What the hell happened? The guy seemed all right to me, and I told her so.

"No, Max—*you don't fucking get it.*"

"All right. I guess I don't." And there was no talking to her at all on the ride back to Roseland Avenue.

But the touchy encounter produced an altogether unexpected effect. When Livy stepped out of the shower a half hour later, it was as if she'd swallowed a brick of Spanish fly or some other powerful aphrodisiac. She gripped my dick and steered me toward the bed, where she seemed to want to devour me whole. It was the best session we had in weeks—and none was ever bad.

"So what in the world happened in that crazy house of yours?" I asked afterward when I lay there smoking a cigarette.

"Sure you want to know?"

"Hell yes, I want to know. Why wouldn't I want to know?"

She stared hard at the ceiling.

"He molested me."

"Who?"

"Who do you think?"

I got up on my elbow and looked at her. She was wearing the mask again.

"*What?* You're saying your father—"

"My two sisters, too."

"Jesus Christ." So *that* was it.

"The entire family knew about my father. And it wasn't just us he was after. It was some of the other girls, too, my cousins, our friends. . . ."

"The lousy bastard. Didn't anyone try to stop him?"

"Oh, he was sly. It was all broom closets and basements and stairwells when nobody was looking. And none of us knew that it was happening to the next person. We all thought it was just *us*. Divide and conquer, as they say."

"What a fucking creep."

In my brain I conjured up incestuous scenes. I got angry. Then horny all over again.

"What—what did he do to you?"

"Put his hands all over me. Kissed me. Groped inside my clothes. Some other wonderful stuff."

" 'Some other wonderful stuff'? Like what?"

She turned her head away.

"Like what? Did he fuck you?"

She wasn't talking. In my mind's eye I tried to picture Enrico Tanga in that compromising position, but I had trouble with it.

Was Livy dishing out the truth? Of course she was! She had to be! Why would she lie about something like incest?

"Why didn't you tell me about this before?"

She made a face.

"But it wasn't just that vileness that came between him and my mother when she finally found out. It was everything else. The fact that he was from the wrong side of the tracks. That he's a lowlife from Newark, as she liked to call him. That he wanted his daughters to stay home and wait on him hand and foot like a Sicilian nobleman rather than get an education. That he wasn't interested in becoming anything better than a carpenter. That his grand ambition in life was to sit around the house and drink wine and eat pasta. . . . You should have seen the *fights*. Once, when my mother locked him out, he tore down the front door of the house out there on the compound. I mean literally *ripped it off its hinges*. I was never so scared in my life. We actually hid under the beds thinking he was going to murder us. Thank God for the police. If it wasn't for them, I might not be alive right now. Maybe none of us would. And she claims that my little sister, Mary-Jo, was the result of a drunken rape one night after they'd come home from a party. . . ."

Okay. So I'd screwed up. It had been a piss-poor idea to coax Livy into a reunion with her father. Next time I'd keep my big mouth shut.

A gang of kids was screeching with delight at some game it was playing down in the street. The late-afternoon sun slanted across the twisted blue sheets, creating an effect that was ineffably sad, like everything else in the whole wide world.

"Now do you get it, Max?"

For that day, there was nothing left to say.

15.

"My mother has a nose for things, too. Whenever my father comes into the picture, she's not far behind, even if we haven't talked for a year. Don't ask me how she does it. She doesn't even know where I'm living."

Sure enough, not long after we saw Livy's old man, the telephone rang and damned if it wasn't the missus.

Livy shrugged after hanging up. "Well, since we're at it, you should probably make the queen's acquaintance."

By now I knew that I had damaged goods on my hands—not that any of us on earth are in one piece. But it was as if Livy felt compelled to demonstrate to me the balancing end of the sick equation.

The offices of T&C Realty were located on the second floor of a row of tony storefronts above the twin movie theater in the posh suburban village of Millburn. Mrs. Tanga had managed to extricate herself from her marriage and start up her own company, which had grown into one of the most successful in the county.

It was a Thursday evening. Office hours were already over for the day. The anteroom was empty except for several heavy gray desks whose surfaces were covered with fat directories and multiline telephone sets. Livy knocked on the door of the inner sanctum.

"On the phone—I'll be with you in a minute!"

Her mother's voice was brassy and hard. Stenciled on the door were the words "Clara Tanga, Licensed Realtor." Translation: She was the big chief.

From the other side of the door we heard fragments of the one-sided conversation, all delivered in a no-bullshit, imperious tone. A few minutes passed. Livy and I stood there gawking at each other.

"Let's get the fuck out of here," she whispered, though she didn't go for the exit.

"We came all this way. Why not stay?" After making the acquaintance of Enrico, I was more curious than ever.

Moments later, there were a few hard, purposeful footsteps, then the door swung open.

The figure that appeared was diminutive but strikingly attractive in her spiffy businesswoman's suit and just-so bob haircut. Large emerald-green eyes were the dominant note in her finely chiseled face. Once upon a time this woman had been a beauty, and she wasn't all that bad now—shit, I'd nail her in a heartbeat. The apple had certainly not fallen far from the tree.

We shook hands. Clara offered us a pair of chairs. At once static electricity crackled between the females.

The conversation was all about people they had in common, business acquaintances and such—no mention of the family whatsoever. All the while, Livy's mother checked me out from the corner of her eye, very unobtrusively to be sure, but I caught her at it all right. With my beard and long hair, I couldn't imagine that I'd be the Chamber of Commerce's cup of tea.

"So what is it you do again, Max?" she asked, all phony smiles.

"Livy mentioned something, but it seems to have slipped my mind."

Musician, writer, etc. Big mistake.

"I see. . . . Now I'm just curious, so I hope you don't mind my asking—*do you make any real money at something like that?*"

The question was like a hard slap in the face. It's a bitch that most times you don't catch on to the full intent of a remark until it's just a little too late for an appropriately smart-assed reply.

I yammered out something about millionaire rock stars and Nobel laureate novelists by way of self-justification, conveniently neglecting to mention my own nullity of income.

The purpose of this exchange was for the business tycoon to gauge exactly what her daughter had in this new boyfriend of hers. Not much, she had to be thinking, though the congenial expression never left her lips. For all I knew, she approved. I glanced at Livy. Smoke was puffing out of her ears.

"I'll call you," Mrs. Tanga nodded at her daughter. "We'll get together for dinner sometime."

Uh-oh. Mother was going to offer daughter her *opinion* of me. What else could it mean?

"Have you heard from your father?" Clara asked, just as we were about to make our escape.

"A little while back. . . ."

"Well, well, well—he actually picked up the phone? *Hah!* I can hardly believe it! If you ever need anything, you make sure you ask *him*. That skinflint can spare a few bucks! What does *he* have to spend money on? The son of a bitch never sends me anything for Mary-Jo as it is! And he's got that new girlfriend paying his way already, so I hear!"

This was a new one on Livy; I saw the surprise register in her eyes.

"I'll tell you all about it later, don't worry," Clara told her daughter like a conspirator. "Anyway, better *her* than me."

Her disdain for her ex-husband was palpable, and it wasn't mere jealousy. It was more like pure hatred. The attack left me feeling a trace of guilt. After all, what was I but a sponge, too? It wasn't like I wanted it that way, but. . . .

"So how about it—think your mom liked me?" I joked when we were on the sidewalk.

"My mother doesn't like *anybody*, including me. Sorry to disappoint you, Max."

Livy looked a bit green around the gills. She complained of a splitting headache before we even neared the Millburn city line. This time she didn't make a grab for my cock.

The next morning. . . . Livy points to her dry, cracked lips and gives a shake of her head. Her eyes were squinched in agony. I roll over off my pillow and move my face close to hers.

"What is it?"

"Water. Get me some water, please. . . ."

Her teeth are clenched. She can't seem to open her mouth.

I ran into the bathroom and filled a cup. The liquid had the desired effect of loosening her jaws and tongue. Like a doctor, I ventured a look inside. Milky-white pustules covered every centimeter of the moist walls and roof of her mouth—a downright ghastly sight. The angry cankers made the slightest movement of her mouth an agonizing torture. Since any attempt at speech broke the sores open, there was nothing the poor girl could do but lie helplessly in the dark. I spent the day running back and forth to the bedroom with any palliative I could think of, from camphor to cracked ice.

Not a goddamn thing worked. For days the lesions remained intractable, resistant like some new strain of stubborn virus to every conceivable ministration. When the pain got to be too much for Livy, I stripped off my clothes and crawled into bed beside her.

Finally she couldn't take it anymore. There was nothing else to do but seek professional treatment. I packed her into the car and drove her to Livingston to see Doctor Brownstein. He took one look and pronounced it the worst—and strangest—case of oral canker sores he'd ever seen, and he'd been an oral surgeon for twenty-five years. He did his best to close them with oxygen blasts but without success; an attack like this had to run its course. Since the doc couldn't figure out why the plague had appeared in the first place, he advised Livy to go home, take a few aspirin, and try to relax. . . .

16.

At the end of the month, the latest Visa invoice arrived. The insidious thing about charge cards is that you tend to forget you've used them. I don't know exactly what had been going on in Livy's head when she'd made all those extravagant purchases, but as they say, the chickens had come home to roost.

When I caught a glimpse of the total, I almost passed out on the spot.

"Jesus fucking Christ—$2,175! That's a lot of jack, baby."

Livy made a dash for the utility drawer and came back to the kitchen table with a pair of scissors. Then she turned her purse upside down, opened her wallet, plucked out the offending plate, and proceeded to cut it into strips before my eyes.

"What the hell are you doing?"

"Just making sure it doesn't happen again."

"Good idea. You don't want to have to deal with another bill like that monster."

"You must be joking! I don't know how I'm going to deal with *this* one."

"What do you mean?"

"There isn't a penny in my checking account."

"What? *What?*"

"Just what I said. I'm flat broke."

"I don't get it. Then why did you go out and buy all that stuff?"

"Because I had to."

"But I mean, how did you expect to *pay* for it?"

"I thought maybe you'd toss in something to help."

"*Me?* I mean I would, but—Liv, I don't have two fucking nickels to rub together, you know that."

"But you've been living here all this time free of charge."

"Free of—what's that got to do with anything?"

It was the first time I'd ever heard anything close to an accusation from Livy's lips.

"Then let them come and take me away. What can they do to me after all—throw me into debtors' prison?"

All the overused clichés when it came to women swarmed my brain. Irrational. Flighty. Unfathomable. Completely unreasonable. Man, I didn't get this one at all. But when you're in love, what are you supposed to do? You stand back and see her as the greatest of natural wonders, to be admired and feared at the same time, but never understood.

Nevertheless, Livy's dereliction felt like a noose tightening around my neck. I had another pang of guilt over shacking up with her all this time and not coughing up a red cent for my share of the ride. On the other hand, she'd never asked.

I pulled her onto my lap. The luscious curves of her flanks melted into me like butter on hot bread.

"So what can we do? We'll just have to find some way to deal with it," I whispered, jabbing the tip of my tongue into her ear.

"Yeah? How?"

"I don't know, but we will. Don't we always?"

"I guess. . . . Maybe I can go out and walk the streets. Think I'd be able to drum up any business?"

"I don't see why not. Hey, June Miller did it for Henry."

I had a laugh over that bit of literary lore. Livy didn't. She was thinking hard about something else. What it was she wouldn't say. Before I knew it she was straddling me.

As always when confronted with an unpalatable reality, we went out and celebrated, convinced that it would all be better tomorrow. That night we selected the Lotus Flower on Bloomfield Avenue, our very favorite Chinese joint, the most expensive of the lot. We shared the steamed dumpling appetizers. Sautéed beef with asparagus stalks for her. Jumbo prawns with lobster sauce for me. A bottle of Pinot Grigio—we went the whole route. I used some of my dwindling stash to pay for it.

Livy's fortune read YOU WILL ALWAYS BE LUCKY WHEN IT COMES TO MAKING MONEY.

That made her happy. "And you know what's really weird? These things are always right!"

Mine was more cryptic: TOMORROW IS NOT ALWAYS A NEW DAY. SOMETIMES TOMORROW IS THE SAME AS TODAY.

I felt vaguely goaded to do something about Livy's oversized tab, but when push came to shove I did nothing. Nothing at all. In life, it's always easier to do nothing unless you feel the heat. And who could know, ultimately, when the heat would be turned up? Despite all evidence to the contrary, I always believed in the last-second reprieve. . . .

Like that leaf in the muddy river, I went on drifting. Some afternoons, agitated by an uncontrollable sexual mania that went beyond my desire for Livy, I jumped into the Impala and drove over to the triple-X theater at the Willowbrook Mall, where I laid down a fin to watch a double bill of suck-and-fuck films. Surrounded by losers, perverts, and dirty old men, I let myself be carried away on a sea of celluloid fornication. When it was over, rather than duck into the rancid john and jerk off, I'd bring a Louisville Slugger of a hard-on and the idea for a spectacular, acrobatic sexual position—such as the female standing on her head like a meditating Yogi—back to the apartment and try it out on Livy. She was always willing.

But I couldn't afford the flicks every day. To kill time, maybe I'd sit for an hour in the laundry room watching our clothes tumble monotonously behind the window of the dryer. Or listen to my old records on the stereo. And of course there was always the public library only a short half block away, where I could murder hours by the cartload dozen while wandering through the stacks picking up every last obscure title.

It was there, in the Mystery section, where I stumbled blindly and fortuitously into the world of Georges Simenon. Life will always bring a man at the right moment to his appropriate destination. Not only were those short novels (the non-Maigrets only) hypnotic and riveting on their own merits, but I sensed a powerful affinity with each of the hapless protagonists who'd been trapped like a rat in some situation beyond his control. I went from one intriguing title to the next—*The Train*, *The Innocents*, *The Man on the Bench in the Barn*—with the uncanny certitude that I was perusing—even living out—one more version of my own life, even though the dramas were being played out on the other side of the world.

Because despite the fact that I could walk away from Livy anytime I wanted to—and I didn't *want* to—I had the growing sensation of being caught, like a fish swimming blindly into a seine. . . .

17.

Livy's canker sores eventually disappeared, but her Visa invoice didn't. Nor did any of the others—water, gas and electric, telephone, etc. When the first notices of serious delinquency began to arrive by mail, then the dire warnings, to be followed by the telephone calls at all hours from company reps indifferent to the reasons why Livy's fiduciary obligations could not be met, there was no longer any avoiding the inevitable—which was to own up to the fact that money was owed and that it had to be paid.

Though we tried to do just that—avoid the inevitable. For weeks running we refused to pick up the phone when it rang. Any piece of mail not carrying a return address—the telltale sign of the bill collector—was immediately tossed unopened into the trash. We even tried staying away from the apartment for as long as possible, walking the streets, hiding in the library, loitering at the diner, hitting the cheap afternoon movie matinees, or watching the American Legion baseball games at the diamond behind the apartment building in the musky twilight.

But no matter what you do, you can't avoid the machine forever. After Livy was threatened with legal proceedings by registered mail, she decided the time was ripe for action.

I sat at the kitchen table and eavesdropped while she dialed her father and put in a request for a bailout loan to be made as soon as possible. He hemmed and hawed, but finally gave in. Maybe it was guilt over what he'd done to his daughter in the past that made him loosen his purse strings—or maybe he wanted to get his paws on her again. Whatever it was, the following evening I ducked out for a walk before Enrico came around with a check for seven hundred bucks, a sum that would have the effect of turning down the heat on Livy and me for at least a short while. A very short while.

That night as we lay in the dark listening to the traffic pass on the avenue below, Livy sobbed quietly.

"At first I thought that you'd take me away from all this, Max. I really did. That's all I ever wanted—somebody to take me away from all this."

It cut me to the quick when she said things like that. There was such pathetic sorrow in her voice it damned near tore the heart out of me. What made it all worse was that I wasn't going anywhere myself.

"Everything will be all right," I tried to convince her, though I didn't believe it myself. They say that having money is the root of all evil, but I could never figure out why. Everybody knows that the truth is just the opposite.

18.

"It's hard to explain how and why, but . . . something's wrong," I stammered out to the willowy, middle-aged blonde sitting on the other side of the dented metal desk.

"Try to put it into words. Just try, in any way you know how."

Ms. Bentford's translucent blue eyes radiated genuine sympathy. *For a shrink, she's a fucking knockout,* I was thinking, all the while struggling to translate my psychic discomfort into something halfway intelligible.

My heart was beating like a trip-hammer. I took another hit off my cigarette. What the fuck was I doing here? What urge had driven me to seek out low-cost counseling at the community mental health center? Whatever it was, it had been powerful enough to bring me to this tight second-floor office on South Fullerton Avenue. In those days, with the demise of religion, there was great belief in "the Couch" as a cure-all for soul sickness. Over the years I'd been attracted to the idea of a fix-up by a trained pro (since I strongly suspected I was in need of it), I'd read widely in the field, from the classics like Freud and Jung all the way up to the quacks like Janov and Laing, but now that the moment of truth had arrived, I was tongue-tied. Max Zajack was a man, for Christ's sake, and men should be able to handle their own baggage. I *was* a man, *wasn't* I? Damned right I was! But where I'd expected a cathartic moment of insight when I finally submitted my case for examination, all I found instead was the ugly reality of the drab office and the dullness of the muggy afternoon.

"Well, you see . . . my life . . . it's not—it's not really *going* anywhere. . . ."

Lame. Impotent. And not really the truth—it *was* going somewhere, and that somewhere was straight down the toilet—but it was the best I could do.

"I see," said Ms. Bentford. "Maybe it would help if you told me a little about yourself. What your life is like right now, for starters."

Well, that was something I could do. I laid out the facts as dispassionately as I could: That I was busted and out of work. That I was living with Olivia Aphrodite. That I was in love with her. That anything I'd attempted as a creative artist—which hadn't been all that much, truth to tell—had come to naught. That lately I'd been harboring nebulous fears about . . . *everything*.

"I know it doesn't really shed light on what's bothering me. . . . so I guess I don't really know what the hell it is."

"Does it comfort you to know that all the people who come through that door feel pretty much the same way?"

It didn't. And what did I have to feel lousy about, after all? Wasn't I merely the victim of my own laziness, my own inability to cope with the world as it was? And whose fault was that? Nobody ever asked me to think of myself as an "artist," nobody told me to walk off the one thousand and one jobs I'd held, nobody had forced me at gunpoint into a ditch of debt. I was young. I was healthy. I could work. Most of my life lay before me—maybe.

And, too, I had Olivia.

So what the hell was my problem?

Though nothing got resolved, I walked out of there feeling a little better than when I went in, if for no other reason than that someone was trying to understand. I even found myself speculating on the personal life of my shrink. Married? Kids? Available? It was a good sign that I could think about fucking. But of course I always thought about fucking.

The sliding-scale fee for my initial consultation was a scant five bucks. I asked the receptionist if I could pay later. Presently without income, I explained. Okay, she said. People do it all the time.

It came as a jolt when I reported for my six thirty session a few weeks later and discovered that Ms. Bentford was a footnote in the agency's history.

"I don't get it," I complained to the receptionist. "I saw her five times, and she never indicated that she'd be leaving."

"It was a last-minute decision, I'm afraid. In fact, she's left the state to open a private practice. We were all quite surprised by it, actually."

"Damn. . . ." I was utterly crestfallen. That's the way it always went. Find something half decent and before you know it, it's gone. And Ms. Bentford and I were just beginning to get somewhere.

"Mrs. Dintenfaus will be taking on Ms. Bentford's patients."

"Who?"

She pointed to an open office door, where a pig-faced, bespectacled figure with a functional crop of dyed red hair sat hunched over a fat textbook. She glanced up at me and frowned. I didn't like the looks of the bitch at all. If you're putting your fate into a woman's hands, she at least has to look like a flesh-and-blood human being.

"You know what? I'm going to think it over."

"Are you sure? Mrs. Dintenfaus is the head of our agency. She's considered one of the best in her field."

"Maybe later. . . ."

"We would rather not have our patients to go away dissatisfied with the quality of our service."

"It's not that. It's not that at all." I waved my hand. "As a matter of fact, I'm feeling fine. Great. Better than I have in months. Those sessions with Ms. Bentford did the trick."

"All right. . . ." The receptionist sounded skeptical. "If you need further help, please don't hesitate to come back and see us."

"I won't."

She looked disappointed. Before I could make it out the door, she consulted her ledger.

"Your total invoice is thirty dollars. Will you be paying today?"

"Tell you what. Drop it in the mail and I'll be sure to take care of it."

I was getting used to telling that story. A little too used to it. I turned on my heel and bolted.

19.

We went through that mini-loan from Livy's old man like it was lunch money. When the dust settled and the change was counted, we were still in arrears straight across the board. And she couldn't go back to Enrico for more.

"Now what?" I asked when we'd polished off the hummus and pita (a dish Livy'd learned during the course of her relationship with Basil).

"You tell me, Max. I'm all out of brilliant ideas."

"Well, you still are gorgeous," I said, thinking of having her for dessert.

"We can't go on unless you help me, Max. I can't carry the load all by myself. We're both going to have to do something, and fast."

"Maybe we overextended ourselves."

"But I need nice things. I can't live in a rathole."

"Well, this place isn't exactly what I'd call skid row."

"It's not exactly what I'd call the Taj Mahal, either."

She was bummed. What she said was certainly true, but I was beginning to see that I was on Mars and she was on Neptune when it came to how to get by in life, to say the least. Me, I could make it on a lot less than Livy could, for sure. But I was in. I was going to have to hold up my end now, no matter what. Writing and music and philosophy and books and all the rest of it were going to have to go on the back burner while we tried to crawl out of the pit we'd dug for ourselves.

That Livy scored first wasn't exactly a surprise. Whenever a hot piece strolls into your place and asks for a job, you'd be crazy not to find something for her to do, and fast. What did surprise me, however, was what she snagged: the position of administrative assistant at Temple B'Nai Jeshurun in ritzy Short Hills.

"You sure you're up to this?" I said after Rabbi Chaim Rosenberg formally phoned the offer in. "Don't you think you should have waited it out for something else? I mean, what the hell do you know about Judaism?" What was more, with her wild and impulsive nature, she would have been my last choice to lock up in an office.

According to Livy, all her neighbors growing up, as well as most of her mother's clientele, were Jews. She was conversant with their calendar and customs, and she felt a kinship with the faith, if not in blood then in sentiment. The salary was decent, too—don't let's forget that. And besides, it was only for a short while, until we got back on our feet.

There was another thing. She knew how to handle Jews. The religious types at the temple would be a piece of cake. She'd certainly *slept* with enough Jewish men.

"Oh, yeah?"

There was Peter Feldman, and David Lorenberg, and Donald Robinson. Those were just the guys she could recall off the top of her head.

"I thought you had a thing for Arabs."

No, Basil was the only Arab she'd ever had. There were lots more Jews. What did it matter? They were all Semites. And the thing with Don Robinson was quite serious. He was the son of a doctor. Very intelligent. Very ambitious. But sexually he had his quirks.

"Oh, really? You never mentioned him before. Sexual quirks, you say . . . such as?" I felt myself getting turned on.

"He believed that the woman's anus would dilate when she had an orgasm. That he could feel it when he put his fingers in there. That when he—oh, I don't want to get into this now."

"But I do!"

"Some other time. Besides, you haven't come up with anything yet and unless we pay the rent, we're going to be out on the street in ninety days." (A new warning about the consequences of unpaid back rent had arrived in the mail the day before.)

"If you want, I'll split if that will help," I offered lamely.

"No! Just help me out. That's all I ask!"

Done. And now, for the first time in my life, it was time to upgrade—no more loading docks, no more factories, no more low-wage crap. Above all, no more daydreams of artistic grandeur.

I began to religiously comb the "Help Wanteds." At the library I dug out a manual on proper résumé format and stretched my meager white-collar experience across the page until it looked like something nearly legitimate. Amazing how resourceful an unresourceful bugger can be when his back is to the wall.

Besides the ubiquitous agencies with names like A-Plus Temps and Office Power, I mailed out envelopes full of my credentials wherever there was a fit—and even where there was no fit that I could perceive, my strategy being that some scattered buckshot is bound to hit the bull's-eye.

To my surprise, I didn't have long to wait.

The smoker's rasp on the telephone belonged to an employment counselor by the name of Bob Tarlecky. His Hanover Technical Affiliates had been contracted to deploy sharp, language-adept editors for a long-term project at the new American Telephone and Telegraph headquarters down in Somerset County, and would I be interested at the salary of twelve dollars per hour?

Twelve dollars an hour! Was this joker kidding? Twelve smackers was more than I'd ever brought down—or dreamed of bringing down—in my working life. Fucking aye, I was interested! Visions of a fat bank account that would allow me to coast—for years, maybe—doing nothing but indulging my creative penchants bloomed in my excited brain. What made it all the more enticing—and unbelievable—was that Tarlecky had no interest in interviewing me beforehand, so desperate was the telephone monster for help.

"When do I start?"

"They really need bodies in there as soon as possible. Would it be possible for you to start on Monday?"

Monday? *This* Monday?

My hopes for a grace period during which I'd lie around and read and fuck and drink and mentally "prepare" myself for entry into the corporate world were dashed into flotsam against the hard rocks of exigency.

"Well . . . sure."

"Good. Now let me explain something to you, Max. I see from your résumé here that you've never worked for a big company before. You have to understand the mind-set at AT&T. Be deferential at all times—they like that. Toeing the company line is the ticket. As long as you're a team player, you'll do fine. Mind your own business, work hard, if you have any problems, don't bother management—*call me.* Got it?"

"No problem, chief."

"Good. If it works out, you can expect to be there two, maybe three months. Ivan Holland is heading up the project you're assigned to. He'll sign your time sheet, which you then forward to me. Paychecks are issued every two weeks. You're eligible through us for a full health insurance package at forty dollars per month. Any questions?"

"No."

"Good luck to you, Max. And welcome aboard."

20.

And then it really was true—the honeymoon *was* over. That Monday morning Livy and I were to go our separate ways for the first time. Some major turn on the highway had been negotiated—where it would take us was anybody's guess.

I shaved, using a red, ball-like gadget that heated the cream as it spurted out of the Barbasol can. It was a sort of bon voyage gift from Livy, who looked like a fashion model in a new ensemble she'd snuck out and bought when I wasn't looking. As usual, it was dark and form hugging, and a flaming orange-and-black scarf that was knotted at her neck set off the whole shebang. I hadn't noticed those high suede pumps on her feet before, either.

Dressed to fucking kill, I thought as I watched her primp and preen in the bedroom mirror. The sight was enough to stir my prick to attention. I pushed it into her ass.

"Let's do it," I proposed, "as a sort of farewell bang."

"You'll mess my makeup," she whined, disengaging herself. "Maybe when we get home. And if you don't get a move on, you'll be late."

Which, of course, was the point. *Let the bastards wait.*

But off we went nevertheless, she in her taxi dancer's outfit, me in my only blazer, tie, and worsted wool trousers, an outfit befitting a young man going places. . . .

I jumped into my rusted-out beast and drove. The signs for exclusive country clubs and gated communities I passed along the highway made me feel like a chimpanzee being rocketed to a distant planet. The folks living in these Somerset Hills were the genteel set, Jacqueline Kennedy Onassis and her ilk. They played polo and hunted foxes—where the hell did I fit in down here?

Headquarters for the communications monolith was a gargantuan pagoda-like concrete-and-glass complex that had killed off hundreds of acres of virgin forest in one of the Northeast's most expensive counties. A little sick at heart, I followed Tarlecky's instructions and turned into a gaping maw that led into the underground parking facility, in the process dodging a gaggle of carefree Canadian geese that I suddenly envied. The elevator was packed tight with grim-faced, cologne-scented men and perfumed women in Brooks Brothers suits. By the time I reached the main concourse, I knew I'd made a fucking terrible mistake. My palms were clammy from sheer claustrophobia. A rivulet of sweat rolled out from under my armpit and made its way toward my elbow. I was a prisoner on his way to the gallows. The thought of a drink crossed my mind.

I don't know why I didn't turn back. For one thing, I needed the jack. I felt a little guilty, for another—I'd been given a long free ride by Livy. But even that didn't explain my passivity at the open elevator door.

What did, at the bottom of it all, was the uneasy sensation that I had no choice in the matter, that I was being nudged from behind by some supernatural imperative, some invisible finger of *fate*, and no matter what I did or didn't do at that moment, I was condemned to lose my illusion of *will*—that I was punier than the puniest rat flea that subsisted off the scum of the earth, and that the course of things was being decided by some entity much greater than my frail self. . . .

So like Bukowski entering the U.S. Postal Service or Melville at the customhouse or Kafka and his nameless insurance company, I reported like an automaton to the front desk, to be inducted into the ranks of corporate America.

All around the vast hall the products and accoutrements of the coming new age were on display—videophones . . . computer terminals . . . fantastic futuristic telephone receivers of all shapes and sizes. The walls were covered with stunning murals, oil paintings, watercolors, etchings, and drawings. Looking closer, I realized that I was actually face-to-face with the original handiwork of Dalí, Matisse, Braque, Picasso, Chagall, Bonnard, as well as the masterpieces of lesser-known but equal talents—and that I was the only one who seemed to notice. That's the thing about big money—incomprehensible money—it buys everything, including the sweat of genius; it turns your living room into a wing of the Louvre. It was surrealistic—not to mention sad—to think of what some of those wretched beings went through in order to produce their work, then to watch the philistines pass by, oblivious to the struggle.

Hundreds of bodies came and went. There were terse telephone conversations between the receptionist and an unseen presence regarding me. They made me wait a long time. Finally I was handed a card laminated in plastic—DAY VISITOR, it read—and told to clamp it onto the lapel of my jacket and keep it there at all times.

A uniformed guard appeared and escorted me up to Ivan Holland's office on the third floor. Ivan was an affable teddy bear of a man somewhere in his forties. His sleeves were rolled up past his elbows and his tie was slightly askew. For the early hour—eight thirty—he looked like he'd already been hard at it.

We shook hands. He showed me to an empty chair next to another guy.

"This is Lars Peterson," said Ivan. I shook hands with him, too. Lars was about my age, a bit soft in the gut, with a mop of unruly Swedish-blond hair. What I liked about him right away was his casual duds—rumpled sports coat, unpressed olive-green khakis, soft boots. Since he was smoking, I lit up, too.

"You fellows will be working together on a long-term, top-secret project I've been overseeing here since last June, so before we start anything, you're both going to have to sign a nondisclosure agreement. The parent company is considering divestiture for some future point in time, and my task force is taking a close look at how Indiana Bell—a prime example of one of the unit companies—would fare in a deregulated environment in a hypothetical scenario when the national telecommunications superstructure has been deconstructed. . . . Got it?"

I had no idea what the fuck the man was talking about. I glanced at Lars. I doubted he did, either. Ivan went on talking. The practical upshot of it was—as far as I could make out—that we were to proof earnings projection printouts from the parent company against actual earnings from the field—whatever that meant.

After we affixed our John Hancocks to the promise not to leak company information, Ivan led us through a maze of corridors to a compact, windowless room. On the oblong table sat enormous stacks of two-by-four computer printouts, pads, pencils, and paper clips.

"All right, fellas, go to it. If you need anything, you know where to find me."

With that, he disappeared, closing the door behind him. Lars and I shrugged at each other. We went to it.

Soon it became patently obvious that not only did Lars and I have no clue what we were up to, but that it didn't really seem to matter in the least. For days on end we never set eyes on Ivan (he was forever "tied up in a meeting"), and when he did come around, it was to cryptically order us to stop what we were doing and await further instruction, or resume what we were doing until further notice. Any and all activity in this joint was shrouded in mystery, and even after gabbing with the other inmates at the lunch table, we never got a clear idea of what anyone here actually *did*, aside from attend those all-important meetings. What we couldn't help but notice was that each and every employee of the Big Telephone Machine carried a single sheet of paper at all times while in transit in the halls. But aside from the comic value to Lars and me, we stayed in the dark on what the business signified.

To stave off boredom, we played games with the dictionary ("Okay, for three points, what does 'transpontine' mean?"), strolled with a sheet of paper in hand (so as to make it look like official business) the length and breadth of the complex, killed time in the company library, smoked pack after pack of cigarettes, and watched television in the lounges during the interminable afternoons. Since no one ever showed up with a long-distance invoice, Lars yakked it up on the phone with his girlfriend, Cecilia Swan, who was living down south (they'd met at the University of Georgia some years back), for hours on end. After all, he figured, the telephone company doesn't bill itself.

As with all meaningless activity, pointless habit soon got the upper hand. Our absurd labors were a river emptying into an ocean of Monday-through-Friday, eight-thirty-until-five-thirty days, during which we rarely glimpsed the light of day. . . .

But the money was rolling in, and just in the nick of time. Within weeks Livy and I made good on many outstanding debts. I was even able to send off a check to Mrs. London for that apocalyptic astrological reading and get her off my back once and for all. For a minute or two, I felt pretty damned good about being flush for the first time in my life. When I sliced open the envelope that held my check, I could hardly believe I was bringing down good money—over $360 a week after taxes—to sit on my ass all day and shoot the shit with Lars.

Corporate America made sense to me now—it was a royal scam, a cushy gig for anybody who could find his way in, *the* place to be, especially if you wanted to do nothing.

But before long a strange restiveness set in. I was nagged by the thought that I hadn't actually *done* anything of any significance whatsoever throughout the long workweeks. I was accomplishing less, in fact, than when I laid around the apartment devouring book after book and occasionally turning out a new tune. And if you weren't doing something you liked in life, well, what good was the money? What good was all the money in the world if you didn't want to be where you were? Now that I had a regular wage, I was responsible for a million and one expenses I didn't have when I was hard up against it. Like the rent on Livy's apartment, for example, and the gasoline sucked up while traveling back and forth to work (a fifty-mile round trip), and my new wardrobe, and the dry cleaning, and the ten-dollar lunches with Lars. To boot, rather than bother with preparing our own meals, Livy and I found ourselves in a different restaurant damned near every night. Before I knew it, I was living paycheck to paycheck all over again, with not a shilling to spare. . . .

Everything in life is money. You can try your damnedest to ignore it, but you're nothing without it, an untouchable. With it, you're damned, too, but for different reasons. Like most things on this earth, it's a no-win situation.

21.

Once you relinquish your dreams—the dreams that bubble up from the deepest wells of your real self—you're finished, you're dead; it doesn't matter how much jack you're bringing down. We were earning bread, Livy and me, but worms had appeared in the loaf of our success. By the time the dead leaves had broken off the tree branches, I'd been gripped by a depression that had me near paralyzed before I could even make it out of the apartment in the frosty mornings. Because by now I knew for sure that in the process of holding down a regular, respectable job and making money the old-fashioned way, I was trashing my life.

"I've been thinking . . . I have to get back to trying to do something," I announced to Livy's naked back as I watched her dress for a morning meeting with the rebbes.

"What are you talking about?"

"You know. What we always planned at the beginning—write, music, travel. All of it. *Any* of it."

She shrugged. I kept an eye on her remarkable deltoid muscles, another part of her I always admired.

"Who's stopping you?"

"Well, with these fucking jobs of ours there's no time."

"So what do you want me to do?"

I laughed. "I didn't ask you to *do* anything. But there has to be some way. . . ."

She swung around and fixed me with a look of scorn and pity—a look I hadn't seen before.

"Let's not kid ourselves, Max. We tried all that, and we didn't even come close."

There was no arguing her point. "Yeah," I went on anyway, "but maybe it'll just take more time. That's the way it is for some people. Think of all the late bloomers who took years, decades, to develop into genuine artists."

"Like who?"

"Well, like Cézanne, for one. Like Whitman, for another. And even Dostoyevsky didn't become Dostoyevsky overnight."

"*Decades?* Who's got decades? Jesus, Max! I can't talk about this now. I have to get to the office. You do, too."

"Yeah, sure. . . . But think about it, okay?"

She stepped into her shoes and checked herself in the mirror. "I can't *think* about that shit anymore. I have to *think* about the rent. Remember the rent?"

I didn't know what I wanted to say. Maybe there was really nothing *to* say. I felt like I was out in left field by myself. As if Livy had bailed on me. As if she didn't take me at all seriously anymore. As if I'd been born to shake up the world and had been sent out to do the job minus the weapons.

I was angry. In a rage. Always in a rage. Livy paused in the bedroom doorway, swinging her alligator-skin purse.

"Know what, Max?"

"What?"

"This is all just more pipe dreams."

"Yeah, well, you can say that for just about anything. Or anybody."

"I gotta go, Max."

"See ya later. . . ."

I watched her sashay out the front door. When she closed it, I fired up a smoke, my first of the day, and mulled over the conversation in the silence of morning. Then I climbed out of bed, showered, and reported for duty.

A long with a flagging spirit, I'd developed another nasty ailment—heartburn. At first I blamed the condition on Livy's hot, rich southern Italian dishes. But when the burning persisted after I laid off the spicy red sauce, it got to be a real nuisance, reaching the point where I could do little during a severe attack but lie on my belly in a vain attempt to quell the hot streams of volcanic acid running up and down my esophagus.

"You should probably see a doctor," suggested Livy after my gastric suffering became a daily phenomenon that threatened to incapacitate me altogether.

I thumbed through the phone directory and made an appointment with one Doctor Bovasi, who had an office around the corner. When my turn came, he studied me first through his spectacles, and then asked me to take off my shirt and sit on the examination table.

"Open your mouth and say 'Aaahhh.'"

He pushed at my stomach. He prodded. He poked and kneaded. He interrogated me on my medical history and family background. From time to time he mumbled, as if carrying on a private conversation with himself.

"Too young for esophageal cancer. . . . Maybe a spastic colon? But you don't present the requisite symptoms. . . . Peptic ulcer? I don't think so. Hmm. . . ."

When he was through, he folded his arms and squinted at me.

"Mister Zajack, is something bothering you?"

"Bothering me?"

"Problems on the job? At home, maybe?"

Sure, there were problems. But to lay them out for Bovasi would take hours. Besides, that's what shrinks were for, and I told him so.

"I see. . . . Well, complicated or simple, I recommend that you eliminate whatever's bothering you from your life. It's my opinion that you won't lose your indigestion until you do."

The good doctor's counsel cost me twenty-five skins, and since he found nothing physically wrong that I could report to my health insurance carrier, it was going to come out of my pocket. . . .

The next evening Livy arrived at the apartment without her long, luxuriant hair.

"What the fuck happened to *you*?"

"I'm going into the real estate business."

"You're going to do *what*?"

"With my mother. Monday after next I start showing houses. Then I start taking classes for my license. . . . Anyway, she thinks that short hair is more *functional*. More mature, know what I mean? What do you think? Myself, I think it looks pretty good."

"What about the temple?"

"I'll handle that."

Eventually the shock wore off, and we talked. Seems that, unbeknownst to me, Livy had been in touch with her mother after we made that visit to her office. In fact, relations between the women these days weren't as icy as they used to be. Maybe they were coming to understand each other after all. And now Mrs. Tanga had decided to take her daughter under her wing. It was about time to get serious about life, according to her. Time to put away childish things once and for all. It was certainly high time to forget about piddly shit like writing stories and novels. Livy let slip that it was her mother's opinion that I, Max Zajack, should have been ashamed of myself for sitting around strumming the guitar *at my age*, and that the best thing I ever did was procure a legitimate position. As a real estate agent, Livy could make some *real* money. She didn't want to be stranded behind a desk drawing up rabbis' schedules for the rest of her life, did she? Glorified secretary was no position for a sharp young woman! Besides, what could Livy do with twelve grand a year? Especially if she wasn't going to get married! If she wasn't going to get hitched to a professional man and start a family, she'd better start thinking about how she was going to make a living to support herself—a good living!

I didn't like it. The thought of Livy fast-talking prospective suburban homeowners didn't work for me at all.

Goddamn her mother. That interfering bitch.

"I don't know, Liv. Are you sure about this? Do you really think you're cut out to sell houses?"

"Why not? Everybody else seems to be able to do it."

"Yeah, but—do you really think you can handle working with your mother? That might be tough for anybody."

"What are you trying to say, Max? That you don't think I'm *capable*? Is that what you're trying to say?"

I challenged her. She was immovable. She definitely intended to tender her notice to the temple. I couldn't come up with a good enough reason to stop her.

That night in bed it was like making love to someone altogether different. It's always a thrill getting inside a new woman, but without Livy's magnificent black tresses something was missing. I kept my mouth shut about it. I knew from experience that despite her beauty Livy was sensitive about the way she looked. . . .

22.

Over the weekend Livy went out with her new MasterCard and charged a crate-load of outfits geared toward presenting her as the ultimate businesswoman. I thought the entire escapade was foolhardy and ridiculous, but I tried to be *supportive*. What the girl was going to do she was going to go ahead and do no matter what I said—I'd seen enough by now to know that. So I wished her the best.

Days pass, one disappearing into the next without a clear line of demarcation. On Saturdays we're asked to log overtime on Ivan's project. In our briefcases Lars and I lug in six-packs of cold beer, and instead of proofing the computer printouts—because by now it's clear Ivan is completely oblivious to what we're doing—we plant ourselves in front of the color television set in the lounge and take in basketball games or boxing matches while getting sloshed at double time.

One day Ivan blows in and informs us that the entire project has been put on hold until further notice. For weeks we sit on our asses playing cards, reading the newspapers, even dozing when the tedium gets to be too much, awaiting that elusive "further notice"—but it never comes.

At long last an anxious middle-aged fellow who looks like all the others arrives and requests that we pack up our personal belongings immediately and follow him. The pied piper introduces himself as Edward Winklewhite, manager on the district level. We're working for him now.

"What happened to Ivan Holland?" Lars asks as we troop through the corridor.

"Ivan's project here has been terminated," Winklewhite answers in a cryptic monotone. "He's returned to his home office in Indiana."

There's something like superior self-satisfaction in his voice. Lars and I shrug at each other. Winklewhite offers no further explanation. We don't ask for one. This is the way things are done inside the Big Telephone Machine.

Winklewhite shows us into the elevator and pushes the button for floor number five. Of course we've heard about what's up there—the executive suites. Well, well, well—we're about to be called on the carpet after all! Our asses are about to be fried! No doubt Lars's daylong phone calls to Georgia is the evidence against us. Or maybe it's the beer cans we toss all over the lounge.

We're ushered into a conference room, where the centerpiece is an enormous oval table flanked by a dozen leather-cushioned swivel chairs.

"The members of the board of directors seem to have trouble operating the control panel in this room," says Winklewhite, wringing his hands nervously. He reaches down and pulls out a console from beneath the lip of the table. "They've requested a new operating manual so that when they come in for a meeting, they're not all out to sea with this darned thing. . . ."

When he gingerly depresses some of the shiny buttons, it's as if he's activated the functions of a spaceship—lights flash, bells ring, buzzers sound, the wall panels move up and down and side to side. A maddeningly placid voice, just like the one inside the lunatic computer in *A Space Odyssey*, coolly addresses us.

"*Sorry. You have not followed proper procedure. Please try again. . . .*"

"See what I mean?" Winklewhite pleaded like a helpless old woman.

Without warning, a movie screen emerged from the ceiling and lowered itself magically toward the plush carpet.

Lars elbowed me in the ribs. "Now all we need is the popcorn. . . ."

"Or the porn."

Winklewhite did not find us amusing. In fact, the fellow seemed to be altogether devoid of a sense of humor. On top of everything, he was completely exasperated by now with the recalcitrant control panel. He threw up his hands and left us with a leather-bound copy of the outmoded user guide, a stack of pads, and a box of pencils.

"It's all yours, fellows. I expect it'll take you a few weeks to work up a first draft."

With that he turned on his heel and disappeared.

Lars let out a soft whistle. "A few weeks? Shit, we'll have this fucking thing knocked off in a matter of hours!"

"Tell me about it!"

"Then what do we do?"

"Same thing we've done for the past seven months—play with our joints."

You could say Lars and I had the hang of corporate life. What made our gig such a golden peach was the fact that we were

just a pair of independent contractors working for a man—
Tarlecky—we never saw, directly beholden to nobody inside the
Big Telephone power structure itself. Even better, we had the
brains to realize that we had it made, and Winklewhite seemed to
have forgotten all about us after that first day. Every once in a blue
moon it happens—you hit the jackpot, and always when you're
not expecting it. Those were pretty good days. . . .

Livy was out the door early every morning, running from here
to there, showing Tudor mansions in Roseland and ersatz palaz-
zos in Short Hills to shady mobsters, rich men's wives who had
nothing better to do with their days, and doctors, lawyers, and
executives looking to escape Manhattan. The image of my girl as
a hard-nosed businesswoman was at odds with my idea of her—
and hers, at least some of the time—as a Sylvia Plath or Anaïs
Nin in the making. But who was I kidding? Like I said before,
in both the long run and the short, life is a matter of dollars and
cents—artistic pretensions don't amount to a hill of horse dung.

But there were no sales for her yet.

"Mother says it will take some time, and that the market is a
little quiet right now. Besides, I have to bone up on my real estate
law if I want to pass the test for certification."

"How long before that happens?"

"A few months, at least."

"Will you draw any salary between now and then?"

"She didn't say."

"Well, don't you think you should ask?"

"Look, Max, this is my *mother*, for God's sake! Give me a
break here!"

"As long as you know what you're doing. . . ."

"I know what I'm doing!"

———

Lars had just gotten through showing a smoker from a friend's recent bachelor party on the board of directors' private movie screen when Winklewhite barged in. Without a word he picked up our decoy working user's guide and scanned the penciled-in deletions and corrections.

"Looks like you fellows have been hard at work here! I'll bet by now you've completely mastered this contraption."

"We sure have!" the two of us answered in unison, like proper bootlickers.

The manager slammed the binder shut and flashed a smile full of miniature yellow teeth.

"Wonderful! We'll have this printed up, posthaste. Now if you'll just follow me. . . ."

We won't need to take anything, Winklewhite assures us, everything we'll need is at the next location. We pass several ominously closed doors en route to the apex of the building itself and directly into the nerve center of power—the chief executive officer's suite. This is where Branford Gladstone White III calls the shots for the American telecommunications industry, where company policy affecting the entire planet is formulated, where deals are cut, and heads are made to roll.

It was as quiet as a cemetery. The scent of a holy reverence— the reverence for power—hovered in the atmosphere. Lars and I were shown to a pair of maple desks in an alcove behind the station of White's personal secretary herself. She glanced superciliously over her shoulder at us, then picked up the telephone and began a discreet conversation. In the meantime Winklewhite disappeared. We were never to set eyes on him again.

More stacks of computer printouts. We are to crosscheck information on certain Big Telephone personnel from across the country. The categories are marital status, age, children, number of years with the company, universities attended, political party (if known), and *dates of surveillance*. Each page was stamped CON-FIDENTIAL—PROPRIETARY USE ONLY.

"What do you figure the point of all this is?" Lars wondered out loud.

"Your guess is as good as mine."

"But how the fuck did we land *up here*?"

"You got me."

"Think maybe they're keeping an eye on us?"

"What for?"

"Who the fuck knows. . . ."

It did seem awfully weird that two nobodies from the outside would be planted squarely in the sanctum sanctorum. Were we being used for some kind of experiment?

The strangest thing about the great American corporation is that one hand never seems to know what the other is up to, no-body ever tells you what's going on or why, and the results of your labors remain completely unknown, vanishing into the air like so much smoke. And for all that uselessness and waste, the paychecks are the fattest, the benefits the juiciest, the buyouts and retirement packages the sexiest. All you have to do is check your identity at the front door and do whatever they say.

23.

Despite the free rein we had, the Big Telephone Machine wasn't working out for Lars. Unlike me, he was never quite at home with the idea of sitting around collecting a paycheck for taking it easy. He was really after a job as a journalist, a sportswriter, which is what he'd done down south after college, but he hadn't been able to land anything up here, and he was growing antsier by the day. Even visits from his Southern belle didn't help. Sometimes he wouldn't show up at the office for days on end, especially after a long weekend. Lars drank, and having to board with a spinster aunt (he was supposed to be looking after the old lady since her health was shaky) drove him to it in excess. Whenever he had the opportunity and a fresh paycheck, he had the propensity for going off on blind benders. He'd swill it down anywhere and everywhere—in bars, at the racetrack, even in his living room, for days running, until he couldn't drink one more ounce. Then he'd pass out and sleep for a day or two. Where he'd end up, he himself sometimes couldn't say.

Once in a while I'd join him for part of the ride, hitting the rat's-nest dives on Eighth Avenue or a strip joint in the financial district (before the neighborhood went upscale), or I'd keep him company in his aunt's parlor while he made short work of a quart of vodka or knocked down a case of Miller High Life or Budweiser, or Heineken, his absolute favorite. When there was a decent fight card in Newark, we'd hop in the car and pay general admission at the gate. . . .

One morning I take my seat behind the blond desk and go to work on a fresh mountain of printouts. Nine A.M . . . nine thirty . . . ten. No Lars. At ten fifteen I hear a muffled groan. I roll my chair back just in time to catch my pal stick his head out from beneath his desk.

"Hey. . . . It was a rough fuckin' night, Max. . . . I'm gonna try and sleep it off down here. Do me a favor, will ya. . . . Keep your eyes peeled for the man, okay?"

He crawls back into his hole, and within minutes he's sawing wood. That's what it had come to for Lars. . . .

We wrapped up what we'd been ordered to do, but nobody showed up with another assignment for us. Lars spent all his time on the telephone with his Swan, who had moved north, gotten her own apartment, and was waiting to hear about a job in the city. I filled ashtrays while working my way through a stream of magnificent tomes—*The Tale of Genji, Magister Ludi, Journey to the End of the Night, She*, Simenon after Simenon. While sitting at that desk I managed to circle the globe and zigzag across vast stretches of time, all in an eight-hour day. Lao-Tzu was on target when he said, "Without going out of your door, you can know all things on earth. Without looking out of your window, you can know the ways of heaven. . . ."

And as somebody else said, all good things must come to an end. Sometimes they come to an end in the guise of good news. Mister Richard Grayson summoned Lars and me to his office in Personnel one afternoon in early April to inform us that as a reward for our outstanding service and contributions to the company, we were under consideration to be inducted into the ranks of the Big Telephone Machine itself—he was prepared to buy out our contracts with an offer Tarlecky couldn't refuse. There'd be less money for us at first, but more in the way of benefits, including the once-in-a-lifetime opportunity to become part of the grandest, most powerful corporation in the entire civilized world.

I was shocked. I didn't know what to think. As we all rapped in Grayson's office, it soon became apparent that Lars and I had no real choice in the matter at hand. Either we accepted this shift in our status or we hit the bricks; there was no middle ground. It was always safer to be enfolded in the bosom of Ma Bell than exposed to the whims of management when those inevitable cost-cutting measures were taken, according to the personnel manager; independent consultants were always the first to go. . . .

As Grayson droned on, I thought it over. Why, if we didn't go along with this scheme, we wouldn't even have a crack at unemployment compensation—for that you had to be laid off, and here we were being offered a choice position! It was nothing new—the bastards had you coming and they had you going.

My brain churned like a bottled frog as I watched Grayson fiddle with the official forms. My gut did a seasick lurch when he slid them and a pair of pens across his desk.

Well, shit . . . it couldn't be all that bad to become one of "them," could it? Would it kill me? I'd made it this far on the job, hadn't I? And I still needed a paycheck in order to survive, right? There had to be worse things in life—like polio and schizophrenia and terminal cancer—than taking on a job you didn't want, no?

I didn't give myself the chance to think further. I took the pen and scrawled my name on the dotted line. Lars did, too. With that simple gesture we became the company's property.

As I dragged my carcass into the office that Monday morning I wasn't sure whether I was dead or alive. On the radio coming in I caught a news report about a Texas Rangers pitcher who suffered a mental breakdown in the clubhouse after one of the first games of the season. Tenuous as the grip on my own sanity had been through the years, I felt some sort of strange identification with the poor devil, who was straitjacketed after lapsing into a catatonic state and hauled off to a psychiatric ward. . . .

D2391 was my new work location. It was one more dull room with nothing in it except for battleship-gray desks, chairs, and credenzas. The assignment meant farewell to the executive suite forever and on to the prosaic reality deep inside the twisted guts of the Big Telephone Machine. And it meant something else, too. A real boss. After all the months of unsupervised shenanigans and tomfoolery, I was going to be working for somebody I could actually *see*.

Her name was Amy Williams. She was gangly and mousy and she wore glasses that didn't help her looks. Even before we said a word to each other I detested her face, which was creased by the lugubrious frown of the drone. *Where was Lars?* was the first thing I wanted to know. Transferred, to another department, on another wing of the complex. My new partner on the job—which was to consist of a massive revision of AT&T's internal mail procedures, something tantamount to rewriting the U.S. Postal Service's operating schemes—was an acne-scarred, blubber-bellied, mustachioed lump of shit in a three-piece suit.

"Max, meet John Oleonski," said Amy. "You two will be seeing a lot of each other. You'll be seeing a lot of me, too."

I gave Oleonski's limp paw a pump. I was seasick all over again. I wanted fucking Lars back. The question of how long I'd be able to last in this cell scudded through my brain. The fact that it was tight and windowless wasn't going to help.

Ms. Williams showed me to my desk. It happened to be cheek by jowl with hers. Not six feet away sat Oleonski at his, which faced mine squarely. A bad setup. Horrible. Oleonski stared at me. He smiled inanely. The long fingers of dread wrapped around my throat. . . .

Time itself grinds to a halt in D2391. I glance at my watch every two minutes. Each second is a small eternity—and it's *only the first fucking day.*

The boss disappears. Since there's nothing whatsoever to do, I pull out a volume of Hamsun. But Oleonski won't allow me to read in peace. He wants to get acquainted. He wants to be my buddy. He wants to talk about ice hockey, which I loathe, and his favorite team, the New York Rangers. This dick follows the Rangers from city to city whenever he can. He loves disco music, too. The Bee Gees. Some group named Meco. He remarks on how lucky we are to have landed this job. Yeah, sure. What a fucking bore.

Ms. Williams returns with a gargantuan volume entitled *Intra-Company Mail Procedures for the American Telephone and Telegraph Corporation.* This is the behemoth we're going to do battle with. Sitting side by side at my desk, Oleonski and I look it over, the ultra-fine print doing a dance of death before my eyes.

Pursuant to Section 101.35A of the American Telephone and Telegraph Corporation's Code of Operations, all mail not designated U.S. shall be stamped "For Company Use Only" and may only be processed in official AT&T mail areas unless otherwise designated by a person at the divisional supervisory level or above; such mails may only be distributed to company personnel at the first or "A" level and may not leave AT&T premises under any circumstance unless so permitted by personnel at district level or above, providing such designated personnel have obtained written permission to approve such permissions from a supervisor at least one level above their present designation. . . .

The boss's telephone rings. She says hello. There's a long, earnest conversation. When it's finished, she walks over to us. As quickly as the manual appeared, it vanishes, having been deemed not yet ready for revision by some authority with jurisdiction over our affairs. . . .

As the days grind on, Ms. Williams makes known the rules of the game. She doesn't like the smell of my cigarette smoke, and she'd appreciate it if when I lit up I'd take myself out into the hallway or the nearest lounge.

"If you're going to kill yourself, do it outside," she sniffs. If we have no immediate assignment on our desks, we are to *sit quietly and wait* for the arrival of such assignment—no reading, no writing, and telephone calls kept to a strict minimum. If this means that Oleonski and I sit idly at our desks for the full eight hours while we wait, then so be it.

When in an unguarded moment I swing my legs onto the top of my desk, she hisses like a snake.

"Shoes on the desk is not a very cool thing to do, Mister Zajack! Kindly remove them!"

What a sour bitch. Like a coward I immediately pull my size tens off the planner.

Choke on it, you miserable whore.

The bizarre image of that ballplayer lapsing into madness explodes like a Roman candle in my brain. It could happen to me, too, and don't I know it. You don't have to make it too far in years to realize that the catastrophes and disasters are lying in wait around every corner, and that at some point you're going to become a victim yourself.

A sheen of flop sweat appears on my palms, and it stays there all day long, leaving the wet impressions of my hands on everything I touch. A knot of tension coagulates in the left plane of my trapezius muscle, lodging there like a tumor. A fiery splash of acid rises up in a wave from the netherworld of my belly.

The walls of the narrow room are closing in on me. I'm beginning to feel just like a rat—a rat in a trap.

24.

Livy was deep under the covers when I got home.

"What's up, baby—early day at the office?"

"I quit."

"You *quit*? What the hell happened? I thought tricks in real estate were, like, spectacular?"

"It's my mother. I don't know what ever gave me the idea I could work with that woman!"

"I told you so, didn't I?"

"Don't start with me, Max!"

"All right, I won't."

"If only she'd left me alone! I cannot *take* being told how to do every single thing all day long! I can dress myself, I can feed myself, I know how to comb my own fucking hair!"

"You actually resigned?"

"After she instructed me on how to conduct myself with Mister and Mrs. Lowenstein—kowtow to them, tell them how wonderful their son the doctor is, because that's how she makes her commissions, after all—I told her I was through and wasn't coming back. Besides, I hate real estate! Selling houses is the most boring job in the world!"

"What do you know. . . . I'm stunned."

The telephone rang.

"Don't you dare pick that up, Max! The last person in the world I want to talk to is that bitch!"

She began to sob.

"So now what?" I said. It was a question we'd asked each other a thousand times already.

"How the fuck should I know? Maybe you can take care of things around here from now on. I'm tired . . . *really, really* tired. . . ."

I ripped off my tie and soggy shirt like I did every day after the office. I felt nothing, nothing at all. I sat on the edge of the blue sheet and watched Livy sleep, waiting for that to change, but it didn't.

Later that evening we had a surprise visitor—the lovely Cecilia Swan. It was the first time in all these months I got a look at Lars's girlfriend. The great thing about being young is that everybody is perfect, at least for a short while, and she was no exception with her long blonde tresses and killer body. But the best part of her was her Southern accent. Something about that down-home sound completely disarms me. . . .

Cecilia Swan is all shaken up, there are tears in her baby blues and her hands are shaking. It seems that Lars has been on a wicked shitter ever since being officially drafted into the ranks of the Big Telephone Machine. And when he's stewed, he bangs her around, and she's got the bruises to prove it: the mouse under her right eye, and the black-and-blue marks his knuckles left on her arm when he took a wild swing in her direction this morning. Frankly, she's scared to death he's going to *kill* her. Since she has no friends up north, she didn't know where else to go for help. Actually, it's a miracle she found our address.

"You can hang out here for as long as you need to," I assure her—with a quick glance at Livy.

Livy nods, but I can see she's not in ecstasies over the prospect.

"All I want is to rest for a little while, then I'll be out of your hair. Lars doesn't know where I am, see. It just makes me feel safer to be here, at least until he sobers up. And thanks, thanks a lot, you two, y'all sure are kind and considerate. . . ."

I show her to the bedroom, where she collapses like a rag doll.

"Some friends you have," Livy sneers when I come out to the breakfast nook. "Low balls from the wrong side of the tracks—every last one of them!"

"I didn't know anything about this, Liv! What am I supposed to be, a goddamn mind reader? Besides, what's wrong with helping somebody who needs it? And this girl needs it!"

"Well, I don't want her here! This is no pit stop for your greasy friends!"

"What the hell's gotten into you, Liv? You were never like this before."

But Livy isn't up to answering questions. She'd much rather fume and rant and act the injured party. Our early morning fuckfest is completely forgotten now.

Was she *jealous*? Was that it? I hadn't seen the signs of it before. I sat on the couch and watched her funk deepen. It wasn't lost on me that Livy's volatile moods were appearing with increasing frequency these days. Aside from the real estate calamity, I was at a loss to explain them, but more and more often I was feeling like a stranger in my own backyard.

We didn't have to wait long for Lars to show. Not a half hour later he was pounding on the door like a madman, hollering and cursing.

"Is she here? Is this where my little Swan came to hide out?

LET ME AT THE BITCH, MAX! LET ME AT THE LITTLE WHORE!"

The last thing I wanted was the one of neighbors calling the police, so there was nothing I could do but open up. Lars looked like shit. He smelled like shit, too. There was barf all over his clothes, which looked like they'd been slept in. He staggered into the apartment and dropped into Livy's peacock chair.

"Look here, Lars," I began, with Livy glowering over my shoulder, "we have to have a little talk. You shouldn't punch Swan around, she's just a gi—"

His eyes were crazed with the fury of the mean drunk. *"Don't tell me what the fuck to do, Max!"*

"Listen, man, I'm not telling you what to do. I'm only trying to—"

He toppled out of the chair, then made a leap for me, throwing an off-target haymaker in the process. I was just winding up to punch back when his bird of paradise flew out of the bedroom. One look and they threw themselves into each other's arms.

"Swannie, baby. . . ."

"Lars! Are you all right? I missed you *so much!*"

I shrugged at Livy. It was okay after all. Since we were all hungry, we figured why not make an evening of it. . . . Within minutes we were in Livy's Nova, on the way to a restaurant. It was a good sign that the lovebirds slobbered over each other in the backseat. But Lars reeked to high heaven—by now it was obvious that he'd broken off a log in his pants—and before long he was snoring like Rip van Winkle.

Livy retched. "I want him out of here! If he's not out of here in five seconds, I'm going to throw up all over the dash!"

I pulled a screeching U-turn and burned rubber in the direction of Roseland Avenue.

After nudging the car into its spot, Livy ran straight into the building without a word. I dragged Lars out of the backseat and dumped him into his own vehicle, then turned to Cecilia Swan and patted her on the shoulder.

"If you need anything, honey, the door is always open."

"Thanks for trying, Max, it was sweet of you, honest. But I think you're going to need some help yourself."

25.

The worst part of most suffering is its utter banality. Like an itch that refuses to go away, you scratch and claw at your wound until it festers and infects and oozes its ugly pus. But unless you throw yourself from the roof or blow your brains out, the world sees nothing, knows nothing, understands nothing of your torment, whatever your torment may be. Because it's not as if you're on the battlefield of war for a glorious cause with your senses all alive. No—it's just you and you alone with your commonplace misery, your garden-variety toothache. Day and night it gnaws at you, until finally you have to laugh at yourself—if you've got a sense of humor left. . . .

Whatever had me by the tail was growing more vicious by the day. No sooner would I hit the ramp to the highway leading me to the Big Telephone Machine pagoda than I began to hyperventilate. My epidermis erupted in hives. My heart tripped over itself with panic. *I was about to lose my marbles.* And for what?

All day long Oleonski and I stared at each other across the little room, while over at her desk the bitch pored over reams of company red tape, scribbled notes, and typed page after page, outline after outline, painstakingly honing the strategy with which we'd eventually attack the mail regulations. We still had no work to do and no indication when it might come down.

"Sometimes," said the boss, "these things can take months. . . ."

It was the most asinine thing I'd ever been part of in my whole life, worse than swabbing toilets, a bigger joke than the loading dock. At that point I would have rather shoveled shit than sit there all day long with those two zombies. When it occurred to me that my reward for all the waiting was going to be the privilege of sinking my teeth into a gigantic bureaucrat's manual, I nearly gagged.

Earning money was nothing but a waste of precious time. . . . Why, I could sit there forever serving the Big Telephone Machine and never have a blessed moment's peace of mind! No wonder the world was full of miserable people! Whether it was the farm, the factory, the office, or the tower of power itself, if a human being was not following his deepest, most natural inclinations, if he was forced into the truss of unfulfilling labor, his existence was fated to be a hell on earth. Where the flower is not watered, it is sure to wilt. . . .

Still, I tried to tough it out. Maybe the situation would improve . . . maybe, by some miracle, Williams would be replaced or transferred, maybe I'd get to supervise myself again, maybe Oleonski would get fed up with living in limbo and go find another gig. Because I couldn't understand how the bastard could be content rolling his number 3 pencils back and forth across the desktop for hours on end, or for that matter how the boss could possibly get a rise out of revising the modus operandi for envelope sorting.

But more time went by and nothing changed. I grew surly. Whatever I said in the little office was meant to piss off and provoke. I compared all Big Telephone Machine employees to sheep moving blindly toward the slaughter. I advocated anarchism. I planted myself firmly in the corner of the terrorists who blew up corporate facilities.

When she got completely exasperated, the boss bared her fangs at me. "Then what are you *doing* here, *Mister* Zajack?"

A good question, but I had an answer for it.

"Paying the rent. Same as you."

"Lots of people would kill to have this job," Oleonski chimed in. "I know I would. But then maybe that's the difference between you and me. I've got ambition. I want to go places in this company."

I cursed them under my breath. I thought of remarkable figures who'd walked out of their straight jobs on the spur of the moment, vowing to live new lives—Sherwood Anderson, who blew off the factory, the country club, the Chamber of Commerce, his wife and kids, and was found wandering amnesiac in another city hundreds of miles away . . . Henry Miller, who after taking up with his second wife, told his superiors at Western Union to stick it where the sun don't shine (and they could keep his last paycheck, too) . . . and Raymond Chandler, who almost took a flying leap off the roof of a Los Angeles skyscraper before waking up from the American Dream . . . and I wondered whether I would have the balls to join their illustrious number.

Then, one late April afternoon, all of a sudden it *was* too much. Too much of Oleonski waxing ecstatic over the price of the Big Telephone Machine on the stock exchange . . . too many of the bitch's baleful stares . . . too much silence in that tiny cell. . . . too many agitated voices babbling inside my head . . . too much priceless time spent collecting a paycheck . . . and all with the spring sunshine beaming outside the windows beyond my reach.

"Where are you going, Zajack?" the boss demanded when I got up without a word and, briefcase in hand, went for the door.

I walked in a nimbus, my limbs heavy and numb. I looked around. It was weird—there was nothing to mark that I'd ever done time in this place.

Ms. Williams repeated her question.

"Enjoy your future, fat boy," I whispered as I passed Oleonski's desk.

"*What?* What did you say?"

With that I was gone. As I hurried to the elevator I began to breathe a little more easily. I was free, free as a bird. There was nothing anyone in the world could do to stop me from taking that walk.

I pressed the button and waited. While I waited, I prayed that nobody would come and try and make me change my mind.

26.

The point was that there was enough cash to last for a while—weeks, months maybe, if we lived frugally. No one—not Ms. Williams, not Oleonski nor anyone else from the Big Telephone Machine—called to find out what happened to me; it was as if the gears of the bureaucratic machinery itself needed time to catch up with the fact that one of their own had flown the coop.

Weeks later the phone finally rang. The voice at the other end of the line was lifeless, incorporeal. It belonged to John Jones, an assistant to Grayson, the guy who hired me.

"Mister Zajack, a few questions. Will you be returning to your position?"

"No way!"

The man paused and cleared his throat. Either he wasn't used to being answered so directly or he had all the time in the world to file his report.

"May I ask the reason why you've decided not to return?"

"You certainly may," I said. "*Boredom*. Utter and complete fucking boredom."

Not a chuckle, not a sigh—nothing. I could hear some papers rustling in the background.

"I see. Boredom, mm-hmm. . . ." I could hear him writing something down.

"Anything else you'd like to know? You caught me in the middle of taking my morning crap."

"No. . . . I thank you for your time."

"You're quite welcome," I said, suddenly feeling sorry for the poor fellow. He had to be thinking that he'd gotten the King of the Nuts on the line, even if David Berkowitz aka Son of Sam had been recently apprehended.

"One last thing. Please return your company identification card to us by mail at the soonest possible convenience. And have a pleasant day."

With that conversation, it was officially over.

Blowing out of the Big Telephone Machine without looking back convinced me that I possessed the spunk and daring to make a life-shattering move, to throw all caution to the wind, to step off the plank without looking down. But soon enough the glow wore off and the specter of doubt reared up and stuck out its horny tongue at me: Had I walked out of there simply because I couldn't take it? Because I feared for my sanity? Because I was skittish of any form of success? Because I refused to accept responsibility for my life? And one more thing—*what the hell was I going to do now?*

I was going to give the creative life one more try, that's what. . . . I'd make an artist of myself or I'd go out on my shield! If I gave it the supreme effort, who could tell what I might accomplish? What was it Thomas Edison once said? "I'll never give up, for I may have a streak of luck before I die!" That's the stuff I was made of, and I'd prove it to the world!

But again I did nothing. Within a matter of days it was apparent to me that Livy and I were back at square one, that we were stranded in the same boat all over again, and that neither of us had the faintest notion how to right the vessel—which was in danger of capsizing.

Like a blanket of fresh snow, a new gloom descended on me. It took the form of a stultifying lethargy and an unease about what lay beyond the door of the apartment on Roseland Avenue. Whenever I crossed the threshold, in fact, a wave of chilling anxiety swept over me. In the supermarket or at the mall, this fright could transform into sheer panic at certain unpredictable moments, until the only remedy was staying holed up in our crib. . . .

Something strange had stolen into the bedroom, too—a dissatisfaction on Livy's part that changed the way we fucked. With all her screaming in the early days, I'd always assumed we'd been hitting the high note. Now I learned that it hadn't been true after all.

"I can never come with you inside me," she revealed one night after we'd just made it.

What the hell was all her rumpus about then? So now, before shooting my wad, I'd roll off and let Livy frig herself to orgasm while I sucked on her tits. The goose bumps all over her flesh was the evidence that she'd brought herself off. Then I'd pry her legs apart, climb back in the saddle, and take it home. It was a little out of the ordinary, maybe, but if it made her happy, so what? It was okay by me. . . .

This shift in sexual technique for some reason gave me a perpetual hard-on. Maybe it was the incredibly erotic sight of Livy getting herself off. Maybe it was some need to prove my dwindling manhood. Maybe I had nothing better to do with myself. . . . but more than ever, all I thought about was sex. With the Polaroid Instant camera she purchased when we first met, I snapped nude pictures of Livy in all sorts of lewd poses. She returned the favor and snapped me at full mast, my stiff cock saluting the ceiling, a shit-eating grin on my face. Then we set up the instrument to record ourselves in the act. Afterward we propped the photos on the bureau and admired our work. I'd subscribed to *Playboy*, and went out and purchased *Penthouse* and *Club International* whenever I had a few bucks to spare, because I could never get enough of the spectacle of the naked female body. Sometimes when I'd study the glossy pictorials, Livy would watch over my shoulder, fondling my cock as she did so, nodding approval over this model or that.

"What if we brought another girl in to join us?" I suggested.

To my surprise, she didn't flinch.

"Maybe. . . ."

For some reason I'd always suspected that she'd nursed secret desires in that direction. I entertained orgiastic images of a ménage à trois, with me plowing both Livy and our partner to the point of exhaustion. Whenever we talked like that, it ended up in a bang that went on for hours. . . .

But there was a price to be paid for my fantasies, especially afterward, when the euphoria was gone.

"All you want is a blonde-haired, blue-eyed, empty-headed California bimbette."

"That's ridiculous, Liv! Where the hell did you get that idea?"

"You're more interested in those films and magazines than you are in me!"

"No. . . ."

"You like their artificial tits more than mine!"

"No way—yours are perfect!"

"You make me feel like I'm *nothing*!"

"I don't mean to, I swear. . . ."

"Why don't you just get the hell out of here and leave me alone! Go on! *Go!*"

My Livy was becoming increasingly erratic. The slightest trifle could ignite a fracas. Without warning she smacked me with her open hand. My instinct was to retaliate, but before letting her have it, I came to my senses: *What the fuck are you doing? You can't hit a woman!*

After she left the bedroom, I'd hear the shattering of a glass or plate in the kitchen sink . . . a rodomontade of the vilest oaths . . . the slamming of doors . . . desperate shrieks that rattled the walls of the building. . . .

Then she'd come back for another round.

"I *hate* you, Max . . . !"

"No you don't, Liv. You're just talking." And I'd laugh, like she'd just told me the biggest and best joke I'd ever heard in my life.

"No, I'm serious—I hate you, you rotten louse!"

More laughter. I could hardly stop myself, and that would incite her all the more.

Hours later the skirmishes would fizzle out, as always, with the two of us in the rack all over again. I promised to change, to treat her better. I made declarations of undying, everlasting devotion, and she did, too. Then we'd hump. Afterward we'd lie on our backs gazing dumbly at the ceiling. . . . We could hear the girl who lived on the other side of the wafer-thin wall pleading with one of her late-night pickups, growing angry, breaking down . . . then sobbing—long, wracking, pitiful, heartbreaking spasms. I wanted to knock on her door and fill her in on my own predicament—that it wasn't so different, but that I wished she'd stop bawling anyway, that she'd stifle herself or at least move over to the other side of her flat because her agony was wearing me down. But I couldn't. All I could do was stay where I was, with Livy next to me, and blow empty smoke rings into the blackness. . . . stay there and absorb that anonymous girl's tears, like rotting wood drinks in the moisture that will one day break it apart once and for all. . . .

The stray moments that endure, the things you remember: a lonely siren down on the avenue. A fugitive gust of wind bumping against the window, like an intruder trying to get in. A renegade creak in the floorboards. The cheap Chinese fan, suspended a little off center, above the headboard of the bed. The grandeur of a woman's exquisite, naked buttocks as they move heavily, slowly, toward the open bathroom door in the half-light from the streetlamp. The sheer misery of her god-awful beauty. . . .

The night you vowed to yourself that one day, when you found the courage of the warrior in yourself, you would leave. How you could never find it. And you stayed.

27.

Instead of writing, Livy and I camped out at the public pool. It was a cracked cement crater built back in the early fifties, after the last great war was decided and the men who'd fought it wanted nothing more than to keep their wives pregnant and sit on their duffs enjoying the security of peace. It only cost a couple of bucks per visit, and from morning until evening you could lie in the shade of the maple tree and watch the world go by. . . .

Livy, looking as tasty as ever in her black bikini, soaked up the sun. Meanwhile I gorged myself on volume after volume in an attempt to forget our fix and convince myself that in doing so I was learning to write. There was more Simenon (always him for what ailed me) . . . Emma Goldman's *Anarchism* . . . Abelard's *The Story of My Misfortunes* . . . *The Arabian Nights* of Scheherazade . . . Lao-Tzu's *The Way of Life* again (it was the only philosophical tract I'd ever read that made a lick of sense) . . . the works of Chuang Tsu (even better) . . . Raul Hilberg's *The Destruction of the European Jews* . . . Jacob Wassermann's *The Maurizius Case* . . . Ludwig Lewisohn's *The Case of Mr. Crump* . . . Lin Yutang's *The Importance of Living* . . . *The Autobiography of John Cowper Powys* . . . Nietzsche's *On the Genealogy of Morals* and *The Antichrist*, one of my favorites for its language alone . . . Dostoyevsky's *The Eter-*

nal Husband . . . Balzac's more obscure canon—*Sarrasine, Facino Cane, Christ in Flanders, A Passion in the Desert, Seraphita, Louis Lambert*, and the incredible *The Magic Skin* . . . John Fowles's *The Magus (A Revised Version)* . . . Mishima's *Confessions of a Mask* and *Sun and Steel*. . . . Flaubert's *November* . . . and finally, a marvelous discovery, the works of the Yiddish writer Isaac Bashevis Singer.

Every page of those books spoke to me in a different way. There was fodder for the body, the mind, the soul. Since I had no money to travel, they transported me around the world. And, if nothing else, they served as a buffer against the purposelessness of my existence—of existence, period. After sucking up *Genius and Lust*, Norman Mailer's brilliant reinterpretation of Henry Miller's stuff, I summoned the brass to write the celebrated author my observations and comments. Some months later, to my astonishment, a gracious reply arrived from the great man himself, praising everything from my critical insights to the power of my writing, and informing me that in the interests of tweaking the master he was taking it upon himself to forward a copy of my missive to Miller out in sunny California, since old Henry was not entirely happy with what had been written about him. . . .

I read the slip of paper again and again to make sure I wasn't dreaming or imagining things. I carried it around in my pocket and pulled it out several times a day. So there—I'd show 'em all! A letter from one of the world's great minds! If that didn't prove something, then nothing would! For days I walked on ether. It turned out I *was* some kind of writer after all! Maybe only a scribbler of letters, true, but I'd take it—it was better than nothing. An acknowledgment from a bona fide genius meant everything to someone floating around like a turd at the bottom of the commode. And maybe, just maybe, I could find my way out of this morass yet.

When my eyes needed a rest, I sat back and checked out the ass. There was always plenty of it, mostly succulent teenagers, around that swimming pool. For a short while at least, the devils were at bay. There's something in the summer sun that heals. All a guy needed was a little hope. . . .

But by the week my bank account dwindled: $1,000 . . . $850 . . . $500. Sometimes, standing in line to make another withdrawal at the savings and loan, I would look into the bovine eyes of the teller, the same featureless woman who happened to be tending the window every time I came in, and I would wonder what she was thinking, what she figured this tanned and relaxed young good-for-nothing was up to when every other man in the world was at his job, or who it was he owed. . . . But she never asked, and I never let on.

Then Livy and I take a turn for the worse. A simple disagreement will suddenly flare into something far more vehement. Worse, I never quite know when an explosion is coming, or what happened to set it off. Once the fuse is lit, there's no turning back—the eruption has to follow its natural course.

If madness is the complete loss of rational control, then Livy and I had taken our first steps across the Rubicon. It begins when she tosses the contents of a glass into my face—maybe during a tiff over the bills, or the fact that we still aren't married and she's not pregnant. Next thing I know, I'm trailing her, screaming like a maniac, from one room to the next while she overturns tables and chairs, smashes glass, hurls dishes and records, topples bookcases and shelves. In short, she destroys everything that lies in her path, and I watch with perverse fascination, unable to stop her, unable to do anything but try to feebly defend myself when she accuses me of every sin under the sun—shiftlessness, stupidity, unfaithfulness, evil. She slaps me in the face, and I've grown deranged enough to slap her back. . . . She calls me a vile name and I call her a rotten, no-good cunt. . . . She tells me to go back to my prosecutor's wife; I tell her to go back to her mother, or better yet, her *old man*. . . . She orders me out of the apartment forever; she never wants to see my face again for as long as she lives; she couldn't care less if I did myself in right there in front of her. . . . Like a loon I laugh in her face. With what's left of my pride I take her up on her invitation. I blow out of the place, slamming the door so hard the walls vibrate. . . . On the front steps I stop. I think it over. I turn and walk back up the stairs to give her another piece of my mind, but she's locked and bolted the door. I kick at the thing, left-hook it, right-jab it, head-butt it, spit at it for good measure. *Let me in, you fucking whore! No? All right then, have it your way, if that's the way you want it! I'm gone, I'm out of here, I'm history! You can take your pathetic life and jam it up your cunt, you castrating bitch!*

In a blind rage I crawl the streets for hours on end, my heart trying to blast its way out of my rib cage, my soul roiling with the fury of the misunderstood. What have I done but adore the woman? Nothing! *Then what the fuck more does she want from me?* Since my pockets are empty and I don't have car keys, I'm utterly stranded. There's nowhere in the whole wide world worse for your misery than the antiseptic lanes of suburbia. Better in your wretchedness to face the mean streets of the ghetto than the sterility of the split-level, the two-car garage, and the perfectly manicured lawn, where the cold-fish eyes regard your forlorn, starving, unshaven face with suspicion, even downright loathing. . . .

For a long time I sit on a curbside bench on one of those side streets, waiting. But for what? For the next bus? To decide once and for all whether to check out of this cruel world? Occasionally a clean-cut pedestrian happens by, glances at me, shakes his head, passes on. No, the ultimate question is whether to light another cigarette. . . .

Evening steals in. Stirring myself from my trance, I get up and walk again. Up on the boulevard I search for any open door—a lunch counter, a diner, a shot-and-beer joint. Hours pass before last call is announced or they tell me to beat it like any common tramp. Inside my head the voices rage. *Is she insane—or is it me who's over the edge?* Maybe, if I just married her, everything would be different. Or if I gave her a baby; everywhere we go she fawns over the little bastards. If only I were more docile . . . more aggressive . . . more this, more that. *If only I were somebody else.*

Back on the street my stomach cries from hunger. The storefronts—five and dimes, Laundromats, travel agencies—seem to mock my longings to be elsewhere—Tangier or Timbuktu or Tibet. They've rolled up the sidewalks, all right, and aside from the patrol car cruising to ensure the public safety, there isn't a soul to be seen—after all, tomorrow is a workday.

Sometimes, if I've got a few coins on me, I mount a bus and ride in the backseat until the driver tells me that I've missed my stop or to move my ass along. Other times I succeed in getting farther without knowing how I've done it, halfway to Baltimore or Pittsburgh, say, and have to find my way back somehow in the middle of the night. . . .

Always, in the end, when I'm too blasted to stick out my thumb and hitch one more ride, there's nowhere left to go. I tap softly upon the door of 5C and hear soft, ominous footsteps. She throws back the bolt, turns the lock, and scurries back into the bedroom before I cross the threshold. I attack the refrigerator and gobble up anything in there, though these days it's usually not much. Then I buck myself up for the inevitable.

The bedroom is awash in the glaucous light from the streetlamps and the TV repair shop's iridescent sign across the way. Even from the doorway I can tell that her eyes are open, angry, pained. On the table at her elbow are empty drug vials and liquor bottles.

I sit on the edge of the bed.

We should talk.

You don't love me. If you did, you wouldn't do to me what you do.

That's not true.

We can't stay together.

I know.

You're no good. You've always been no good. You're nothing but a piece of shit.

Probably you're right.

You're destroying my life.

I'll try to do better. Honest to God I will. I promise.

Why? What's the point?

I don't know. I'm just so goddamn tired. . . .

Where have you been? Where did you go?

Everywhere. Nowhere.

What are we going to do?

Try again tomorrow, I guess.

It grinds on into the early hours—three, four, five o'clock, when the refracted rays of the rising sun wrap themselves around the gauzy drapes. There's no point to this talk, to any of it, but every inch has to be covered, every last tangent, until exhaustion is all that's left.

When we can't thrash it out anymore, I crawl in beside her. Strip off her nightgown. Stick it to her good.

28.

Even though we were staring down yet another collapse of our meager finances, Livy decided that we had to have a dog. The notion seemed to grow out of her longing for a baby, though she denied it. It seemed to me the lesser of two evils—no question a canine would be easier to care for than a human being. Maybe a mutt would make things better between us.

She insisted that we drive out to the pound, in the event there were any cuddly pooches we might rescue from the gas chamber. The experience was a depressing disappointment. I'm not sure what Livy expected to find in those awful pens, but it certainly couldn't have been the mangy, feces-covered creatures that howled at us so piteously from behind the chain-link. When the attendant offered us a broken-down German shepherd and an ugly wire-haired mixed breed scheduled for execution in a matter of days, Livy turned and hotfooted it back to the car.

We sat there contemplating what to do next. "You and me, we're doomed," she said.

"What are you talking about?"

"You idiot. Haven't you noticed that everything we touch turns to. . . ." She shook her head.

"It's just a run of bad luck."

"No. It's me. It's my whole life. It's us."

"Come on, Liv, you're being fucking melodramatic."

"Then why does this always happen?"

"What? Doomed mutts? They were doomed before we got here. We can't rescue every doomed mutt on the planet, baby. But if you think we should go back and save those two, then I say let's go back and save 'em."

She shook her head violently. "We can't."

"Sure we can."

"No. It's too late."

"I don't get it, Liv."

"Drive. Let's just get the hell out of here!"

Doomed. That was a new one on me. The idea of being doomed did not appeal, but I had to admit that maybe she had something there. Nevertheless, every time we went near a mall, Livy made us scour the pet stores with their yipping puppies, cackling jungle birds, and scurrying rodents until she found what she wanted—a pocket-sized gray-and-white dappled Shih Tzu that looked out at us from its cage with pleading eyes.

"That one!" she gasped. The dog seemed to be pointing back at us with its paw. Within seconds a salesman had it sprung free. The thing squealed with delight and frolicked at our feet.

"He *likes* us, Max," Livy cooed.

"All dogs like you if they think you're taking them home, Liv."

"Tough to resist, eh?" said the salesman, eyeing Livy as she stooped to let the dog lick her nose. "A real heartbreaker, this guy is. . . ."

He grinned at me, assuming that as the man of the couple, I was the one with the money. If I could have gotten away with it, I would have decked him.

Livy, who'd never in her life owned an animal of any kind,

wasn't quite sure what to do. She daintily touched the Shih Tzu with a mixture of awe and fear.

"You sure about this?" I questioned her out of the side of my mouth. "Maybe we ought to think this over some. . . ."

"Oh, Max—you have to take chances in life!"

"Tell you what," the clerk butted in. "List on that pup is three-fifty, but I'll let you have him at two-fifty—today only, AKC papers and all. You won't find a better deal anywhere. Look at him—the little fella is dying to go with you. You're not gonna turn down that mug, are you?"

If there was one thing I detested it was the hard sell, but Livy was totally oblivious. Her mind was made up. She looked at me imploringly—*I wasn't going to deny her this, too, was I?* If we couldn't afford to (translation: if *I* didn't *want* to) get married and have a child, then couldn't I at least let her have this harmless toy?

Even as I was pulling out my wallet for the down payment I knew the whole thing was completely daft. The expenditure itself was like a new rupture in the hull of the sinking *Titanic.* Oh—and we needed a leash and collar and dog food and dishes and flea powder, too. Should we add them to the tab? Sure, why the fuck not. . . .

Minutes later we were transporting our whimpering cargo back to the apartment.

"Don't worry, little guy, it'll be all right," I assured him as I patted his cardboard transport. It was a new low for me—I'd resorted to lying to a dog. . . .

We settle on the unlikely name of Blake, after another of my idols. Like his namesake, Blake turns out to be a bundle of raw life force, a two-pound firecracker who gnaws on everything in sight (including wicker chairs and Persian rugs), hides beneath the bed and sofa as part of a game, and pisses and shits wherever and whenever he so desires without the slightest warning. Just as I suspected, the thrill wears thin very quickly for Livy. Within a day or two she's cursing the dog, begging me to do something about him before she murders him, and finally ignoring him altogether.

The care and feeding of Blake quickly falls to me, and since he's a fractious son of a gun, it's a twenty-four-hour ordeal. Livy refuses to be left alone with him—I'm not sure what she thinks he'll do to her—so my sole purpose in life now is looking after a miniature mutt that was her idea in the first place. Since it's slightly embarrassing for a grown man to be seen walking a lady's lapdog during the daylight hours—and since my fear of the outside world is worse than ever—I take Blake out for jaunts after dark, when we can meander freely through the tiny parks around the neighborhood.

One night when I'm having a smoke on a bench and Blake is sniffing the grass, I hear a voice.

"What a precious dog!"

"Thanks," I say without thinking.

The color of night is heavy, like the black curtain in an old-time movie theater. I can't see a goddamned thing. Then, like a ghost, the lady passes from somewhere in the darkness into the light of the moon. She's nothing to look at. Squat. Unevenly cropped hair. Thick glasses. Age indeterminate. Her mouth has that torque to one side you sometimes see in hard-core alkies or old whores. Blake trots over; he takes to her at once. The lady goes to her knees, caresses him, kisses him, whispers sweet nothings into his ear—it's a puppy bonanza.

The mystery woman is beside herself over the pocket-sized creature. She'd like nothing more than to take Blake straight home with her, and if he wasn't Livy's property, I'd hand him right over. Does she live nearby? Yes, just around the corner. We'll be back again, I assure her, and no doubt she'll be seeing Blake around town. . . .

Back at the apartment I make a nest for him out of a cardboard box and place it next to the sofa in the living room. But the cur is restless, hyper, like a toddler—which he is, of course—throwing a tantrum. I try to soothe him, cajole him to sleep, but his mind is set on the bedroom. No matter what I do to distract him, Blake makes a beeline for the boudoir at every opportunity. After a few minutes of the fray, I'm ready to send up the white flag. So what if he sleeps in bed with us? But Livy won't have it.

"I don't want him in here!"

"Don't give me any shit! *You* were the one who had to have this pooch! Now all he wants is a little affection. What the hell's gotten into you?"

"Keep him out of here!"

"Damn it, Liv, I'm trying, but he's just a baby. He's afraid to be alone."

"I don't give a damn! Keep him away! I don't want a beast sleeping in my bed!"

All right, okay already, Jesus *Christ*. When I shut the door on Blake, he sends up a heartrending shriek. Like a yo-yo, I travel back and forth for hours attempting to reason with him. "If you stay out there, it'll be better for all of us, take my word for it, little guy."

Finally, totally whipped, I stretch out across the doorway and block his entry with my body—but he still won't take no for an answer.

"Oh, for Christ's sake! Can't you even control a two-pound animal?" Livy calls from the bed.

"You try it then, baby! Come on! Be my fucking guest!"

I push the ball of fur back into the living room each time he mounts a new charge for the interior, and his ass-first slide across the shiny floorboards transforms the pathetic scene into a ridiculous one.

"For God's sake, Max, *please.* . . ."

A note of desperation has shown up in Livy's voice—it's as if she herself identifies in some strange, ineffable way with the hapless, whelping animal, and it's *me, me* yet again who is the agent of her torment.

A hard lump forms in my throat. *I'm about to lose it here.* I sweep Blake up in my arms and carry him out to the living room, where we curl up on the rug and spend the night—and every night afterward.

A few days later, driving back to the apartment with bags of booze and groceries, I brake at the light near the park. Someone—an escaped mental patient, a psycho case off her medication—is creating a scene near the azalea bed. She's by herself, convulsing on a bench, her head bobbing, tears rolling down her cheeks. She rants, she raves, she pounds the planks with her fists, gesticulates wildly to no one.

I look closer. It's the lady who took such a shine to my dog.

The signal changes. Someone behind me leans on his horn. It's all clear to me now. The world is against her, too.

29.

Blake developed a cough. At first it was nothing much, but within days it turned into a spasm that wracked his entire, diminutive torso, buckling his legs in mid-caper, and robbing him of his typical high spirits. All day long he did little but lie around and mope. His watery eyes told me he was sick, and that it was serious.

"He has to be seen by a vet," I informed Livy.

"So take him already."

"We don't have that kind of jack. As a matter of fact, baby, we haven't even paid off the pet shop—in case it slipped your mind."

"What do you want me to do—rob a bank? Make a decision, Max—I can't think of everything!"

I opened the telephone directory, closed my eyes, and lowered my finger into the listings for veterinarians. After examining Blake, Doctor Goodson made the diagnosis that the animal was suffering from distemper—in other words we'd been sold a defective piece of goods by the pet shop and had the right to a refund.

The doc prescribed some medicine, but frankly, the prognosis wasn't good. With enough long-term therapy distemper could be licked, but it was going to cost. On the other hand, when you're attached to a vulnerable creature, what does money matter?

I forked over sixty bucks and brought Blake back home.

"What do you want to do with the dog?" I said to Livy.

She didn't know. She had no suggestions. She ducked into the bedroom and stayed there while I tended to the puppy. In the end I knew there was only one thing I could do.

Late that night at the park entrance I was stopped in my tracks by weeping and the gnashing of teeth. Blake's ears pricked up.

You motherfucker—you're unclean!

I don't give a goddamn shit what you say about me!

Cunt! Cunt! Cunt!

Sometimes I can hear God. Understand? You think I don't know what I hear? I hear the voice of God!

No. You're nothing. God wants nothing to do with you. You're a cunt. A motherfucking cunt.

If you don't stop swearing at me I will tear my skull from my shoulders, rip it off before your eyes! You don't believe me? Try me— watch me. All you ever do is watch me anyhow. I'm sick to death of you watching, watching, always watching me. Your filthy eyes everywhere! Your eyes everywhere like the devil's! You are the devil!

Trash!

Satan!

Whore!

Streetwalker!

Slut!

Two souls were locked in a battle to the death, their ranting a mad poetry that made no sense and struck a perfect logic at the same time. By now I knew who it was.

She's perched on her favorite bench. *"Blake!"* she cries, coming out of her demented trance when she spots the little mop scrambling along the sidewalk in the shadows. *"You don't know how much I've missed you!"*

All at once her mania subsides. Magically she comes back to herself, and a shy smile appears on her lips. The dog pirouettes at her feet, licking her hands.

I took the bench opposite, set fire to a Marlboro, and watch the two of them devour each other. What's the hurry, after all? Where do I have to be? Why not let the poor maniac have one last night of pleasure before she's carted off to the bughouse forever? Frankly, Blake would be better off with her than with me, and I'd let the crazy gal waltz off with him were it not for certain hard monetary realities that have to be reckoned with.

Like a prison guard I grant them a half hour together. When it's time, I gently pull the pooch away.

"You'll bring him back tomorrow, won't you? Please? I have to see him or I'll die!"

I'm going to lie, I've got no problem with that, in order to give hope, to help her through the night of her demons. What else can I do? Soon enough she'll be back in the asylum anyway, climbing the walls with the other bedbugs.

"Sure, of course. It's obvious how much you love him. How could I keep the little fella away from you? I'll bring him back tomorrow night."

She plants a kiss on Blake's slavering mouth.

"Till tomorrow, honey pie! Sweet dreams! *I love you!*"

I thought I'd already hit the depths, but this was something altogether different, putting on a disabled human being. It was actually fascinating to me—how much lower could I sink? Walking out of that park, I felt as if I just committed murder.

———

ivy can't bear to accompany me to the pet shop. She locks herself in the bedroom and refuses to come out to say farewell to Blake, the cute little doggie she couldn't live without. Whose fault is this entire mess? Neither of us says a word. Maybe it's all gone beyond words.

A brutal, stifling July day. . . . As I drive, I talk to my companion, who's shut inside his box, his shiny button eyes peering up at me helplessly through the air vents.

I didn't mean to do this to you, buddy, you gotta take my word for it. But it just wasn't going to work out between the three of us. It's a disaster, Blake, nothing short of a fucking disaster. It started out as love between that girl and me, and now I don't know what it is. So under the circumstances it's best if you go back to where you came from so you won't have to bear witness, so you won't have to bear the brunt of our misery. Maybe somebody will come in who can take proper care of you, somebody who'll have the jack to cure you of your disease. Maybe somebody who can give you a proper home, with kids and all that. I'm so goddamn sorry, Blake. . . .

Aside from a lone whimper, the dog is quiet, resigned. When I set the box on the counter, I can hardly open my mouth.

"I . . . I . . . I have to return this animal. . . ."

I show Doctor Goodson's report to the clerk. He reaches in and lifts Blake out of his transport.

"Mm-hmm. Distemper, you say? All right then. . . . Sheesh, he's a cute little guy. Sure you don't want to hold on to him? Maybe we can refund your vet bills."

"I really can't. See, my girfriend's allergic. . . ."

What the fuck does it matter what I say? That lump is in my throat again.

"Have it your way. Just give me a minute to do the paperwork."

Those few ticks of the clock are an eternity in Hell. I lay my hand on the pup's fuzzy head, but I can't bring myself to *look* at him—that would be the true Judas kiss.

Finally the moment comes to return Blake to his cage next to the Labs and cocker spaniels. I'm rooted to the spot. I watch as the clerk hoists his frail body and places it inside, then turns his back and resumes his position behind the counter, as if he's just stacked a can of beans onto a supermarket shelf.

"Sir? Excuse me . . . would you mind stepping aside?"

Sure. . . . I have to move along. I'm blocking the way. . . .

But before I go I just want to make sure he's all right. I shuffle toward Blake's prison just in time to see him push his snout through the bars.

He's looking for me, his master, the guy who's been feeding him and sleeping with him, the guy who took him to the hospital when he was under the weather. When our eyes meet, he sends up a shriek that freezes me all over again.

I was going to say a final good-bye—but I can't, I just can't. It'll be better this way, if I don't prolong the pain.

I turn and bolt for the exit. All the way down the mall concourse I can hear the dog's plaintive howling, until I push through the doors. . . .

Out in the car I drop my head onto the steering wheel and sob like a baby. A little old lady carrying a shopping bag stops and stares.

"Are you okay, young man? Do you need some help?"

"No thanks, ma'am. Nobody can help me now."

30.

Neither Livy nor I ever brought up Blake's name again—it was like the dog never existed. Only when we passed a pet shop did the debacle come back to us, and then only in silent embarrassment.

The fiasco was one more ugly, ignominious flop for the two of us. Livy was right: no matter what we did or tried to do, it was doomed. We'd been mysteriously cursed, it seemed, and we didn't have what it took to cast off the evil spell.

The refund for the return of Blake to the pet shop only postponed the inevitable. Within a couple of weeks we were down to our last few dollars and cents, and there were no paydays on the horizon. In a desperate stroke—one I thought was nothing short of brilliant at the time—I drew the last thirty pesos out of my account and handed it over at the corner newsstand for a roll of lottery tickets. The prize was a whopping $1.5 mil, to be parceled out over a period of fifteen years. Man, it seemed as if every week I read about some slob who turned his life around with the purchase of a single lousy ducat! With thirty to play with, I had to be a lock for five hundred bucks at least! And even if I took home only fifty—the lowest possible jackpot—I would recoup my original investment and be a twenty spot to the good.

After all the shit, our luck had to turn at some point, didn't it? According to the transcendentalists and yogis, there was no reason it couldn't happen, especially if enough bolts of positive energy were projected into the ether. And when was a man's luck likely to turn? When he was on the bottom rung of the ladder—precisely where I stood.

When I rushed home with the newspaper the next morning, Livy and I huddled over it with the roll of chances. This week the winning combination was 765412. A number with a nice, lucky ring to it.

"Come *on*, Max, what do we have? Hurry, hurry, *hurry*, I can't stand the suspense!"

"Stand still, baby—here we go: 337863 . . . 980011 . . . 666799. . . ."

No, no, and no, but we still had twenty-seven shots at it: "290655 . . . 912607 . . . 875420 . . . 152859 . . . 831760 . . . 653098 . . . 773205. . . ."

"Jesus, Max, you sure can pick 'em. . . ."

"Don't fucking jinx me!"

But she was right—so far not even two stinking numbers matched. . . . By the time we reached the last ticket—521090—it was obvious that we'd been had again, that somebody else was going to waltz home with that cool one point five, that we were going to have to face the future with the last few pennies in Livy's passbook—if she still had one.

31.

You're weak, she tells me over and over again whenever we bicker, which is damned near every day now during the long, hot summer. You're worthless, you'll never amount to anything, my mother was right about you. You've dragged my life into the gutter.

I make a feeble attempt at standing up for myself, but there's not much left of me anymore. My agoraphobia has reached the acute stage—according to Livy's text on abnormal psychology, my case would be categorized as extreme, with shock treatments and antidepressants the antidotes. Livy takes to bed with her vials of pills and bottles of liquor. If the mood hits her she might stay there for days. And yet she'll almost always allow me to bang her, even if her mouth is sealed shut from a full-blown attack of cankers. Yes, for us there is always the elixir of sex. One Saturday night, with Belushi and Aykroyd performing a skit on the portable black and white, she begs me to give it to her straight up the ass. . . .

Sometimes, after forcing myself to hike around the block for a breath of air, I'll walk in on her while she's dancing with her shadow to the strains of some sappy tune. Her favorite is "You Don't Bring Me Flowers" by Streisand and Diamond. God, how I detest that glob of pure syrup. . . . I could kill the bitch for doing this to me, because I've given her everything, all I have to give, all the fuel that's in the tank. If I could, I'd lay the world at her feet. But I can't. Not that it's not inside me, it's just that the world won't allow someone like me to subdue it. It's not that I don't have the desire to be a great artist, it's just that I haven't found that being inside me yet. When we started, Livy thought I was capable of becoming something, but I haven't become anything, I've gone backward, I've deteriorated into an insect. So maybe the solution is to off myself, which is what you do to bugs . . . and before that, her. Yeah, what I'll do is, I'll slice her splendid throat from ear to ear some night when she's sleeping. . . .

Watching her sway to the cornball music is heartbreaking, in some way that defies words. Maybe I don't murder her because I've already done it, and she's nothing but a ghost.

This is what we do to each other.

Whatever arrives in the mail is bad. And it's always the same thing—countless demands for money. *Why is it they never let one of those monthly statements slip by?* The telephone calls have started up again, too: Your rent money is late. . . . You're delinquent on your electricity bill. . . . An invoice for such and such is still outstanding after repeated notices, and we have to ask you to make good *as soon as possible*; if not, the matter will be turned over to the appropriate agency. . . .

Finally comes the ominous knock on the door. . . . Livy and I have trained ourselves to be as quiet as mice, to do without shoes, to tiptoe over the floorboards as if they were hot coals. On the other side of the peephole stands a burly man in a rumpled sack of a suit, his tie knotted tight despite the heat and humidity. The rat's eyes in his blubbery face are mean, lifeless, devoid of fear, as if his bounty hunter's trade has drained him of any last residue of human sentiment.

He raises his fist to knock again. I step back and motion Livy to flatten herself against the floor, where I drop down silently and join her.

"This here's Bob Smith, from the Travis Collection Agency. . . . You know what I'm here for. And I know you're in there, so you may as well open up. I got all night to wait."

Ape-man has a voice to match his mug. Like soldiers in a foxhole under bombardment, Livy and I hold our positions. We stare into each other's eyes in the gathering darkness. I'm dying for a cigarette but don't dare risk lighting up. Fifteen minutes pass, a half hour. My heart's racing like a motherfucker. Once in a while, just to remind us he's still out there, Mister Smith raps hard on the door. Occasionally he spits out a curse—a gross, filthy epithet that shivers us. After night falls decisively we hear the heavy bang of his footfalls down the five flights to the street. A note slipped beneath the door informs us that we'd better cough up *or else*. . . .

We've won this battle, but he'll be back again, and we know it. We are fated to lose the war.

The scenario is played out once, maybe twice, even three times a week. Sometimes the goons from the collection agency threaten to break down the door. Unless we make good on the double, our credit is on the verge of being shot forever, they want us to know. Next they'll have the utilities shut off.

Since most of the debt is in Livy's name, she decides she has only a single recourse at this point—to declare personal bankruptcy, a subject she's been boning up on during the long, idle days.

It's as close as a wet straitjacket the morning in August when we have our appointment at the Caldwell law office of Samuel Richter. *Mister Richter was* so *nice to me on the phone,* Livy tells me more than once—she's quite taken with his bedside manner. I insist on tagging along since two minds are better than one when it comes to deciphering legalese. She's reluctant, but I insist. She pours herself into a scarlet cocktail dress that makes her look more than a little like a high-priced streetwalker. The strategy— seducing the fellow—is dubious at best, but I decide not to voice my opinion. Whatever works.

She prances into Richter's office like the queen of the hive.

"Olivia Tanga," she announces to the receptionist.

The girl doesn't look up from her typewriter. "I'll let him know you're here." She pushes the intercom button.

"Miss Tanga to see you."

"I'm on a long distance call," answers the unctuous voice at the other end. "Tell her I'll be with her in a few."

The cocksucker makes us wait in the anteroom for the better part of an hour. "Miss Tanga," he says, extending his hand when he finally deigns to make an appearance. "—And this is?"

"Max."

"Olivia, Max—why don't you two come on in and have a seat."

He's disappointed. It's obvious he hasn't bargained on seeing a guy—me—in tow. Guess Livy didn't tell him about yours truly. We drop into a pair of vinyl-covered chairs that immediately stick to our sweaty bodies.

"Now what did you have in mind again? Something about declaring Chapter Eleven, was it?"

The lawyer's grayish-pink tongue flicks like a lizard's over his neatly trimmed mustache. His framed credentials hang on the wall directly above his head: Haverford College. The University of Pennsylvania School of Law. Very impressive, and he can't be much older than me. Probably has a lovely piece for a wife, too. No wonder he's so goddamned cocksure.

Richter adjusts his glasses and looks us over from head to toe. He isn't very impressed. Not at all. And since I showed up, any thought he might have had in the back of his mind of hosing Livy has to go by the wayside. I know what he's thinking: *I'll wait forever for these two losers to pay me for my services. Whatever they want me to do for them ain't worth the time.*

"Let me tell the two of you something right up front," he barks, rocking back and forth in his swivel chair. "Declaring Chapter Eleven is no laughing matter. You do that and you're courting a plague of troubles. Like, for instance, your credit is a distant memory for years to come. Like anything and everything you have in your possession is up for grabs. Like you have no financial identity whatsoever. Are you prepared to accept what all that signifies? It means that without a wad of cold, hard cash on hand at all times you won't be able to buy your next meal."

Out of the corner of my eye I watch Livy deflate like a tired balloon. All of her dolling up for this meeting has been for naught. "But I thought—"

Richter stares hard, first at me, then at Livy. "Want a piece of free advice, you two?"

This isn't what we had in mind, but the lawyer is going to pontificate anyway.

"You look like you're capable of a healthy day's work, both of you. Why don't you just go out and hustle up a couple of decent jobs? The classifieds are full of them. You'll save yourselves a hell of a lot of anguish in the long run, take it from me. The kind of debt you're showing here"—he taps with his manicured finger on

Livy's papers—"shouldn't be overwhelming if you're willing to apply nose to grindstone."

By now my sweetheart is boiling. Her nostrils flare and her cheeks are beet-red. I can guess what's going through her brain—that she's been had by this crummy shyster after he promised her help over the telephone.

"So you mean you're not going to *help* me?" Livy demands.

Richter shakes his head no. "Not worth the time I'd put into it."

"So this is how you sucker girls into your office! YOU SNEAKY SON OF A BITCH!"

She leaps out of her chair and goes flying across Richter's desk, fingernails raking the air, fangs bared to strike. All of the lawyer's shit goes airborne—paperweights, pens, files, law books. The smug look on his face suddenly vanishes—he's so petrified with fear, he just might crap his pants! It's comical, but I'm not laughing. . . . While I wouldn't mind seeing my wildcat rip this jerk-off's gullet out, there would be consequences. Nasty consequences, such as an assault charge we could ill afford. Like a linebacker I tackle Livy before she makes it to Richter's body, grab her by the scruff of the neck, drag her spitting and screaming toward the door.

I beam a phony smile over my shoulder as Livy struggles to escape my stranglehold. "Nothing happened here, man. . . ."

The attorney's hair was standing on end. "SHE'S FUCKING CRAZY! GET HER OUT OF HERE BEFORE I CALL THE POLICE!"

"Thanks for your help!"

"THE INVOICE WILL BE IN THE MAIL, DON'T WORRY!"

Livy breaks free and makes a run for the street. At that moment I don't know whether to punch Richter out or blow him a kiss.

"Want some better advice, pal?" he says, his sharklike eyes darting back and forth in their sockets.

"Yeah?"

"Run."

I couldn't quite figure out how Richter knew, but he was on to us, all right. What would have been hard to explain was that it was tough enough for me to make it out of doors on any given day, let alone take a job. He wouldn't have gotten it at all.

I was having trouble sleeping at night. There's no worse torture in life than not being able to rest in peace. No sooner would I crush out my cigarette and shut my eyes than the nightmares would begin their demented march through my brain. Hideous creatures—half man, half beast—with drooling jowls chased after me, pinning me like a cornered rat into cul-de-sacs. . . . Mobs of cannibals accosted me in the street, wrestling me to the ground, then tried to eat me alive. . . . After scaling the facade of a skyscraper for some crazy reason, I'd look straight down and freeze with terror. . . .

In the morning I write this down:

At any moment World War III is going to break out. I'm standing on the windswept, arid apex of a mountain in the Atlas range overlooking the vast Sahara. How the hell did I get here? I can't say exactly what I'm waiting for, but from the maniac thrashing of my heart I understand dimly that there is about to be a cataclysm of unparalleled proportions. The blood pushes itself like an untamed river through my veins. . . . those

*fugitive gusts swirl all around me, snake their way through
my cranium. . . . Suddenly, out of nothing more than a flashing pinprick of light, a hydrogen bomb detonates on the floor
of the great sand valley below. Rising up like a gargantuan
mushroom, the desert shudders, the planet itself rocks, the
blue sky takes on a full panoply of flaring color.*

*The mushroom unfolds, enveloping the entire universe.
Even in my frenzy of panic, I realize with complete lucidity
that there's no chance, no chance whatsoever for me. . . .*

I'm jolted awake by dread. Lying in a pool of cold sweat. The
world around me is utterly quiet, except for the faint wheeze of
Livy's breathing. I reach for the cigarette pack, light up, drag deep
to soothe my quaking nerve endings.

I pinch myself. Have I already crossed over to another dimension without knowing it?

Am I real? Am I sane? Have I ever been sane?

32.

The single job I was able to land was newspaper delivery boy. Every morning at five I reported to a street corner in Verona to pick up my stacks of the *New York Times, Wall Street Journal, Daily News, New York Post,* and *Star-Ledger,* which I then loaded into the car and tossed into the driveways of the suburban homes all around the tree-shaded neighborhoods off Bloomfield Avenue. The truth was, throwing rags was the only job I *could* handle given my extremely fragile state of mind—by the time the sun was fully ascendant, my chores were through for the day and I could retreat to the safety of my cave without having to be seen by or interact with other human beings.

There was nothing like being alone in the world before even the birds awoke, nothing like the cool mornings of late summer, when you could cruise with the windows rolled down and the breeze blowing through your hair. For once in your life, you could say you had it all to yourself, including the streets. My first stop was Dunkin' Donuts, where I'd grab a tall java and treat myself to a gooey donut or two. A few of the regulars were already on hand—nut-jobs released from the nearby state hospital, a toothless bum who always sat in the last counter seat near the ladies' restroom hoping for a glimpse inside, an off-duty whore or two, early-morning delivery guys like myself. Some of us even got onto a first-name basis.

But I never lingered. The objective was to get rid of my cargo, and pronto. If I was through by eight, it was a good day; any later and the complaint calls poured into the boss's office. Tom Lopato took those calls very seriously, since he had a wife and brats to support. He certainly viewed me with a jaundiced eye—never before had he had an underling who wanted to quit early in the morning so he could spend the rest of the day working on his novel.

If he knew that I wasn't actually doing any *writing*, he would have considered me certifiable. After a brief apprenticeship served under Vinny Salerno, who was giving up the route to go into the office-cleaning business, I was on my own, wending my way through the lanes of the wealthy, where the professionals, corporate execs, and Wall Street marauders and kingpins were ensconced with their attractive families, their Beemers and Volvos and Audis, and their built-in swimming pools. From where I sat, the world seemed full of riches that I neither coveted nor could conceive of. *Where does all that money come from?* That question often bugged me as I gazed on the stately Tudors and Victorians and Georgians that bloomed more commonly than flowers, so commonly in fact that the outsider was in danger of taking them for granted. More than once, in a cracked, magical fantasy of putting an end to my misery, I plotted a knockover of the finest of them, slashing the throats of their owners, and splitting town with my pockets fat. Why didn't I act on it? With my luck, I'd never have made it as far as the state line. . . .

Livy landed a new gig, too, as hostess of a swanky eatery over in West Orange called La Portofino. Her hours were the exact opposite of mine; when I was nodding off to sleep in the evening, she was reporting for duty. By the time she pulled in at three or four A.M., I was ready to set out with my paper bundles.

Between the two of us we managed to begin another climb out of the black hole of debt. For a while, things were hunky-dory again. In the mornings when I got in after doing the route, I slid into bed beside her, jabbed my strong early-morning hard-on into the palm of her hand, and off we'd go. Afterward we'd sleep like babies, until it was time for lunch.

One morning, however, something different happened. Instead of heading straight for the rack after tossing the heavy Thursday editions, I sat down at Livy's desk in the living room with my smokes and coffee, picked up a pencil and began to write. . . . Before realizing it, I'd filled up a page, then two, then three, with the voice of a Soviet gulag survivor, a guy I'd worked side by side with cleaning johns for the transit company some years back, way before Livy. Juxtaposing his harrowing account with a black-comic account of my own adventures at the time, I realized suddenly that I'd begun composing the novel that had been fermenting beneath the surface waters of my brain for a long time—months, maybe years, but whose structure and tone had always eluded me. On the other hand, maybe I'd just been *afraid* of writing the damned thing for some reason I didn't understand. Or maybe I had simply no defenses left against the notes of my own song. Whatever—in a burst of pure inspiration I saw the finished book in my mind's eye, understood how it was supposed to be laid down, and though I realized that I'd begun somewhere in the middle of things, I had the feeling that I'd be capable with this newfound certainty of working my way fore and aft to finish the job.

Miraculously, the cement block I'd lived with for so long was history. The hours vanished—I forgot to eat or piss or shit—as I knocked off page after page with the unbridled joy of a kid with a new toy. At the end of the day I had a dozen pages. But more important, I'd discovered something about myself.

When I told Livy about it that evening over dinner, she was skeptical.

"What makes you think you'll be able to pull it off? You've never been able to do anything before."

"Shit, I don't know—but this time I just have the feeling it's going to be different."

I couldn't blame the girl for her lack of faith. I hadn't done a damned thing since the day we met to justify her belief in me. And that belief went extinct long ago.

The next morning I was at *The Old Cossack* again, as I was the day after that and the day after that. Utter and complete desperation had spawned it, but I saw clearly now that my hopelessness had freed me at last to talk. If nobody ever saw the fruits of my creation, what did it matter? I held the lowest job on earth, that of overgrown delivery boy—I couldn't really sink much lower, even in my own eyes. The important thing was that I'd found my tongue, even if I was only rapping to the four walls in a room somewhere in the barrens of America.

When I finally paused long enough to catch my breath, I checked out what I'd written.

The next day we boarded a train from Poland to God-knows-where. It wasn't so awful as the train to Auschwitz, because now at least we had seats, even if they were only long slabs of bare wood. The journey was long, and the diet of weak tea and moldy bread didn't make it any easier. It was terrible, but food is food. Anything is food when you're starving. You can even learn to live without an appetite. Besides, I was in such a state that I didn't know if I was dead or alive. It was a bad dream that never seemed to end.

Traveling across the endless expanse of Russia, I began to realize the enormity of what had happened to me and to the world. Everything was in chaos. The train seemed to have no schedule, and that fit right in. It would stop here and discharge some, arrive there and pick up others, all without rhyme or reason. Out the window from time to time you could see columns of the displaced—refugees, prisoners—marching with their heads down while the soldiers of the Red Army whipped them on. It occurred to me that it was strange that they didn't ride in the train, too, since we were all bound for the same destination. . . .

In the car, my fellow prisoners were ill with every kind of disease. I hoped that I'd contract one of them, a deadly strain, so that the end would come, and swiftly. A crazy way to live, no? But even that privilege was denied me.

It was like the Tower of Babel in there. Even though I spoke a dozen languages, there were dialects I couldn't identify. As luck would have it, I knew Russian, which was becoming the common denominator in all conversations, especially when it came to taking orders. Those guards didn't have an ounce of patience. You understood or you didn't. And woe to you if you didn't catch on! No one wanted to be out in the snow, and it was falling without letup. It was then I knew that the priests had lied. Hell wasn't a fiery place; it was a never-ending blizzard! It got so it was impossible to see anything even an inch out the window. The flakes were as big as babies' fists and hurtled out of the sky like millions of missiles. We all thought this way—if you didn't watch your step, you might be out there. We were

freezing inside, but still it was better not to complain. No-
body knew where we were going, but we all had our premo-
nitions and forebodings. . . .

I leaned back in my chair and looked out the window at the
blue sky. Not half bad, really. Not half bad.

33.

During this rare interlude of peace I was able to pile chapter after chapter of *The Old Cossack* on top of the desk until I reached one hundred pages, then two hundred, then three hundred. Around that time I began to smell pay dirt—damn if I wasn't actually going to *finish* a *novel*. It might be the worst book ever written in the English language, it might best be consigned immediately to the wastebasket, it might not ever have a single reader aside from its author—but at least it would be *finished*. Maybe that was more than most people could say for themselves. Maybe, too, it counted for something—I wasn't sure what, exactly—but just maybe it did. And maybe my life was salvageable after all.

In the meantime, I'd taken my eye off Livy, which was something I should have been swift enough by now not to ever do. I hadn't assigned any meaning whatsoever to the slinky dresses she wore when she left for work, not paid any attention to the later hours she kept (she was going out afterward for a drink or an early breakfast with some of the La Portofino waitresses), not noted any radical changes in behavior. But when she started talking about "Fred," my ears pricked up.

Fred happened to be the manager of La Portofino. He was just some guy, she explained, a dark-haired, nondescript fellow who wore glasses and talked with a peculiar accent.

I'd like to meet him sometime, I said.

No need to do that. Why would you want to do something like that?

Don't know. Sometimes I just like to meet people. No harm in that, is there?

After that, Livy grew elusive on the subject of Fred. But now and then details would trickle out. That accent of his was a Boston accent. He had an ex-wife and a handful of kids living somewhere in New England. He had to be forty, forty-five years old if he was a day.

Then this: Fred had done jail time.

For what?

For fraud or embezzlement, something along those lines, she didn't know for sure. Anyway, what did it matter?

And how did she find all this out?

He'd told her. How else would she find out?

Oh. And when did he get around to dropping that bit of juicy information about being in stir?

After hours. When some of the La Portofino staff happened to be sitting around having a drink.

I see. . . . And how is it Fred was able to come by a job handling considerable sums of money if he has a felony record?

He has friends in Jersey. They helped him when he got out of the joint. The poor man needed a break.

Ah, friends. You seem to be awfully interested in Fred's welfare.

She neither confirmed nor denied my accusation. What's going on between you and Fred? I asked point-blank.

No answer to that one, either.

Livy? What the fuck is going on?

The fact that I was writing on a daily basis—I'd returned to composing songs, too, in the afternoon hours—seemed to strain relations between us all over again, just when I was getting into a groove. Whenever Livy would see me hunched over the desk, a spiteful glint would appear in her eyes. "You and that novel," she'd sniff. It never occurred to me that she might be jealous of my progress. After all, I was still right here with her, wasn't I? And wasn't she with me? From the very beginning we were in this thing together—weren't we?

A day or two later a real humdinger breaks out between us when I'm clearing away the lunch dishes. What brings it on? It's no longer easy to tell—not that it ever has been. Today it's a range of little crimes, starting with the way my upper lip hangs over the lower, which she mimics mockingly. And that I never pay any attention to her. That I've freeloaded off her long enough. That she needs her freedom, which is stifled by my mere presence. That she can't go on functioning as my sounding board for ideas on that piece-of-shit book I'm trying to write. And that old standby, that I'm a weakling. Nothing but a weakling.

I let the dirty dishes fall to the table with a crash. "Fuck you, then! I've had it! Wanna see how much of a weakling I am? I'm leaving! I'm getting the fuck out! Swallow that!"

"Go! Get the fuck out! See if I give a damn!"

Like rabid dogs we go at each other while I skulk through the apartment grabbing up my meager belongings. The altercation escalates as I make trip after trip with my shit down to my bomb. By now a crowd has begun to gather on the sidewalk to watch.

Just as I slam the trunk shut on my bags and boxes, Livy's tune abruptly changes.

"I can't believe that after two years you're just going to walk away! How dare you! After all I've done for you! I took care of you! I stuck with you through thick and thin! You louse! You double-crosser! *You cold-blooded killer!*"

The mommies with their prams, the neighbors, the pedestrians out for a walk in the sun, are all being treated to a good eyeful. There's nothing so fascinating as misery, especially when it's not your own. . . .

As for me, I'm beyond humiliation, even when Livy cracks me over the head with my dog-eared copy of *The Brothers Karamazov.*

"You motherfucking son of a bitch! I HATE YOU!"

"Good-bye, Liv. I hope you're happy now. I hope your life will be a bed of roses *with Fred.*"

I jump in behind the wheel, jerk in the key, and turn it over. Just as I'm about to hit the gas, Livy flings herself across the windshield with a banshee wail.

"You can't go, Max! I can't live without you! I thought you loved me! Please! DON'T DO THIS TO ME!"

This is insane. She's ripped open her blouse. Her naked, perfect tits are mashed like plums into the smudged glass.

"Livy, what the *fuck*—"

When I roll up the window, she claws at the glass, foams at the mouth. By now the busybodies have drifted closer to suck in every sordid morsel.

"MAX, PLEASE!"

"We can't keep going through this shit, Liv, I just can't take any more. . . ."

"PLEASE, MAX. . . ."

Her hysteria is doing something to me, softening me up. But if I don't make the break now, at this very moment, I'll never have the balls to do it.

The car lurches into reverse, throwing Livy off the hood and onto her knees on the asphalt.

"IF YOU LEAVE ME, MAX, I'LL KILL MYSELF! I SWEAR TO GOD—I'LL KILL MYSELF!"

The throng waits to see what I'm going to do. Will I have mercy on the damsel in distress, or will I prove myself to be the demon from hell she accuses me of being? I extend the middle finger of my right fist toward the newsbags, but it's not enough to chase them off.

"Liv, come on, don't do this. . . . We're making asses of ourselves. . . . Get up from there. . . . Do you want one of these jerks to call the cops?"

"I DON'T CARE! I DON'T CARE WHAT HAPPENS TO ME NOW! *I'M GOING TO KILL MYSELF*, MAX!"

Oh, for fuck's sake. . . . I switch off the ignition; what else can I do? Then I swing the door open, get out, and pull Livy to her feet.

"This is crazy, you realize that, don't you? Completely fucking whacked!"

But it's not the time for reasoning with Olivia Aphrodite. All right, I tell her, if it means that much to you, I'll stay, but things have got to change. I put my arms around her, whisper in her ear, and that's enough to break up the block party. . . .

During the fallout, for some screwy reason, it's me who ends up apologizing, me who swears that everything will be better if she just gives me one more chance. I know that I have no choice but to go back up to that apartment, I can feel its magnetic force like the undertow of the ocean, I realize that Livy and I are shackled together hand and foot and that whatever unknown power holds sway over our fates, we have to wait on its dictate, and its dictate alone. . . .

Unloading my crap from the car and lugging it back up five flights of stairs is like a journey down the Amazon—it always kills the better part of the day. Nothing is ever resolved or better between Livy and me after those drop-dead drag-outs, but we are condemned to repeat them time and again like junkies powerless to break the habit. When the war wears on into the wee hours, I'm little better than a zombie, bleary-eyed and hungover, as I go about my deliveries the next morning. I toss papers at the wrong houses, miss addresses altogether, even fall asleep at the wheel. When I come to, the car is rammed nose-first into the curb and the kids on their way to school are staring at me as if I just dropped in from outer space. Sometimes I can't even drag myself out of bed until ten o'clock or later. . . .

One morning, after pulling into the driveway at 717 Redman Terrace and dropping the *Times* and the *Journal*, I back my heap into another vehicle by mistake. The crunch of the collision is sickening. I jump out—it's a spanking new Mercedes-Benz 300SD. Without morning light I couldn't see the goddamned black Nazi-mobile sitting there behind the mailbox. My vehicle is as clean as a whistle, not so much as a scratch—like it would make much of a difference. The Benz wasn't so lucky. I'd blasted out a headlight, punched a hole in the fender, and smashed the grille. Totaled. The damage was a lock to run into the thousands.

Standing there like an idiot it dawns on me that the street is quiet except for the drip-drop from one of the Benz's hoses . . . that no one has poked his head outside to investigate the commotion . . . that no doubt they're all still sleeping cozy in their beds. . . .

I think it over fast. No way I can afford to pay out of my own pocket for the repairs to that vehicle, same as I can't afford to watch my auto insurance rate rocket through the ceiling—my last payment is two months overdue as it is. Ditto for a careless driving citation. And, I figure, if the man in the mansion can afford a Mercedes in the first place, he can pay to have the dents pounded out of it. And so I do what I have to do—step on it and blow out of there.

Back home in bed, I wait for the cops to show up at the door and nail me for leaving the scene of an accident. But I no longer really give a fuck about anything, except for avoiding prison and the psychiatric ward—I have a gnawing, irrational fear of both. *If they only knew that Max Zajack is a freak on the loose, then they'd come and throw the net over me.* But they don't. They never do. Cruising those deserted streets with my newspaper bales under cover of darkness I'm like a lost creature from another dimension, drifting through the outer limits of my own tortured mind. Sometimes planet Earth plays along with my delusions via the radio waves. Like the morning I heard this coming out of the speakers:

"Now we're getting reports of scores, hundreds dead at the People's Temple in Jonestown, Guyana. . . ."

"And just where is Guyana, Joe, for the sake of our listeners who might not know?"

"Guyana, Bill, was formerly known as English Guiana, and it's located on the northeastern tip of South America. She's a relatively small country at 83,000 square miles, with a population of 763,000. A large part of that population is of East Indian extraction, and the major religions observed are Hinduism, Islam, and, of course, Christianity. . . ."

"That's quite interesting, Joe, really quite fascinating. . . ."

"And our reports are indicating that the heaps of corpses are already bloated, distended from the poison those poor people either chose to or were forced to ingest."

"Just horrific, just horrific. I can't begin to contemplate the agony—"

"And now, Bill—excuse me for interrupting—I'm being told that a preliminary official count indicates that at least 350 people are thought to be dead at Jonestown."

"Can you tell us exactly where Jonestown is located?"

"I'm sorry again, Bill, but I'm getting a description now of row after row of bodies ringing the central pavilion at Jonestown, one stacked on top of another. It's a scene only Hieronymous Bosch could conjure . . . 500 . . . 735 . . . Would you believe 800 bodies? . . . 875?"

"My God. . . ."

"Authorities are now saying that at least 912 people committed mass suicide by drinking cyanide-laced Kool-Aid at Jonestown, and let's pray that's as high as this death count climbs!"

"How could it happen, Joe?"

Before Joe has the chance to answer, the radio transmission is cut off, leaving me without an explanation for the surreal hecatomb thousands of miles away. I feel for all those dead people. *Because I know what it's like to give up the ghost.*

I aim and hurl another gazette. Drive on.

34.

A few mornings later Livy never made it home. There was no answer at the restaurant when I called, so after getting rid of my newspapers I drove over to La Portofino and did a search and destroy through the parking lot—not a vehicle on the premises, no sign of Livy's Nova.

I'll be damned—the bitch beat me to the punch and flew the coop.

Back at the apartment, I was at a loss for what to do. I couldn't write. I couldn't sleep. I couldn't eat. All I could do was pace the floor smoking cigarette after cigarette and look out the window every few minutes. Once or twice I nearly phoned the cops, but at the last second decided against that course of action due to some gut instinct that told me not to get them involved.

In the late afternoon I buzzed the restaurant again and was informed that Livy had taken the night off. Was the manager on the premises? I believed his name was Fred something or other?

Sorry. Fred wasn't in tonight, either.

Another long night, this one utterly without sleep. My mind races in ten million different directions. But knowing Livy as I think I do, I have no fears for her safety. No, her sudden disappearance has something to do with *me*, I can feel it in my bones.

Like a human oscilloscope, I pitch back and forth between rage, pity, yearning, jealousy, and sentimentality. If she comes back, I'll change. No, I won't, either. Fuck Olivia Aphrodite—I *hate* her. No, I don't; I *love* her. It's my fault that I don't understand her, she's said it herself countless times. No, fuck that shit—when I get my hands on her I'll murder her, the two-bit whore.

At two the next morning I down a few beers, catch an hour or two of restless shut-eye. Seeing double, I drag my ass out of the rack and head out to make my deliveries. When I get back, still no Livy.

Finally at nine A.M. she bursts in, looking fresh as a daisy, a mask of defiance on her face. I jump up from the kitchen table to confront her.

Where the hell have you been?

Out.

There's something different about her, some *aura*, but I can't put my finger on what it is.

No *shit*. Out where?

None of your business. Since when do I have to tell you where I go?

Some remnant of wholesome human self-regard prevents me from telling her that I was concerned for her well-being.

Who were you with?

None of your business.

What do you mean none of my business? I fuck you, don't I? Doesn't that give me some kind of right? Or have you forgotten about that?

Give me a break, Max. I'm tired. And while we're at it, let me ask you a question: do you really give a damn about me? Why kid yourself—you don't. You care more about yourself and your books and songs than you ever cared about me.

Oh, is that so? Well, would you mind telling me who puts up with your fits of fucking insanity? Who is it that sleeps out on the living-room floor like a dog when you're on the rag? Who dances like a marionette when you call my tune?

Whose fault is that? Anyway, you never had it so good! Without me where would you be? Living in another dump somewhere, cleaning shithouses, eating off food coupons, without a pot to piss in! Better yet, you'd be on the street, where you really belong anyway! On the *street*, where you came from! And if you don't like it, there's the door! Who's stopping you from walking out? Leave! See if I care! I WANT YOU OUT OF HERE!

You want me out of here? Would you mind telling me who it was begged me on hands and knees down on the street to come back or you'd die! Who was it, Livy? *Tell me!* Open your mouth now, you cunt! NOW YOU'RE GONNA TELL ME WHERE YOU WERE AND WHO YOU WERE WITH!

All right! Have it your way! I was with Fred! *FRED!*

Oh, *Fred!* And did you FUCK Fred, you fucking cunt?

With that single word—"Fred"—hanging in the air like a guillotine, she kicks off her shoes and makes a break for the bedroom. Even in my blind fury everything about her gets to me— the sheer black stockings, the skintight dress, the tilt of her chin, the sway of her hips. But I'm not finished with her, not by a long shot. I follow her, firing off interrogations, demanding answers. As she pulls off her clothes I smell the air for traces of another man. I can just picture her on her back, taking Fred's cock, letting him do everything, rolling over for him like a bitch in heat.

Livy, did you *fuck* him?

What does it matter if I did?

Are we getting somewhere now? Is this an admission of guilt? But no, she refuses to give me the ultimate satisfaction of saying yes.

I dog her to the bathroom, but she locks me out. I pummel the door with lefts rights lefts until my knuckles bleed. Soon the shower comes on, stays on, and before I know it I'm not cursing Livy anymore—I'm cursing myself like a raving lunatic.

I n no time flat something goes wrong for Livy at La Portofino. She pulls into the apartment on Roseland Avenue at daybreak, retires to the boudoir, rips off her clothes, and slips between the sheets. All without a word to me. By the time I'm on my way to a rendezvous with the overstuffed Friday editions, the bedroom door is fastened airtight.

This time she holes up in there for days—no admittance to me, no admittance to anyone. I can live with that—I've been rolling like a locomotive through *The Old Cossack* and don't at all mind the quiet and privacy. From time to time Livy opens up to place a sullen order. There are tears in her eyes. Her canker sores are back with a vengeance; would I run to the pharmacy and fetch some medication? And bring some strong cough medicine, too—anything with codeine in it. And aspirin, don't forget aspirin or some other painkiller. And while I'm at it, how about a bottle of Le Grand Marnier?

Do you want something to eat? Aren't you hungry after all this time?

No. I'm not hungry.

Does she have to report in to the restaurant anytime soon? Nope, all finished there. Does she want to talk about it?

Her answer is a hard stare at the wall.

Another day passes, another night, then one more day, before I lose track of time. I camp out on the sofa while Livy indulges her need for solitary confinement. In the morning when I stroll up to the corner newsstand for my cigarettes, my gaze is drawn to the faded letters painted into the bricks of the three-story building next door:

FLY-BY-NIGHT MOVERS
FLORIDA AND WEST COAST SPECIALISTS
OR ANYWHERE YOU WANT TO GO
DELIVERY IN 24–48 HOURS

The advertisement fills me with incredible, romantic longing. I can see it all: the turquoise waters . . . the eternal golden sunshine . . . my ass at the base of the palm tree without a care in the world. If I had the balls to split for somewhere, I would. But I don't. I don't know why I don't. There's even less of me than there was two months ago. For consolation, I tell myself that one place is as good as another—it doesn't matter in the slightest where I am.

When I walk in, Livy is sitting up in bed staring morosely into space.

You want to know what happened, Max? she whispers.

Yeah, let me have it. I take a seat on the corner of the mattress.

I was all packed up to leave you, Max. That Thursday night when I went to work, Fred and I were supposed to take off together for somewhere. Mexico. The islands. You never even noticed that I had a bag with me.

No, I guess I didn't. So what happened?

The bastard never showed. We had the whole thing all worked out. He told me he had enough money to carry us for a year, maybe even two. We were going to have ourselves a high old time.

I nod, but don't say anything. I want to hear more.

I would have married him, Max. In a heartbeat. You were never going to see me again after that night.

All right. . . . I'm shocked, but not surprised. Like a sponge on the ocean floor I sit there taking it all in. Now there's nothing left of me, nothing at all, and I don't even realize it.

So what went wrong? I manage to ask.

I don't really know. . . . Her voice is hard as granite, emotionless. Maybe he emptied the till and took off by himself. Maybe he went back up to Boston, to his wife and kids. I don't know. All I know is, he didn't show. He didn't keep up his end of the deal. The stinking coward dicksucker.

So what am I supposed to do now? Feel sorry for her? I'm exhausted, all worn out. I don't have it in me to do battle with her or anybody else. I can't say that I even feel jealous. I don't feel anything. But I do have a question.

How many times did you fuck him, Liv?

Come on, Max.

I know it doesn't matter. But I just have to know. *I have to know.*

Oh, Max, Max, Max. Use your imagination.

35.

It was Friday. Payday, as my old man back in Philly liked to say. My goods had been delivered, and on time for a change. Had it not been for Livy and her thing with the now-vanished Fred, I would have been feeling pretty damned good. Lately I'd succeeded in making that $120 check stretch a long, long way.

Lopato summoned me into his office. It was a dingy rat's nest tucked between a second-run movie house and a typewriter repair shop on Bloomfield Avenue near the Verona-Montfleur line. I'd never been in there before. The place was piled high with stacks of crusty yellow newspapers. It smelled of cat piss.

"Here's your paycheck," he says, tossing an envelope across the desk at me. "And one more thing—you're fired."

This throws me for a loop. I don't know what to say, so I laugh. It's a funny joke, one of the best I've heard in a long time. But Lopato's expression is flinty—he's dead serious.

"I ain't never had so many complaints about a carrier before in all the years I've supervised these routes. You've already cost me a dozen customers—I can't afford to lose no more. Now get out of here and stay out. I don't want you around no more."

Some primitive instinct makes me open my mouth to protest,

but I stop myself in time. You don't fight it when you're sacked from a delivery boy's job.

In a daze I get up and stumble out the door. Driving back to Roseland Avenue in the wake of my latest defeat, it occurs to me that not so very long ago I'd voluntarily resigned from a job writing for a major daily newspaper in another part of the country. *Now I'm not good enough to deliver the damned things.*

But ironies don't mean a thing now, now that I'm free again. How do I feel about my freedom? I can't decide. I can't decide anything, not whether to ram full speed into the garbage truck directly in front of me or even whether to brush away the fly that's landed on my arm. . . .

Livy's hangover finally wore off. Since she couldn't very well lie on her back forever, she roused herself out of bed and got back to the classifieds. Fortified by whatever she was taking and the endless blasting of "I Will Survive" on the turntable, she grimly went about the task of putting her life back together. In the meantime I kept my head down and plowed through my masterpiece—when I could. After the debacle with Fred, a new strain of madness manifested itself in Livy. The floors of the apartment had to be stained one day; the next the pad needed new drapery. Things—*everything*—had to be turned upside down in order to shake her out of her rut. The upshot was that the writing desk—as well as the writer himself—was booted from the living room to the bedroom to the breakfast nook and back again: anything to keep me and that goddamn book of mine in a state of perpetual turbulence, until the routine became a kind of perverse ritual. Like a stick of furniture that's outworn its usefulness, I complied most times without putting up a stink, even when Livy flew into a rage, cursing and berating me for being a worthless fool. By this time I'd learned that there was no use resisting her when she was in that state and that if I tried to escape, she'd track me down and punish me all over again. During this siege I bucked myself up with the half-baked, completely unfounded notion that the novel was going to be a success and my tribulations would miraculously come to an end. God knows why, but I'm one of those psychos who has always had a powerful, irrational sense of destiny—my dire circumstances at the time notwithstanding—even if that belief could disappear in a matter of seconds when Livy and I threatened to kill each other. Something else—I had no idea how "destiny" was supposed to work, but I was damned curious to find out.

That hunger was just the thing to drive me back into the library stacks, but instead of escape, my goal now was to produce a fissure in the secrets of metaphysical wisdom. Whatever occult material I could get my hands on I sucked down whole, particularly when it came to the astrological, which had always fascinated me. I delved into the horary, the mundane, the karmic. I studied the fixed stars and constellations, midpoints, zodiacal symbology, progressions and transits. I cast horoscopes—for the famous and the infamous, my buddy Bernie Monahan, Livy, and myself, all for practice—in order to understand how they worked, to try and comprehend the abstruse machinations of fate. Since I'd joined the ranks of the unemployed again, I had all the time in the world.

I failed, it goes without saying. No one in this life can grasp what's written in the Great Beyond—if there is such a place. At the heart of existence on earth—a cause and effect that itself is completely unknowable—is mystery. It is mystery within riddle within enigma that governs all things, from the smallest grain of sand to the beauty of the flower, from the relations between yin and yang to the ultimate darkness at the outer reaches of the universe. If the great philosophers claim differently, they're full of it—they don't know a fucking thing.

But if I fell far short of the mark, at least I became conversant in the arcane pseudosciences. And who could tell—a new line of bullshit might come in handy someday for picking up a few bucks. Show me somebody who doesn't want to hear about himself. . . .

Meanwhile, Livy had landed something new. This time she was going to be assistant to a guy who owned and operated a roofing supply company out of the attic office of his house at the south end of Roseland Avenue. Ned Sampras was the prototype of Caspar Milquetoast, she told me when she got home from the interview—she could handle him all right. She started on Monday and the pay was respectable, just enough so that if we lived within our means, we'd be able to go on until—

That was exactly the problem. Our lives were always a matter of until, and until never came.

36.

Livy decided that we needed a vacation before she harnessed herself to the yoke of work again. Better yet, since we were still together after all our ups and downs, since we'd lasted through Blake and Fred, we should make it a sort of unofficial second honeymoon, do it up big. It would have to be someplace cheap, someplace close by, since she was starting the new gig in only a few days.

I didn't want to go. The last place you wanted to be when you were miserable was on holiday pretending to enjoy yourself. And once again Livy had us trying to act like royalty—or at least a middle-class family—when in reality we were nothing more than bottom-feeders scraping by on a shoestring.

Okay, I said. I let her make the arrangements. We packed up our stuff fast. But before we could get out the door, a half-dozen skirmishes had to be fought. First she wasn't going. Then I wasn't going. She hated my guts. I hated hers. It went back and forth like this for hours. Madness. By the time we climbed into the Nova with the suitcase, half the day was gone. I drove with a flask of Rock & Rye between my legs. It was sleeting and snowing and raining, all at the same time. Livy navigated, until we ended up at one of those cheesy blue-collar newlywed resorts in the Pocono

Mountains where the sunken bathtubs were built in the shape of gigantic hearts and every night you were supposed to screw the living daylights out of your new bride or groom. Wherever we went we were greeted as "Mister and Mrs. Tanga." Rather than make Livy happy, whenever that happened she would glance at me with a hint of disappointment in her eyes. Could she possibly want to be legally married to me after the shit we'd been through? After all this time, I still couldn't decipher what was in her mind. She had to be insane. I knew that I was. We were both insane.

Bombed on the cheap champagne that was stocked in the room by the maids every afternoon, we got it on a few times in the tub, and the old magic was back. For some reason at that time I liked to pin her ankles behind her ears—buck-fucking, I once heard someone call it. If I was out of rubbers, I'd wait until the very last second to pull out and blow my wad all over her smooth, hard belly, then drag my dribbling dick across the black hair of her cunt and to the mouth of her asshole. When it comes to sex, that's how men are—we get something in our heads, and we can't rest easy until we do it. I can still see Olivia Aphrodite climbing naked out of the white puffs of frothy bubbles like some mythological Diana emerging from the forest, and my mouth waters at the memory. But if fucking Livy was good, the best part of the trip was driving the snowmobiles in the hills surrounding the resort. Rocketing through the icy winter air in the bullet-shaped vehicles, I felt free. Free of everything, including myself, for a few minutes. Had there been some way, I would have kept the pedal to the gas until I made it all the way to the other end of the earth—China.

At night after dinner it was important to Livy that we listen to the lame comedians and then dance to the second-rate music in the main lounge. Even though I hated it, I did it. I did everything I could so that she'd be happy for those three or four days at least, not so much from a desire to see her happy, but in order to have a few hours of surcease to the suffering that had become our life together.

But in the end, as we were driving away through the early February flurries, I couldn't miss the dejection in her face, and I knew that whatever I'd tried to do hadn't worked.

37.

For ten bucks I had a business card dummied up:

MAX ZAJACK
BIRTH CHARTS
DELINEATION, INTERPRETATION,
CONSULTATION
226–9164

   I cut the astrological symbol for Capricorn (my sign) out of an issue of *Dell Horoscope* and asked the designer at the shop to affix it to the upper right-hand corner. With the addition of that decorative touch, I was in business.

   I dropped the card all over the place, in the Laundromat, the library, at the corner newsstand, and within a few days the phone was ringing off the hook. I was right—people aren't interested in anything so much as they're interested in themselves; if there's one thing that will keep a woman's attention (and my clients turned out to be women almost exclusively), it's talking about her nonstop for an hour or two.

   I scheduled all my appointments for anywhere between nine and five, when Livy was at work. All species of female came to the apartment in search of answers to questions about their past and future. The majority were lost souls simply in need of someone to talk to. Like Minnie the librarian. She was a nearsighted little mouse who was shy to the point of painfulness and who'd never set foot out of her Jersey hometown. Whether it was something she gave off or something I sensed, her horoscope refused to speak to me in any way. While I considered it my duty to be truthful about what I thought was written in the cosmic wheel, I couldn't bring myself to let her leave without some kind of hope, so I concocted a few glowing generalities on the spot.

"Your life is going to take an adventurous turn. Yes, definitely."

"Really? When?"

"Hmm . . . let me see here. . . . Well, in about a year, when Jupiter crosses into your ninth house."

"*God*, I hope you're right about that. . . . Sometimes I'm afraid that I'll never get out of my mother's house!"

"I'm always right, so don't you worry."

"And what else do you see?"

"From the favorable relationship between your Neptune in the fifth and Mercury in the second, that you have quite a fertile imagination. And that there's money to be made from developing it. Poetry, singing, sculpture."

"Really. . . . I never thought. . . . I mean, I *wanted* to believe, but I never had the *confidence* that—"

"That's all it is, Minnie—a matter of confidence," I said—as if I knew anything about it. "If you believe in yourself, there's nothing that can stop you. You just have to dig right in, and whatever you do, don't be afraid."

Even if no such thing was indicated, what was the harm in a few bromides? It was necessary to impart hope; that was the important thing. Because, after all, hope was what they'd come for—even if hope was at bottom an insidious quantity. Better to live without a shred of hope than to live within the hazes of illusion. But human beings always need the quick fix. Without it, there's no use getting out of bed in the morning.

"I'm so glad I came to you, Max! You're making me feel so *good*!"

"It's not me, Minnie—it's right here in the stars."

Of course, just the idea of a jerk in my boat doling out counsel was preposterous, since I was completely and totally inept when it came to handling my own affairs. I only had to think of my relations with Livy to be reminded of that. Still, it didn't seem to matter—in a steady stream they kept coming to have their fortunes told. . . .

One of the more intriguing calls came from a woman announcing herself in a heavy Middle Eastern accent as Shareen. How did she get my number? Laura Dexter, a portrait painter who I'd advised recently, recommended my services highly. Rather than come to my apartment—Shareen had two young children and it was sometimes difficult to haul them around—she wondered would I be averse to making a house call? She would certainly make it worth my while.

We set an appointment for Thursday afternoon. The address Shareen gave me was in a ritzy section of Roseland, across the street from where the Mafia dons had their fortresses. I rolled my heap into the driveway and took in the huge Colonial: three stories with two spacious wings, a shady acre or two out back, a shiny black Mercedes docked in one garage bay—somebody here was nicely covered.

When she answered the bell, I had trouble believing my eyes. Shareen was a drop-dead dusky knockout. Her ebony hair was pulled back from her face, revealing an exquisite bone structure full of lovely angles beneath bronze skin and black eyes that seethed with sex, the sex-fire of a harem girl in ancient Persia. She wore a neck-to-floor shift, but at her slightest movement I could see the outline of her brown nipples and juicy haunches.

She invited me into the airy living room and served coffee. Her kids scampered around like mice until she banished them to the basement to play.

"Now," she said, reclining against the plush cushions on the sofa, *"tell me all about myself. . . ."*

Since I could hardly rip my eyes away from her, it took a supreme effort to pay attention to what I was there to do. I rambled from topic to topic, spouting truisms until I ran out of things to say. It didn't matter. She wanted to talk, too.

It turned out that Shareen had entered into an arranged marriage at seventeen (she was only twenty-something now) in her native Lebanon to a considerably older man. They'd immigrated to America only a few years ago, in order to pursue greater opportunities in his career. Her husband was a surgeon at the Saint Barnabas Medical Center in Livingston, a man under enormous pressure to save lives every single day. Why, he was so busy at the hospital, it was a wonder she or the kids got to see him even once a week.

Sometimes she felt lonely, being marooned here in the American suburbs. Which was why it was so nice to have company. . . . someone like myself to come around and offer intelligent, mature, sophisticated conversation. How much did she owe me again?

She wrote out a check and laid it on the top of the glass coffee table. One more thing. . . . Would I by any chance be able to come again and go into greater detail on her chart? There were certain things she wanted to know, answers she needed to specific questions. Was Tuesday a possibility, maybe?

It was a date. Next time I'd concentrate on her fixed stars and the arcane symbols attaching to her personal and outer planets, the points that truly determined a person's fate. And if she was interested, I'd leaven the mixture with a dash of Vedic astrology, which was so much more effective than Western methods when it came to the exact timing of events.

That Tuesday afternoon the brats were napping when I arrived. Shareen was barefoot and moving around in a clinging silk caftan. When I took my seat in the easy chair, she served me dainty appetizers from a silver tray and iced tea from a crystal decanter.

"You are like a bird of paradise in a gilded cage," I began, consulting my notes. "You are in some danger of being held in restraint, and of being moved to different places at the will of others."

"Yes," she nodded vigorously, "absolutely true!"

"And, as a beautiful woman, you can't help but be seduced by the reflection of your own image in the looking glass. This condition is indicated by the rising degree, which happens to be the ninth of Leo."

Man, I was as full of shit as a Christmas turkey. But Shareen went along with everything.

"You know me too well, Max! Would you mind pointing it out to me?"

She got up from the sofa and stepped around to the back of my chair. A lock of her hair brushed against my cheek as she peered over my shoulder at the chart.

"There—right there. . . . See?"

When I turned my head, our mouths met. Even though I'd

suspected that something like this had been on the lady's mind, no way I thought it would actually *happen*. Within seconds she was straddling me, and my hands were inside the sleeves of her caftan. She had hairy forearms, like most women from the Levant, but the rest of her was fucking incredible. My instinct, since I was in another man's house, was to make it fast, but Shareen seemed oblivious to time and to whether her brats might wake up or whether someone else—who?—might walk in on us.

She leaned back and yanked on my belt. I ran my hands up under her garment. *No panties.* I worked my fingers into her slit, which felt like a bloody cut of steak. She began to moan and grind and caress my balls. By the time she worked her tongue into my ear, I couldn't think straight.

When she went to her knees and tried to inhale my cock, I couldn't think at all. I folded my hands behind my head and let her go for a while. I'd read somewhere that the renowned astrologer Sydney Omarr had to sleep with many of his women clients, but I had trouble believing it. Now I suspected that there was something to it. In fact, I thought raggedly as I watched Shareen's comely head bob up and down on my glimmering pole, maybe this was why a guy became a fortune-teller in the first place.

When I could feel the tide rising, I pulled Shareen to her feet. Before I knew it, I was between the goal posts. . . .

She took her sweet time. At every creak of the chair beneath me I twitched like a nervous animal, but she held me firmly in place.

"Don't worry. My husband is performing open heart surgery this afternoon," she whispered in my ear. *"Now I want you to forget all about him and concentrate on me."*

I wanted to hold out for as long as possible, make her do all kinds of vile stuff to me, but that day I just didn't have the control.

"Where do you want me to come . . . ?"

"Inside, inside . . . !"

Just before I pulled the trigger, I took her hand from around my neck and placed her fingers just behind my sack so she could feel my engine pumping all that semen into her.

When it was over, she slid off and disappeared into another room. Clean and hard and silent—just the way I liked it. She was gone for what seemed to be a long time, fifteen minutes, twenty. When she finally returned, it was to hand me a check, this time for more than my usual fee. I'd never made easier money in my life.

"Can you tell me more next Thursday?"

I cleared my throat. "Whatever you say. . . . Maybe next time we'll tackle your secondary progressions. . . . Yes, I think so. Same time?"

"And I want you to chart my husband, too."

"What?"

"His name is Habib, born April 7, 1935, Beirut, Lebanon, at six A.M."

I jotted down the information.

"You're sure this is a good idea?"

She smiled.

"Of course it is. He needs to know about himself, too."

38.

I hadn't meant to cheat on Livy, but the way I saw it afterward, nobody else with a straight dick in his pants would have been able to resist Shareen, either. Besides, what about *Fred*? What had Livy been up to with Fred on the nights she didn't come home? They hadn't been discussing trends in the restaurant industry, for sure.

My prize client jumped me as soon as I made it through the door that Thursday.

"Shareen, where are your kids?"

"The children are at my mother-in-law's today! And Habib won't be coming for his reading—he's too busy in the operating room. So, Max, you and I will have all the time in the world. . . ."

"You mean I did all that work on his horoscope for nothing?"

"Forget it, Max! You'll just have to do the reading another time."

Shareen was excited, but the situation had me feeling downright jumpy. The huge house was so cavernous—all balconies and alcoves and black doorways—that I couldn't shake the creepy sensation that a body was going to pop out of nowhere like a jack-in-the-box at any second and catch us in the act. Making love to a beautiful woman was one thing, but doing her in her husband's living room was something else altogether—that was playing with fire. But I wasn't about to argue with my hostess. One look at her and I was nothing but iron-hard tusk.

It was another hell of a fuck. I was lounging half asleep against the sofa pillows, the tail of my shirt peeking out from the top of my fly, when the front door burst open.

"Habib!" cried Shareen, flying straight into his arms. "I didn't expect you home so *early*! What a pleasant surprise!"

Lucky for me that my charts and ephemeris were scattered across the coffee table and Shareen was just entering from the kitchen with a tray of refreshments. Apart from the fact that I had my feet up like I owned the place, the scene at least had some little appearance of up-and-up business.

Still and all, I felt myself go red in the face. Habib was a small man who looked a bit lost inside his dark suit and tie. He seemed less interested in his wife than he did in me.

"This is Max. . . . Max, my husband, Habib."

I jumped up and extended my hand. Habib's was tiny, weak, and clammy—the deadly claw of the surgeon.

"I've heard a lot about you," I lied.

"Max was just finishing up the spiritual portion of my reading." Shareen smiled with wifely deference. "He's very good, you know."

"Is that so?" sneered Habib. His pockmarked face flushed with anger.

"Oh, yes! In fact, since you're home early, maybe you'd like to have your chart read. Max could do that—couldn't you, Max? You are prepared to read Habib's chart, aren't you?"

"Absolutely and positively," I stammered. "I've got everything I need right here. . . ."

Habib waved his hand disdainfully.

"Please. Don't insult me. I don't believe in such tripe. Besides, who has time to waste listening to old wives' tales?"

This response seemed to throw Shareen. "I will pay you for the preparation of my husband's horoscope," she said quietly before rushing off into another room.

"You have some nerve, coming into my house and stealing my hard-earned money," Habib hissed like a viper when his wife was out of earshot.

"Well, your wife seems to think—"

"My wife is a child. Look at all I've given her, and still she needs toys to play with."

At the word "toys" he tilted his head backward and looked down his nose at me.

"My advice to you is take your silly charts and stay away from this house!"

Shareen came back with a check for my services, which she handed over to me without a word. I felt a little ashamed taking it, until I glanced at the generous total and the slew of overdue bills back at the apartment crossed my mind.

I stuffed the slip of blue paper into the pocket of my jeans. Then I turned my back on the two of them and got out of there as fast as my feet would carry me.

39.

After that run-in with Habib, my counseling business inexplicably went south. Nobody, it seemed, wanted her fortune told anymore. As fast as it had come, it was gone. Screwing Shareen had turned out to be bad luck.

Until Livy came home one day with an order—her boss and his wife wanted their birth charts analyzed. While I was at it, would I mind accompanying her to their house for dinner some evening? Ned wouldn't stop bugging her to set a date. It was hard to work for someone in close quarters when you were under that kind of pressure.

What the hell. My social calendar was empty. Besides, I was mildly curious about this Mister Sampras. The only information Livy let fly about him was that his personal habits were less than appealing—he liked to pare the nails of his beefy hands while they were having lunch, for instance. It made her want to throw up, but a job was a job.

I dashed off the horoscopes and we drove on over the following Wednesday. Ned's place was the typical suburban deal—a split-level coated with fresh paint, nice backyard full of healthy grass, spacious two-car garage. Not quite in the same ballpark as Habib's spread, but the Samprases were doing okay for themselves. It must have been a good year for roofing supplies.

Bald, glasses, geeky—Ned could have passed for Habib's brother or cousin. All these bourgeois stiffs looked pretty much alike, cut out of the same cookie mold that left them without a mark of distinction whatever their income level. The way I saw it most of the time, they were the real losers in life, desperate to fit in, frantic to "make it" in the eyes of society. For all my failings and weaknesses, at least I wasn't *that*. And if I was a loser— and I had to admit that I *was*—I was a loser more or less on my own terms. Not that it mattered so much when all the marbles were counted. We're all losers in the game of life; nobody gets out of it in one piece—or alive. Anyway, that was Ned. At first glance, there wasn't much to say about him. He smiled, he was congenial, he made us feel right at home. The wife, Helen, was a middle-aged hausfrau with indistinct features who still carried the residue of an accent she'd brought over from Athens thirty years before. She was a hell of a cook, though, serving up one rich delicacy after another. By the time dinner was over, I was so stuffed with lamb, cabbage, tomatoes, and retsina, I could hardly push my chair away from the table.

We moved to the living room and huddled around the coffee table for the main event. I did a perfunctory reading of Ned first, then his wife. They oohed and aahed over my prognostications (for an upturn in business, mostly). Like most people, after the subject of themselves, their main interest is their money.

What could they possibly want with us—a bum and a girl thirty years their junior? I couldn't make it out until Livy ducked into the powder room and Mrs. Sampras went to busy herself cleaning up in the kitchen.

I was in an easy chair and Ned was on the sofa. He was on his sixth or seventh glass of wine by then. There was a leer on his doughy face. He leaned over to me confidentially, his dentures flashing in the lamplight.

"She must be something, eh?"

"Huh?" What the hell was Poindexter getting at? I laughed, being a little kicked in the ass from the booze myself.

"Your girlfriend—Olivia. She's so . . . *hot*. I have to admit—I often wonder what it must be like . . . well, you're a guy—*you know what I mean.*"

He gave a lecherous chuckle. Caspar Milquetoast had been transformed into one more guy on a barstool. *So that was it:* Ned had a thing for Livy, and it was probably driving him crazy. Why hadn't I figured it out before? Lock any man in a two-by-four cell with Livy and he'd have to go nutters.

"You said it," I agreed, deciding on the moment to taunt him. "She's really something else, all right. Sometimes she won't let me out of bed for days on end." After all, Ned had to be as harmless as he looked, right?

Ned swallowed hard and blanched. He didn't bring up the subject for the remainder of the evening.

Before we left, Ned slipped me a check for fifty bucks, twenty-five each for his and Helen's astrological forecasts. On the way home I told Livy what happened when the women were out of the room.

She seemed annoyed to be let in on Ned's dirty little secret. "So what do you want me to do about it anyway? Quit the job? I don't see you bringing home any fat checks lately!"

And of course, I couldn't argue with her. . . . A few days later I'm deep into *The Old Cossack* when the telephone rings. It's Livy.

She's standing on a street corner somewhere in Roseland. I can tell from her icy tone that she's in high dudgeon. She needs for me to come out and pick her up—on the double.

"Where are you, again?"

"How the fuck should I know!"

"Well, how the fuck am I supposed to pick you up, then?"

"Just find me, Max!"

She describes the area around the telephone booth. It sounds like a street corner near the Roseland post office. I jump into the car and within minutes Livy's sitting beside me.

"What happened? Why aren't you at work?"

"I quit, that's why!"

"Why? What gives?"

"The stupid bastard made a move on me!"

"You mean Ned?" I had to laugh. "Well, what's so bad about that? He seems like an innocuous old fart."

"It was the way he did it!"

"What did he do?"

"He broke down and started bawling like a two-year-old!"

"He *what*? He didn't try and grab your snatch or anything?"

"Oh, no! *That,* I might have been able to deal with. Instead, he sits his fat ass on my desk and confesses that he's *in love* with me! That he's been in love with me from the first day I walked into his life. That his wife knows all about it because he *told* her. That he doesn't know what he's going to do . . . that he can't stop thinking about me, and that's all he does, day and night—think about me. He can't even sleep anymore."

"Oh, shit. I see what you mean."

"No, you don't! I was never so embarrassed in all my life! You should have seen me tiptoeing past his wife on my way out the

door! I don't know why the idiot jerk-off fool just couldn't leave things the way they were—I was making money, he was happy. The stupid, stupid bastard!"

"He was *hap*— Liv, what are you saying—"

"Shut up, Max! JUST SHUT UP!"

40.

Livy didn't go back to work for Ned Sampras. I never found out what really went on between the two of them in that guy's attic, but if I owned a ranch I'd bet it that it wasn't the line of jive Livy tried halfheartedly to sell me that day she demanded to be retrieved from the street corner. My guess was that somewhere along the line she'd entered into an intimate relationship—the exact nature of which I didn't know (and didn't want to know)—with Ned in exchange for lucre, and that something had gone wrong; maybe he'd wanted more out of it—or maybe *she* did. Once certain lines were crossed—I was thinking of Fred here, and others for all I knew—what did one more trick matter? Besides, Livy took a perverse pride in being a slick prostitute. . . . What this latest fuckup meant, of course, was that we were without an income all over again, and that somebody was going to have to go out there and hunt down a good enough job so that we could survive from day to day.

Since my fear of the world was temporarily in remission (the condition mysteriously came and went), I gave it a shot, but for some inexplicable reason, my marketability was at an all-time low. I filed application after application for anything and everything under the sun, but nobody ever called and invited me in for an interview. Secretly I was relieved—I was much too absorbed in my book to take on a nine-to-fiver. If I was put out on the street for the crime of financial insolvency, then so be it. I often consoled myself with the thought that I knew of no one in my lifetime who'd been tossed into debtors' prison.

Livy saw it differently. These days a new, reckless determination had shown up in her demeanor. Watching her across the kitchen table, I would speculate on what had fueled it. Was it despair over what had gone sour between us? Or was it Fred she was still pining over? Was it maybe something I was blind to altogether? You never really know where you stand when it comes to the inner life of a woman. There's some basic part of the female that by nature has to keep you—the male—in the dark. If not, then what's the point in being the opposite sex? Whatever it was, she seemed bent on pulling herself by her bootstraps out of the shithole we'd dug for ourselves. Morning after morning she patched herself together in front of the bathroom mirror and set out to beat the bushes for something decent. As I watched her go out the door, I wished her good luck. . . .

Sunday afternoon. After the tolling of the church bells, sleepy boredom. The weather is fine, it's early spring, so Livy and I decide to take a hike through the woods of the South Mountain Reservation twenty minutes away. Afterward, in the parking lot, she stops dead, as if she's seen a ghost. She's eyeballing a man who's standing on an incline of dead grass, hands in pockets, admiring the view of the pond in the distance.

What is it?

She snaps out of her trance and hustles toward the car.

Let's get out of here, she says, sitting rigidly in the passenger's seat.

What's wrong?

No answer, only a fixed gaze at nothing.

As we roll out of the lot, I take a closer gander at the object of her scrutiny. He's not much, a lump of a guy with a middle-aged paunch hanging over his belt and a balding pate. What could he possibly mean to Livy?

The incident is enough to nudge her into one of her remote, melancholic states by the time we reach the apartment. As usual when that happens, she flops on the bed and stares at the ceiling. I find a spot on the floor and wait for what's going to come. Because I know something will—it always does when she gets like this.

I had an affair with him. Her voice is far away, like a burble in a dream.

What? Who are you talking about? I say, though I know damned well who she means.

That man in the parking lot near the woods. Michael Goldfarb. A jeweler.

I hate the way she pronounces the word "Michael." "*Mi*-chael." Why not just fucking "Mike"? Why does she have to be so goddamned *delicate* with it? Women have a maddening habit of being entirely too reverential with their ex-lovers' names, handling them like pricey crystal vases.

Yes . . . I thought I recognized him out there. At first I wasn't sure. It's been years since I've set eyes on Michael.

So why didn't you just go up to him and say something?

Oh, no. No, I couldn't.

Why not? Who is he, the Prince of Wales?

No. . . . It was just too—

Too what?

You know.

No, I don't.

Oh, you know—just too *intense* between us.

What does she expect me to say to that? And why an "affair"?

He's married. Two kids. His wife didn't understand him at all.

Mm-hmm.

Michael treated me like a queen. Gave me things all the time, whenever he came to see me. Flowers. Clothes. Jewelry. Took me to the finest restaurants. He would be at my side the minute he could get away from his family. And I would wait for him. I would have done anything for him. *Anything.*

Another revelation. With Livy, there are always more lovers to learn about, to be compared with. And you never know when you're going to be treated to a lesson.

He's nothing to look at, I know, but what does it matter? Look at you. You're handsome, but you don't love me the way Michael loved me. So when I saw him today, I just—

What?

Remembered. How it was at the end. How it couldn't go on. Because he couldn't bring himself to leave his kids. If it was just his wife who was involved, I wouldn't be here right now.

Livy's eyes well up with tears. She rolls over and buries her face in the pillow.

I stare at the back of her neck. What I should do is take a carving knife and sink it in there, get this over with once and for all. What a grand thing love is.

Instead, after a long time, I get off the floor and climb on top of her, my hard cock searching for a way inside her body.

Get away from me! she howls into the pillow. *Just leave me alone. I don't want you near me.*

41.

Once again Livy's looks saved her. This time she was going to hump tables with a bevy of other cute young waitresses at Gennaro's, a glossy pizza-and-beer joint in West Orange that ran a comedy club in the basement on weekends. All kinds of people passed through Gennaro's—on-the-rise comics, prizefighters, low-level mobsters, celebrities on the way down. Since the customer turnover was phenomenal, she could expect to haul in anywhere between fifty and seventy-five a night in gratuities along with her hourly salary—not bad in a pinch. She started on Tuesday.

A few days later my heap finally died. I persuaded one of the mechanics from the Exxon across the street to help me push it into his garage for an estimate. Autopsy results: shot fuel pump, leaky transmission, ring job needed. There was no point in having the car fixed, and even less money to do it. The beast no longer had blue book value, so I had no choice but to call the junkyard. When the guy arrived he handed me twenty-five in cash and hitched the flecked green dinosaur to his truck. I got all choked up when I watched its dim taillights sink into the river of traffic on Bloomfield Avenue. Gone forever. . . . I'd never see her again. A car can do that to you—the Impala and I had been together a long time.

Since now we had only Livy's Nova between us, I became her chauffeur to Gennaro's every evening. Back at the apartment I banged away at *The Old Cossack* in the heat of the summer nights, the sweat rolling off my arms in clammy rivulets like a boxer in the ring. I was in a delirium now to finish the damned thing and, what the hell—maybe chance it out on the open market.

Some nights my old pal Bernie Monahan would show up at the apartment, and we'd head out to a nightclub to try and pick up women—he was bored with his longtime girlfriend, and one look at yours truly convinced him that I was in even more immediate need of a change of scenery.

But we weren't really trying very hard, and when the bars shut down most of our forays ended in a highway diner over eggs and home fries and coffee, to be followed by long bullshit sessions about how my life had turned into such a minefield.

Bernie had his opinions.

"That one's a fruitcake, buddy. You have to get out of there before something happens. Something *serious*."

"I'm not arguing with you."

"Either she's going to kill you, or you're going to lose it altogether and murder her."

"Not unless one of us ends up in prison or the state insane asylum first. But every time I make a move to break away, she threatens to bump herself off. And I'm not even sure at this point that I could survive on my own, man."

"You really think she'd actually do something to herself?"

"I think she's capable of *anything*, Bernie. God's honest truth."

"You gotta be tough as nails then! Let her know who's boss! That your life is your life. That you won't stand for any more shit from her."

"Yeah. . . . The trouble is it's not that easy."

He shrugged. "How's the sex?"

"Still white hot, believe it or not. I never get tired of Livy. It's like all the madness stokes the fire."

"Even though she probably fucked this ex-con, Fred."

"Yeah. Go figure."

"And who knows who else, right? . . . I don't get it, Max. The whole thing sounds wacky to me. Look at yourself, for Christ's sake! You live by night like a vampire, you can't hold down the lowest job, and you write stuff nobody wants to read."

"We don't know that yet."

"We *know*, if your past history is any indication. The point is, what are you going to do to turn this thing around? You're like a . . . a *worm*, at the mercy of this femme fatale's every whim. Either find a way out or keep the bitch in line once and for all!"

"Sure, Bernie, whatever you say. . . ."

When we parted ways in the early morning, my friend had me half convinced that my war with Livy was one I was capable of winning. One half of me made resolutions to the other. I promised myself a new regimen. I swore a new defiance the next time a conflict broke out. No way I was going to let Livy get the best of me—even if some sick part of me still loved her.

By the time I had to pick Livy up at the restaurant, my kite would do a nosedive and I was completely disheartened all over again. I shuffled inside and nursed a beer at the bar while the waitstaff tallied up their depredations for the night. If the take was good, spirits were high. If it wasn't, there was sure to be lots of grumbling about all the cheapskates they'd had to wait on hand and foot.

Livy made a whole new set of best friends among the workers

at Gennaro's. The best of the best was Mitchell Jeremy. Behind his back Mitch was referred to as the "gay caballero" by some of the he-man wiseguy types who hung around hitting on the waitresses. He sported earrings and makeup long before that crap became au courant. Like most fags in enemy territory, Mitch kept himself and his lifestyle enshrouded in a cloud of secrecy. His jokes were on the inside and under the cuff. His repartee was quick, clever, and bitchy. The guy wasn't easy to talk to, but Livy got along with him famously. Like other effeminate males, he enjoyed trading his maquillage secrets with women, and he and the waitresses had their own clique, from which I was unofficially excluded.

Thus began another round of nocturnal carousing for Olivia. She and her group began hanging out at Mitchell Jeremy's house in Livingston, which had been left to him when his parents retired to Florida. There, according to Livy, they knocked down a few drinks, smoked some weed, and watched a little early-morning television. Whether that was what they were really up to was anybody's guess. It was okay—when she called me off I didn't mind being left to my own devices.

My problems at Gennaro's began with a cat by the name of Siffuzzi. He was young, like me, and one of those privileged souls who never seemed to have to be anywhere or have anything to do. When he had a few under his belt or some blow up his nose, he liked to crow about his Mob connections, which I suspected was nothing more than braggadocio since the real item for the most part kept quiet about it. Livy took that stuff much more seriously than I did—she was always impressed by any mention of La Cosa Nostra. Maybe it was her Latin blood.

At first Siffuzzi was cool, buying me drinks whenever I stopped in to take Livy home, chatting me up about my novel, riffing on the characters who frequented the restaurant. But as time passed, he developed a strange, inexplicable hostility toward me, until his friendly banter had turned mocking, even vicious, and one night. . . .

"Man, that's some deal you got, sittin' around scribblin' shit nobody's ever going to read while your girlfriend slaves to pay your rent."

This was delivered like an observation about the weather. I couldn't believe what I was hearing—which is always the case when something comes out of left field.

"Since when is it any of your business? Anyway, that's not exactly the way it is, Siffuzzi."

"*Bullshit*. I got eyes in my head. I see what you're up to. You're a sleazy fucking pimp, Zajack!"

I turned to face the jerk-off douchebag.

"Who are you to talk about deals? I don't see you doing much of anything but holding up the ass-end of a bar and blowing hot air, Siffuzzi. That chain around your neck must be cutting off the flow of blood to your brain. If you have one."

"Fuck you, Zajack!"

"Are you trying to jump into my shit here, Siffuzzi? What the fuck is your problem?"

"*Fuck you, man!* I'm gonna kick your ass!" He tossed the dregs of his beer into my face. Before I could react, Jimbo the bartender quickly stepped out from behind his station and forced his body between us.

"I want bot' a you outta here! You got a problem wit one 'nother, you take it out back to the parkin' lot!"

What the fuck was going down here?

I was completely in the dark as to what it might be, but as low as I was, I wasn't about to let some two-bit barfly make a fool of me in public. Being humiliated by Livy was one thing. This was something else altogether—a man-to-man thing, all testosterone. So we took it on out there, winging at each other like a pair of common drunks while the staff and some of the customers shouted encouragement at both of us—but mostly him, it seemed to me.

"Knock him on his ass, Siffuzzi!"

"Squash the motherfucker!"

"Don't let that bastard get the best of you, Sifooze!"

Despite the fact that I'd let myself go over the past few years, I was always something of an athlete. I'd played baseball, hoops, diddled around in the squared circle. There wasn't an ounce of fat on me. No way this Neanderthal dildo was going to get the best of me. All my pent-up rage was like raw electricity in my arms and legs. I was out of my mind with fury.

I tried to find fast openings for my fists since I figured I was the less drunk of the two of us. Here and there I landed—near the liver, on the top of Siffuzzi's rock of a skull, on the bridge of his nose. Although he was taller than I was, he was softer and punched like a cunt, wild and undisciplined, with his thumbs tucked into his fists. But no matter what I threw at him, he kept coming at me like an enraged pit bull.

"I'm gonna kill you, asshole!"

"Fuck you! You fight like a little girl!"

I grabbed Siffuzzi and slammed him into the rear fender of a Cadillac. Somehow he managed to trip me on the rebound and I went sprawling face-first onto the black asphalt. He jumped me down there and we rolled under a Dumpster, whaling away until someone cried, "A siren! Somebody called the cops!"

The whole thing was ridiculous and absurd. Why did this thug hate me? *And by the way—where the fuck was Livy?* I don't know how, but I managed to jump into the car and beat it before the pigs arrived on the scene and started asking questions. . . .

I couldn't even remember driving back to the apartment. When I saw myself in the bathroom mirror, I shuddered. I was a wreck—torn clothes, two black eyes, jagged cuts and ugly bruises and abrasions everywhere. Both my hands felt broken. All my limbs were swollen to distortion. I stumbled into the shower and stayed there for an hour. Livy must have gotten a lift home from one of her little friends. She tried to fix me up with hydrogen peroxide and Band-Aids. When I lowered myself gingerly to the sofa, I thought I'd never move again. My only consolation was knowing I got the best of my adversary. If I felt like a cut of flank steak, Siffuzzi had to feel like ground shit.

"Where the hell were you when all this was going on?" I mumbled to Livy through puffy lips and a sore jaw.

"I have a job to tend to, or did you forget about that? I don't have the leisure to camp out in the parking lot and watch you act like a child."

Livy's lack of sympathy puzzled me. It didn't dawn on me until early in the morning when I lay wide awake on that sofa like a giant throbbing wound that there was probably a good reason for it—she was either about to have a thing going—or already *had* a thing going—with that third-rate Mafioso wannabe. What other explanation could there be for the ambush? It had never even occurred to me that Siffuzzi was her *type*, with his pudgy belly and short hair.

Then I thought of Michael Goldfarb, and realized I should have known better.

42.

With bandages on my hands and a bottle of Advil at my side I put the finishing touches on *The Old Cossack*. When the completed 350-page manuscript of my first novel was sitting on the desk in front of me, I sat back and treated myself to a victory cigarette and can of beer. For the first time in years I felt a sense of real accomplishment. And for better or worse, success or failure aside— and I really had no clue which I was drinking to—I couldn't believe that I'd actually pulled it off. Frankly, I was amazed at myself. When I started writing I'd had no idea what I was doing. I scribbled, scratched, and typed, I'd found my way from the dead center of the book to its outer reaches, then back to the beginning in a loopy trajectory, but still, despite everything, including daily strife with the person I slept with and the bill collector at the door, I'd *done* it, and I'd done it without encouragement or hope. And if nothing else, that was more than most of the world's losers could say for themselves. For those few moments on an autumn afternoon, the world looked pretty good again, and it held out some kind of promise.

The next morning I marched up to the stand where I bought my Marlboros and newspapers every day and laid out a buck fifty for one of the monthly magazines devoted to writers. In the classifieds was a list of literary agents. The Vroom Agency in Sarasota, Florida, took on all sorts of properties and at no fee to the writer. A representative list of titles sold over the past few years revealed some books I'd actually heard of, including one that had gone on to become a major Hollywood motion picture. Next I had the original manuscript of the novel Xeroxed at an office supply store, where I also picked up a pair of envelopes large enough to accommodate my bundle to and back from the Sunshine State. Then I sat down and wrote a letter introducing my masterpiece To Whom It May Concern, dropped it into the mail, and forgot all about it for the time being.

Livy didn't have a single word to say about my accomplishment. Furthermore, she had no desire whatsoever to look at *The Old Cossack*. "I'm too exhausted to read after the restaurant" was her excuse. It was as if the novel I'd slaved over didn't exist. When I told her that I'd packaged it off to an agent, she shrugged. Just as well. Since she hadn't been able to complete so much as a single story in the years we'd been together, there wasn't much point in rubbing it in. Besides, it probably wouldn't matter one way or another, because there wasn't the proverbial snowball's chance in hell I'd be able to sell the stack of paper anyway.

T hanks to you, I'm getting laid off," Livy snarled when she got into the car. "Goddamn you, Max!"

It was two thirty in the morning. I'd roused myself out of a deep sleep to pick her up from the restaurant. My head ached. My mouth was full of cotton from the two packs of cigarettes I'd smoked that day. I felt like one of the undead.

"What are you talking about?"

"I'm getting the boot, that's what! They tried to sell me that

business is slow, but it's a crock! I know why this happened: it's because of that stupid brawl you had with Siffuzzi!"

The mist in my brain was beginning to lift.

"*Fuck.* . . . Yeah, but that was weeks ago. And it wasn't my fault, remember."

"People talk, you jerk! Jimbo the bartender complained about you to the owner! You had no right picking a fight with anybody at my place of business, Max! *You cost me my fucking job!* And you know what that means!"

"I'll kill that motherfucker," I growled through gritted teeth as I drove, swerving to avoid the black trunk of a tree that had appeared out of nowhere.

"Watch where the fuck you're going or you'll kill the both of *us*!"

"And besides," I went on, ignoring her and arguing my case, "Siffuzzi was the one who started it!"

"Who gives a fuck who started it, Max! I'm losing my job on account of you! *Don't you fucking get it?* In a matter of a couple of weeks, we're going to be out of money again!"

I got it all right. I knew what the implications were.

When we reached the apartment we went straight to sleep, me on my side of the bed and Livy on hers. Lately we weren't making it so much; after all we'd been through, the thrill was finally gone. The fact was we rarely went near each other anymore. Sometimes late at night I would hide in the bathroom and jerk off to get myself whipped enough to sleep. I had the feeling Livy was doing the very same thing at the very same moment in the bedroom. . . .

When I would finally lay my weary head on the pillow, a single thought coursed obsessively through my brain like the ticking of a manic metronome: *I have to get out of here. Monahan wasn't*

kidding. I have to get out of here: somehow, some way. Before one or
both of us crack. Before there's mayhem and murder.
But how?

After getting the ax at Gennaro's, Livy flatly refused to budge
from the bed. If I thought the two of us had hit rock bottom
before, I was sadly off the mark. Now we were under the rocks.
Now, in addition to her dope and her booze, she kept herself barricaded in the bedroom with the telephone. She held marathon
secret conversations in there, and the muffled quality of her voice
as well as the fact that there wasn't an extension to eavesdrop by
kept me from making a good guess who she might be talking to.
Mitchell Jeremy? Michael Goldfarb? Fred? For all I knew, it was the
dude she was with when we first met—Edward. *Maybe she was*
talking to herself. We never went anywhere or did anything anymore, not even so much as venture out to the movies like we used
to in the early days. Nobody, including the bill collectors, ever
stopped by for any reason. It was as if we'd fallen off the face of
the earth, as if we'd made ourselves into pariahs. Nothing seemed
to matter anymore to either of us.

The rows that broke out between us now were downright
terrifying. A glance, a single word, everything, anything could
set off World War III. Livy would pick up whatever was at
hand—bottle, book, lamp—rear back, and aim straight for my
head. From that point on, at all hours of day and night there
were shouts, curses, the din of smashing glass and crockery
emanating from unit 5C. It was like a madhouse in there.
Sometimes the neighbors called the police, who arrived in a
matter of minutes, banged on the door, and demanded to know
what the trouble was.

"Why, nothing at all, officer! What would give you such an idea?" Livy would respond, all honey and sugar, after pulling herself together for the performance.

"We got a summons about a disturbance in this apartment," one of the uniforms would explain.

"Oh, no, we're fine here . . . *aren't we, Max*? Maybe you should try at the other end of the hall. We've heard some strange noises coming from that vicinity. . . ."

After the squad car pulled away, we'd pick up where we left off. One night Livy pulled a carving knife on me and threatened to use it.

"Go on! Put me out of my misery, I dare you!"

Without blinking an eye she took me up on the challenge and lunged, slicing and slashing like a fiend. She succeeded in gouging my palm and inflicting a few superficial cuts on my arms before I could tackle her and wrest the weapon away. I tossed it over my shoulder, grabbed her with both hands around the neck in a choke hold, and shook her like a rag doll.

"You crazy fucking bitch! You've gone over the edge! I'm going to call the state hospital! They'll bring the straitjacket and wrap you in it so tight you'll never get out! Do you hear me? DO YOU?"

I cocked my fist to let her have it square in the face, but at the last second I woke up. Instead I left her on the floor and fled the premises before I lost all control and committed the capital crime. After hours of trudging the streets, my nerves still jangling like live wires, I jumped an eastbound bus and found myself on the doorstep of Bernie Monahan's pad in Montfleur.

"Sorry to wake you, man, but I'm out of places to go, and wouldn't you know, it just started raining. . . ."

I hadn't seen Monahan in months. He looked me up and down and decided not to ask questions.

"You can have the sofa," he whispered, "but don't wake Gloria." He offered me a beer, but I was too wrung out to even drink. Without taking off my clothes, I collapsed and passed out. My last hope before tumbling into oblivion was that I wouldn't open my eyes again—ever.

In the early morning, when I was on my way into the bathroom to take a leak, I ran smack into Bernie's naked girlfriend, who was toweling off after stepping out of the shower. Gloria blushed as I took in her big, naked brown breasts.

"Max! I had no idea you were here! . . ."

The sight of her was a shock. I never knew Bernie's woman was put together so well. On another day it would have made a dent. But not today. I turned around, went back out to the sofa, and lit a smoke.

Now what was I going to do? I was blown out. Depleted. And I didn't have more than a buck or two to my name.

For a long time I sat there chewing it over. Some say that life is a beautiful thing, but for me the magic was out of it. Maybe the magic was out of it for good. The solution was action. All right, I decided: I'll go back to Roseland Avenue. But I'm going to get out of this thing with Livy once and for all. I don't know how, but I'm going to get myself free.

I pulled on my clothes and slipped out to the street. Then I walked up to the corner and waited for the bus that would take me back to Caldwell.

43.

THE VROOM LITERARY AGENCY
SARASOTA, FLORIDA

OCTOBER 8, 1979

Dear Mister Zajack:

We like your manuscript THE OLD COSSACK, and wish to offer it to market. Enclosed are two copies of our agency representation contract. When you return the signed first copy to us, we will send your work out to seek a publisher. . . . We here at the Vroom Agency feel that you are a writer of exceptional promise and look forward to working with you.

Sincerely,
Henry Barr

I couldn't believe my eyes. I read the letter over again, very slowly this time, pausing to drink in every single word. I pinched myself to make sure I wasn't dreaming. I turned over the envelope and shook. Out came the two contracts and another sheaf of papers containing breakdowns of potential royalty payments.

I pinched myself again. No, I wasn't dreaming. *The Old Cossack* had hit the sock on its maiden flight.

I soon realized that the agency's offer didn't add up to a sale, but still, it had to count for something, right? Didn't it have to indicate that at least one expert thought I had talent—or something like it? Hadn't Mister Henry Barr typed the words "a writer of exceptional promise"? After all the wasted years, the failure, the brain-dead jobs, that letter was a vindication.

In every lifetime there are a handful of days you're destined to not forget. That shimmering early October day was one of them. For hours I was beside myself with a delirious ecstasy bordering on outright disbelief. From the excitement alone I couldn't decide what to do with myself. I got up from the table clutching my letter and contract, then sat down again. I whooped like an Indian. "I've got a friggin' *agent*," I repeated to myself like a moron who knows only five words or a souse who's just hit the Irish Sweepstakes. I skipped from the kitchen to the living room to the bedroom laughing like a hysterical hyena. I phoned Bernie Monahan and whoever else I could think of with the news. I was in a state of shock. In the back of my mind was the anticipation that somehow this completely unexpected turn of events would spring me from the trap I was in. Maybe I wouldn't have to get free. Maybe Livy would even fall in love with me all over again. Maybe it wasn't too late after all.

When she got home from wherever she'd been I leaped up from the sofa and waved the letter at her.

"Look! An agent wants to sign my book! Can you fucking believe it? I can't—tell me I'm not dreaming!"

She grabbed it out of my hand and looked it over skeptically.

"And they're not charging me a red penny! They seem to think this thing has a real chance out there on the open market! Think about it, Liv! The possibility of an advance! This could be *it*! Our ticket to a new life! No more crappy jobs! No more slaving for idiots! We'll get out of the hole and head for Europe and all the rest of it! You can even have a kid if you want to!"

I'm not sure why I said everything I said. At that moment I would have promised just about anything to anybody.

Livy's reaction to my lucky break was curious. The trace of a sneer crossed her lips. After only a few seconds she seemed to lose interest in the letter. Without a word of congratulations, she dropped it into my hands and disappeared into the bedroom.

Now that beat everything. Maybe she was on the rag. Or maybe it was her own failed aspirations. After all, we'd both started out of the same gate, and I'd managed to do something while she hadn't. I felt for the girl. She'd sacrificed for me in the beginning. Had I been in her shoes, I'd have probably felt the same way. Not jealous, exactly, but . . . shortchanged somehow. But after a few minutes I didn't give it a second thought—I was too absorbed in my own good fortune.

That afternoon I strutted up to the savings and loan on the corner, the same institution where I no longer had an account, and affixed my John Hancock to the contracts in the presence of a notary public, who in turn stamped her official certification on both sheets of paper. She smiled at me when I handed over my five-dollar fee—I must have smelled like a man going places. Then I dropped the stuff into the mail, went home, and popped a bottle to celebrate the day.

Livy was looking like a fifty-karat piece of ass all over again. Amazing, what catching a break could do.

"How about a new restaurant tonight, Liv, that Turkish

kitchen over in Weehawken? On me," I said, running my hands over her majestic flanks.

She said yes—I knew she would. After we devoured our exotic feast, I was going to fuck Livy. She would never know what hit her. It was bound to be a great night.

Within a few days I began to figure out that the good tidings from the Vroom Agency hadn't solved all my problems, especially my biggest, which was, as usual, money—the lack of it. With Livy out of work again and unable to collect unemployment compensation benefits—leading me to believe that she'd been fired rather than laid off from Gennaro's—I was going to have to hit the pavement and dig something up all over again no matter *who* thought I demonstrated exceptional promise.

I put off the ugly task. The only thing I wanted was to bask for as long as possible in the afterglow of my little triumph. Dreams of fame and fortune swirled in my head, but when I didn't get immediate good news about *The Old Cossack*, the shine wore off. It only took a matter of days.

44.

This time I found myself behind the check-in desk of the Camel Brook Motor Inn in West Orange, a two-story motel-cum-nightclub that catered to tourists, corporate parties, hookers and their middle-class johns, lounge lizards who got lucky and their pickups, and a handful of geriatric Jews whose families no longer wanted them around and felt less guilty keeping them in a private motel room than an old-age home. Four-to-midnight was the most heavily trafficked shift of the day and the shift nobody else wanted, so of course that was the shift I drew. My duties included signing in lodgers and directing them toward the vending machines, ice chest, nightclub, and nearby restaurants, and handing out extra towels and directions. It was another chimp's gig. The salary was peanuts. The weird thing about it was that the Camel Brook sat no more than a mile from Livy's old homestead, where once upon a time—and it seemed like a lifetime ago now—she and I spent those eerie and poignant Sunday mornings. . . .

Working as a desk clerk was a new one on me, but it could have been a lot worse. There was a portable television in an alcove behind the desk, unlimited coffee, and a cigarette machine. When there was no customer action, I was free to do whatever

I wanted so long as I didn't fall asleep and allow somebody to knock the place over.

The proprietor was a guy named Billy Stankowski. Billy oversaw the daily operations of the Camel Brook, but he never interfered with me aside from asking "How you doin', Max?" whenever he came or went. He was a flabby blimp who just happened to inherit the whole shebang from his folks, Warsaw Poles off the boat who'd raked in a small fortune running the Camel Brook and had since retired to a Caribbean island. Billy Stankowski was one of those dumb-lucky oafs born into the right situation, but I didn't hate him—he was only in his midthirties and already wearing a bad hairpiece.

The boss's constant shadow was a hot little minx by the name of Marilyn. It was hard to tell what she actually did around the place, but if she wanted to attract the attention of men, she was a smashing success. Day and night she traipsed around in stiletto heels and velvet short shorts, showing whatever she could of her killer body without stripping all the way. Long and slim and blonde, there was more than a little something of the tart about her, and for all I knew she'd been just that once upon a time. If so, God bless Billy—everywhere he went there was that primo piece of tail right behind him. At five every afternoon the Polish prince and his princess retired to his penthouse suite on the top floor for a "nap," a habit that bugged the shit out of the maids. "They're disgusting, those two!" the ladies would bitch whenever Billy and Marilyn took the elevator up. One of them whispered to me that Billy's room was like a pharmacy, so crammed was it with birth control devices. To top it off the place was as filthy as a pigsty! Couldn't the two of them at least pick up after themselves? But I knew what the cleaning ladies were really pissed about: *Why Marilyn and not them?*

No sooner had I finished training on the register than Livy began campaigning for an engagement ring. Her disastrous flings with Fred, Siffuzzi, and Edward and her unrequited passion for Michael Goldfarb hadn't dampened her enthusiasm to get hitched, even if these days she all but pretty much detested *me*. Whenever we passed a jewelry store Livy would stop and moon over the merchandise in the window. When I wasn't feeling bad for her, my blood was boiling, especially since we were still flat broke and owed money to everybody—and everybody's brother.

The mere idea of marriage was insane—even I realized that in some recess of my frazzled brain—and so I tried to prod her off the notion. "Remember, at the beginning, how we always said we didn't need society's approval for the way we lived our lives?"

"Let's not start a long intellectual disputation again, Max! If you don't want me, just tell me and I'll find somebody else! I can do it, you know! Make up your mind for once in your life!"

I was beat. I was so fucking tired. Maybe this time there *was* no way out. *Sure, I wanted to get married* . . . maybe it would make everything better. And maybe *The Old Cossack* would do something big and Livy would be happy and content at long last. Maybe then, if we had some money, I could afford to pop one into the oven and distract her from her demons once and for all. . . .

Lots of maybes, but in life you never know. Stranger things had happened. Men had walked on the moon, hadn't they? So I went ahead and out of my first paycheck laid a fifty-dollar payment down on a minuscule sapphire at a discount place in an industrial park in Fairfield. I was supposed to pay the balance off in installments over a six-month period. Until I did, Livy couldn't wear it. What in hell was I thinking?

———

Once I had the hang of the desk, the motel wasn't such a bad gig. On a daily basis I got to study an enormous array of characters out of the world's encyclopedia: upstanding family men on the cheat with their mistresses . . . finely dressed pimps . . . slick distributors of cocaine . . . shady types who laid low and paid only in cash—in other words, guys on the run. There was something pathetic about all of them, but maybe it was just my frame of mind at the time. . . .

When I wasn't busy with check-ins, I stared at the tube— usually hoops, and the best soap opera ever broadcast on an American network—*I, Claudius*. For an hour a week, the chronicle of the decline of the decadent Roman Empire transported me out of my beleaguered self. The sight of that wicked, deadly adder slithering across the mosaic tiles of a Roman bath in the opening credits reminded me that we were all mired in a poisonous slough of deceit and treachery, whether we were gods, nobles—or motel clerks. The only difference between us was that the rich and powerful enjoyed themselves more than ordinary mortals during their time in hell. That program was the single event of every week that I lived for.

With the rest of my free time I'd begun writing again, in five- or ten-minute stretches, on legal pads I found stashed in the bottom drawer of the registration desk, this time a florid pornographic novel based on my own past sexual exploits. There'd been a few before Livy, and what I hadn't lived myself I could concoct out of my imagination—like any horny guy on the street. If *The Old Cossack* was a flop (I still hadn't heard a word about its whereabouts or fate) this new book would give me something to fall back on. Sex, according to the experts, always sells.

From the beginning, it came shooting out of me like sperm from a humongous geyser: anonymous seductions, threesomes, daisy chains, lesbian fist-fuck-fests—my windy literary version of *Penthouse Forum*. And if ultimately the book failed, at least I was learning something new about the craft of writing. The most important thing was that I was *doing* it; in one sense, it was all a writer could ever ask for, and it sure beat the shit out of some of the other ways I'd frittered away time in my life.

If I had a problem, it was at home. Since I used her car now to get to the motel, Livy had nothing to do with herself during the long nights. Apparently she was still unable to write—writing was something she never even mentioned anymore. Livy was an odd duck . . . while she could lock herself in her bedroom for days on end, it was because she knew I was on the other side of the door. Like most beautiful women, she couldn't stand to be alone with herself. Soon enough she'd had enough of staring at the four walls night after night, so she took to dialing the desk whenever she felt the whim.

"I'm bored, Max. Bring my car home."

"Liv, I happen to be right in the middle of a customer here."

"I don't care what you're doing! You've got my car, and I want you to bring it back right now!"

"Look—I can't talk now, I'm telling you. . . ."

By this time the registrant's curiosity was piqued, and he was watching me like a hawk.

"Didn't you hear me, Max? I said bring my car home! I'd like to use the fucking thing!"

"Liv, *please*. . . . Listen. I'm going to hang up now. I'll talk to you about it later."

No sooner did I replace the phone in its cradle than it would ring again.

"YOU SON OF A BITCH! I'M NOT KIDDING AROUND HERE! IF YOU DON'T BRING THAT CAR HOME THIS

MINUTE, I'M GOING TO CALL THE COPS AND TELL THEM YOU STOLE IT!"

I'd force a phony smile while I filled out the registration card. "Yes, thank you," I'd reply politely into the mouthpiece. "Yes, ma'am. Whatever you say, ma'am. . . . And thank you for calling the Camel Brook Motor Inn. . . ."

Most times the person standing in front of me wasn't snookered at all. Livy's voice was so loud coming over the wire he could hear it clear across the counter.

The bitch had me cold. And no way I could get away with not answering the telephone—management would have me fired in a heartbeat.

All night long Livy punched the redial and let me have it until I was damned near out of my gourd. She hollered. She accused. She cursed. She threatened. She bawled. When I finally got home in the early morning, it was even worse. Laying to waste everything in the apartment, she seemed to have reached a new threshold of dementia.

After helplessly watching the spectacle for a few moments, I'd resort calmly to my old threat: "I'm going to call the men in white suits."

"Go ahead! Do it! See if I care! Besides, it's you who belong in the nuthouse, not me! You're pitiful! A maggot! Not even half a man! Why don't you crawl back into the hole I found you in, you creep!"

Sometimes, even then, we'd fuck, with a hatred that made fucking that much better. . . .

Of course Livy eventually won the tug of war over her car; I had no choice but to surrender it. In order to get to my job now, I had to leave the apartment upward of two hours before my shift started, hop the bus on Bloomfield Avenue into Roseland, transfer to another line that would take me into Livingston, then a third that would drop me across from the motel, and hope each would be on time—which of course they never were. My workday now ran anywhere between twelve and fourteen hours, but it was better than hearing Livy scream in my ear all night long. . . .

45.

"He was here," she announced dreamily from the sofa when I dragged my ass in at three thirty A.M. On the floor was a glass of amber booze. The stereo was oozing the Bee Gees' disco abortions. Livy was in a flimsy nightgown that had fallen open at the belly. Her arm was folded behind her head. She looked like the finest courtesan in a French cathouse.

"Who?"

"Michael. . . ."

I was still in the dark. My back ached. The soles of my feet felt as if they'd been pierced with slivers of glass. I was soaked through from the freezing rain. The day had been entirely too long to play guessing games.

"Michael who?"

"Michael Goldfarb. You remember."

The jeweler she'd spread her legs for, the pudgy guy we saw out in the reservation.

"Well—what the hell was he doing here?"

"I don't know. He found out my address somehow."

"What the fuck do you mean, 'he found out your address somehow'? The only way he could find out your address is if you called him and told him your address! And besides, the last time I checked, it was my address, too!"

"Hah! Check your facts! The last time *I* looked, it was *me* who bought all the furniture in this place, *me* who painted it and stained the floors, and *me* whose name is on the lease! You're sitting on *my* chairs and sleeping in *my* bed! I can kick you out of here anytime I want!"

"Every time I try to leave you, you threaten hara-kiri, you two-bit whore! Or has that memory conveniently slipped your mind?"

"Fuck you, Max!"

"I'd invite you to do the same, but you've probably been fucked already today, you greedy bitch!"

"GO FUCK YOURSELF!"

"Is that all you know how to say?"

We went at each other like a pair of bedlamites, until Livy stormed out, repeating her advice to me a few times for good measure before slamming the door.

I collapsed to the floor, my sanity once again slipping into foggy eclipse. It was four thirty in the goddamn morning and here I was twisted into a billion knots. *I'd lost my mind. And where the fuck had that bitch gone to at this time of night? To meet Michael Goldfarb? Donald Robinson? Basil? Maybe Fred? To walk the streets?* Why did I even care anymore?

I didn't know the answer to that question. I didn't know *anything.* I'd deteriorated beyond pain, beyond despair, beyond even madness into a state of scary numbness. Outside a ghostly wind had kicked up, lashing the rain against the windows like buckshot. Listening to the skeletons dance, I stared at the ceiling above my head and demanded of the invisible gods some explanation why I was unable to escape this hell I'd descended into when I wasn't looking. I could blame Livy for everything, but there was little doubt that every single accusation she'd leveled at me was essentially true. I was nothing but the lowest dog turd ever dropped on the face of the earth. *Wasn't I?*

My heart drummed as if I'd just run a marathon. My temples beat with anguish and exhaustion. There was a fifty-pound chunk of granite in my gut. I needed a drink. A *dozen* drinks. I needed an overdose of horse tranquilizer. At that moment, I had doubts—real doubts—whether I was going to make it through this infernal night. What made my fix even more absurd was that I couldn't count the number of times I'd been down the same road already.

I pulled myself up, lit my fiftieth or sixtieth cancer stick of the day, and reeled into the kitchen. I opened the telephone directory and with trembling fingers riffled around until I located the listing I'd made a mental note of some weeks before.

SUICIDE PREVENTION HOTLINE—769–3000
REMEMBER: NO PROBLEM IS TOO BIG
BEFORE YOU GIVE UP ON LIFE,
GIVE US A CALL
COMPASSIONATE HELP AVAILABLE 24 HOURS
A DAY

I dragged deep on my Marlboro and dialed. It rang for a long time. This was the dead of night—where could they possibly *be?* Finally the tired voice of a tired lady spoke up.

"Suicide Prevention. This is Yvette. How can I help you?"

Suddenly I had stage fright. Maybe this wasn't such a hot idea after all.

"Sorry if I woke you. I don't want to give my name, but. . . ."

"It's okay, you don't have to identify yourself. Please. Don't be shy. Talk to me."

"Well, it's like this. I—I think I'm going to either kill Livy or myself. Or both of us."

She was quiet. I wondered if maybe she'd hung up.

"Who?" she asked after a few seconds.

"Forget it. I guess you don't need to know her name."

"But I do," insisted the lady, suddenly alert and aware.

"No, you don't."

"You're wrong. I *do* need to know her name, in case she's in real danger."

"But I'm the one who needs help. Remember? I'm the one who called."

She didn't say anything. In the silence I detected that she was a little confused, baffled even. Maybe she was even frightened by the deadly earnest tone of my voice.

"Well, can you do it, Yvette? Can you help me?"

I could hear her clearing her throat, stalling for time. "Now just hang on. If you tell me again . . . the truth about what you're planning to do to this person, Livy, then yes, I might be able to help you. . . ."

Another fiasco. What was the point? I was snakebit. Everything I tried to do to help myself ended up a rank failure. I looked at the receiver in my hand. I could try talking to Yvette again, try convincing her of my harmlessness. But I didn't. Instead I hung up. I had the feeling it just wasn't going to be my night.

I paid off the balance on Livy's engagement ring the day she landed a new job of her own. The Arch, a semiprivate welfare organization that aimed to rehab hard-core juicers and druggies demonstrating a sincere effort to reenter mainstream society, took her on. A glorified halfway house, in other words. Livy would be writing grant proposals geared toward winning it more money from the government. This was a far cry from working the bars and restaurants. And ironic, too, since Livy and I needed professional help in the worst way ourselves. . . .

With me doing nights and Livy days, we hardly saw each other. Whenever we did, it was only to play out another ugly scene. Occasionally I ended up on Bernie Monahan's couch in Montfleur. But at least we had a new routine, and routines are what keep lives intact.

On weekends—if we were on speaking terms—I garnered bits and pieces of what Livy's new job was like. She spent lots of time on the phone dunning various federal and state agencies for cash. When she wasn't up to that, there were endless meetings about where the Arch was now and where it was headed in the future. From what I could make out, she did very little writing.

She dropped lots of new names. There was Pat Borders, the chief administrative assistant. Wonderful lady, maybe I'd get to meet her sometime. And Ed Blank, a top-notch substance abuse counselor, very friendly chap. There was Jack Brady, the brilliant genius—and former addict and drunk himself—who'd founded the Arch. Jack's name was always uttered with a special reverence.

And there was Duke Johnston. He was the maintenance chief for the Arch facilities down in East Orange, Brady's best friend, and a reformed fall-down lush and smack freak who'd done time for everything from simple possession to burglary to assault and battery and attempted murder. He owed his life to Jack Brady, and he'd do anything Brady asked him to do, including jump off the George Washington Bridge. His life consisted of attending daily meetings—known as "meetins"—of Alcoholics Anonymous, replacing dead lightbulbs, and swabbing the decks of the Arch's headquarters. If you couldn't exactly call these folks *happy*, you certainly had to say they were a family. Booze and junk, as Livy had begun pointing out, were thicker than blood.

All this was quite fascinating to her. Our lives were downright boring and dull by comparison. And there were more where Duke Johnston and Jack Brady came from—real flesh-and-blood characters who'd had it tough in life, who knew personally what it was like to travel to hell and back. (Not like me. Not like me at all.) Livy realized and admitted that she'd had it wrong all these years. The salt of the earth were the ones to be admired, not the children of privilege, not the precious artists, not the rich and famous.

Well, thank God, I told her, *that you've finally seen the error of your ways.*

46.

From time to time I received brief letters from the literary agency asking me to remain patient, as my novel was still in circulation and getting the book to the right editors for a thorough read generally took a great deal of time. Not to worry, the notes assured me, things were happening. Quite courteous of them, I thought. I could hang on all right as long as things were happening. . . .

As for Olivia Aphrodite, she was a new woman. The names of her coworkers were all I ever heard around the apartment now. It was the Arch this, the Arch that—nothing else held the least interest for her.

Even more time passed with no word on *The Old Cossack*. Up and down Bloomfield Avenue the gaudy dressings of Christmas began to appear. The world was entirely red and green and silver. HAPPY HOLIDAYS banners were wrapped around the streetlamps and draped over the telephone lines. For displaced souls like me, the pressure created by the birthday of Jesus Christ was too much. Here I was, barely making it, and now I was supposed to run out and buy gifts for everyone I knew. It was ridiculous. All I wanted—all I'd ever wanted—was to be left alone in a room with my manuscripts and guitar and cigarettes, and once in a while a good bottle. Holidays and the like brought out the worst in the losers and the lost, which was why the season always left me feeling morbidly depressed. I would have preferred to hit the road, but in my beat-up, dejected state of mind, I wasn't up to it, especially without a wad of cash or a car, neither of which I had.

There was going to be a big holiday party, Livy announced, and I was invited through the generosity of the good folks at the Arch.

This came as a major surprise. "Sure you want me there? I wouldn't want to invade your turf, you know."

She shrugged. "I don't care what you do. If you want to come, then come. If you don't, forget about it. I'm not going to beg you to do anything."

Part of me was curious. The festivities were held in the gymnasium of an old public schoolhouse where the Arch was headquartered. There were streamers billowing from the rafters and tables brimming with appetizers like miniature hot dogs, wedges of cheese, and dried-out shrimp. The centerpiece of the room was a huge Douglas fir tree decked out in blinking lights, dangling ornamental balls, and shiny tinsel. In every corner stood clusters of men and women sipping the nonalcoholic punch. As always, Livy was dressed for the kill, tonight in a whorehouse-lavender sarong that squeezed her tight and like-colored pumps. She introduced me to a couple of people, then disappeared into the crowd.

I mumbled a few words, but the conversation was awkward and stilted. I couldn't shake the uncomfortable suspicion that these people knew a lot more about me than they were letting on.

The absence of booze made me jittery. I'd filled a flask with Cutty and tucked it into the deep inside pocket of my peacoat before leaving the apartment, but I hadn't cracked into it yet. You never want to be stranded at a social function of any kind without alcohol—it's like being on a beach without sand. But for these disciples of the Program, alcohol was poison, out of the question, and you weren't going to find a drop within miles. Shit—you couldn't even *joke* about the stuff.

I was slouching by myself in a corner when I heard a gruff "You must be Max."

The voice was a dead monotone. I turned. He was big, 215, 225, dirty blond. Seedy-looking. A deep, angry scar that had been badly sutured ran in a jagged crescent from his Adam's apple to the lobe of his right ear. He sported an unevenly trimmed mustache and a pair of gray overalls.

"Okay, I admit it. What did I do, officer?"

He didn't laugh. Either he didn't get the joke or he had no sense of humor.

"I'm Duke Johnston."

"Oh, yeah? I've heard a lot about you."

His dull blue eyes showed a flash of life. "No kiddin'?"

"No kidding."

That was pretty much all he had to say. He didn't stick his mitt out to shake. Instead, he grunted and stood there gawking at me like a tranquilized gorilla. After a few clumsy seconds, he lumbered away.

Ten minutes later he reappeared on the floor dressed as Santa Claus and handed out gifts to the kiddies. At that point I decided I'd had enough—Johnston had to be the saddest Old Saint Nick I'd ever laid eyes on. I went outside, leaned against the building in the frosty December air, screwed the top off my flask, and waited for Livy.

This Johnston dude has a thing for you, doesn't he?" I said to Livy when we got back to the apartment.

She flushed and turned away. "You're out of your mind."

"I don't think so. It was written all over him. He was scoping the both of us like a fucking vulture."

"So what do you care if somebody else admires me?"

"At least you admit it. . . ."

"Get off my back, Max! For four years I've put up with your crap, listening to you rant and rave about everything and everybody you hate, pretending you're a *genius*, sucking the lifeblood out of me like a leech! At least Duke Johnston can take care of himself! At least he can hold down a job and pay his own rent! He may not be a millionaire or famous, but he doesn't have a pretentious artistic bone in his body, thank God! He knows how to make a *decision*! To him life is black or white, right or wrong, not all anguish and torture—and books! So leave him alone, too, would you!"

"So now you're defending this hunk of shit. . . ."

"And don't call him names! Duke's a man's man. Maybe that's what I should have had from the beginning."

"Oh, is that so? Tell me more."

"I'm not going to explain anything to you, Max. You and I have wasted too much time talking. Talk talk talk, that's all you ever do. I've had enough of your talking and books and philosophy. I don't even want to have to *think* anymore."

"Just be sure you don't bring any more crabs home, Liv."

"Go to hell, Max!"

"I'm already there, in case you haven't noticed."

Just like in the early days, strange things began happening. When the telephone rang, I'd pick it up and hear nobody at the other end. Livy was gone all hours, which she blamed on overtime at her job. The refrigerator was always empty, but since I lived on cigarettes and coffee and Livy never ate a meal at home, there seemed no point in stocking it.

The little old lady who lived in the apartment beneath us moved out and a new couple moved in. They were noisy as elephants when they did, cursing and hollering, smacking into the walls with their furniture, cranking up the volume on their music. Taking possession of 4C was a party that went on all day and half the night.

The next morning I was jolted awake by the blast of a horn—a trumpet or cornet—traveling up through the floorboards. *Fuck my ass*—I'd never heard anything so loud in my entire life. I yanked on my jeans, checked under the bed, and went downstairs to investigate.

It was the new tenant, all right. When I rapped on the door, he refused at first to answer. Instead he went on blowing his brains out as if his life depended on it. I banged again. No dice.

I stomped back upstairs and tried to eat breakfast. The new neighbor was still serenading the heavens. What made the clamor all the more unbearable was that bugle boy was completely devoid of musical ability. He was capable of nothing but flat belches and farts that bore no resemblance to melody and hadn't an ounce of rhythm. It wasn't pop, it wasn't jazz, it wasn't improv, it wasn't anything. A two-year-old child who'd never touched an instrument could have done better. After a few hours of the shit, I thought I'd go bonkers. I couldn't write, I couldn't read, I couldn't think, I couldn't sleep. When I picked up my ax and strummed, I couldn't hear a single note I produced.

When Satchmo finally clamped the lid on his session, I went back down the stairs and pounded on his door again. This time he opened up.

"Yeah? Whadya want?"

I checked him out. A lug with a forehead that was nothing but thick black eyebrows that met in the middle. No light shining in his bovine eyes. He scratched his puffy, naked belly as he looked me over. I tried to peek over his shoulder for a glimpse of the girlfriend. Apparently she was smarter than I was—she'd gone out, probably to work.

"Your trumpet playing is driving me fucking insane." There was no point in mincing words.

"I gotta practice. I don't practice, I don't work."

"You here every day?"

"Yup. All day long. Just me and my horn."

"You don't have a job or anything like that?"

"Nope. Only money I earn is when I get a gig."

"Haven't been working much lately, have you?"

He took the jibe head-on. "Nope. That's why I gotta practice." Just like I thought—dense.

I didn't know what to do. What *could* I do? I wanted to punch the guy's lights out, but what would it have accomplished? Besides, I was still recovering from my last brawl. I had the feeling it would be useless to politely request that he lower the volume. Fuming, I turned around and climbed back up to 5C.

From that moment onward, it was total war. Whenever Maynard Ferguson's asshole started to blow, I had no choice but to retaliate. I was the ugly American, he was Hirohito after Pearl Harbor. I dribbled a basketball on the floor. I donned my old factory boots and hopped up and down like a jumping jack on a pogo stick. When I tuckered myself out, I flipped the stereo speakers facedown on the bare floorboards, threw some early Stones or Zeppelin on the turntable, and maxed out the volume.

But nothing deterred the lummox. When I ran out of ideas, I called the cops.

"If he plays his trumpet or whatever the hell it is between the hours of six A.M. and ten P.M., there's not a thing we can do. The city ordinance reads 'no unnecessary noise between the hours of *ten P.M. and six A.M.*,'" said the desk sergeant.

"You wouldn't consider that kind of racket a disturbance of the peace?"

"Not according to the letter of the law, it ain't. Look, I feel bad for you, sir, but. . . ."

My only chance at a legal recourse was gone. I didn't know how much longer I'd be able to last.

47.

The telephone buzzed at nine thirty in the morning. It was my boss at the motel, Billy Stankowski.

"Don't bother coming in today, Max."

"What's up, Billy? You giving me a vacation day?"

I was trying to make Billy laugh. Guys like me never rate vacation days.

"Very funny, Max. No. No vacation day. We're going to have to let you go, man. I'm sorry."

"*Shit.* . . . What the hell did I do wrong?"

"It was the little things, Max. Especially the coming in late all the time. This place that has to be run like a Swiss watch. I mean, you're okay, but not good enough."

The job itself I didn't give a damn for. It was the paycheck I couldn't do without. That paltry two-fifty a week was the only thing that allowed me to feel anything close to a human being these days. Without an income of some sort, I was fucked all over again, at the complete mercy of my wild woman.

"I'll change, Billy, I swear. I'll get on the bus even earlier." Naturally he'd caught wind that Livy had taken the wheels away.

"Too late, Max. We already got somebody else. See, it was

the other stuff, too. When that crazy girlfriend of yours cuts your
dick off by telephone, it's embarrassing for the customers, know
what I mean? And we can't make a habit of letting you sleep in
the vacant rooms overnight without paying. Max, you're a good
guy and all, but your personal life is more than I can handle."

"I can't deny it's a fucking mess, Billy. The truth is it's more
than *I* can handle."

"Want some advice?"

"Depends on what it is."

"You're probably not gonna like it."

"Well, everybody else has tried. You may as well take your
shot."

"Unload her, man. The sooner, the better."

"You don't get it, Billy. That's because you sleep in a bed of
roses with Marilyn."

"Sorry, Max. Look at it this way. At least you'll be able to collect unemployment benefits."

He had something there. A decent guy. Billy Stankowski was
the only man I never hated for firing me.

L istening in an impotent rage to the shitty horn player in the
apartment below for hours on end was what my life had finally come down to. I had no strength left to fight back; it simply
consumed too much psychic energy. Short of assaulting the guy,
there was nothing I could do to stop him from making noise.
Somehow it didn't seem to be worth going to jail over. The dude
had me licked. Join the queue.

Livy didn't give a damn at all about the situation since she was
never around. As a matter of fact, whenever we did run into each
other, she seemed increasingly preoccupied.

"Max, let's go for a walk."

Another spring was closing in on us that day in April she rushed in all out of breath.

"You mean like *now?*"

Her cheeks were flushed. Her eyes were ablaze. She was standing just inside the door, vibrating.

"Sure . . . what's the big rush?"

"It's just . . . I have something to say to you, and maybe if we get out of here it'll be . . . *easier.*"

Why couldn't she just speak her piece right there in the breakfast nook? I grabbed my jacket and went along with her anyway. We were at the park entrance when she opened up. Red-breasted robins were stabbing at worms in the rolling lawn. The tulips were bursting into bloom. There wasn't a cloud in the sky, which was an unreal shade of blue. Somewhere in the country they were playing baseball.

"Max . . . Max, you have to admit it's not working out between us. It hasn't worked out between us in a long, long time. We need to be away from each other."

It was the first and only time in all these years she hadn't made that same request in a state of extreme rage, so I knew this time was different. Besides, what she was saying was the truth. There wasn't even any point in arguing with her.

I didn't know what the hell I was feeling: rage, panic, anticipation. My gut pitched. It was the break I'd been waiting for.

"I gotta buy a car first," I mumbled, mostly to myself.

"It's okay. Use your unemployment money to get a clunker. As soon as you sell your book, you'll be rolling in the green."

"Right. . . ."

Knowing Livy, there was a man in the wings. I couldn't be 100 percent sure, but I had the feeling I knew who it was.

She couldn't even look at me. "Then it's set?" she asked with more softness in her voice than I'd heard in months.

"Yeah."

I sucked in the fresh air and tried to look on the positive side: at least I wouldn't have to listen to Dizzy fucking Gillespie anymore.

48.

After scouring the used-car ads I turned up a ten-year-old Rambler Ambassador with eighty-five thousand miles for $350. Not bad. Livy lent me the Nova to drive out to Livingston for a looksee. The owner was a jelly-bellied suburban papa jumpy as a cat in heat to get the vehicle off his hands. He grinned and fidgeted while we stood in the driveway. The sweat rolled off his greasy face in big droplets. "I'm telling you, this baby really treated me nice. . . ." He patted the flaking battleship-gray hood. The vehicle was a dinosaur one step from the junkyard. I took it for a test spin with him sitting beside me, jabbering about its merits the whole time. The transmission slipped a little and the rear panel of the passenger's side had been punched in, but I was assured that those things were nothing a couple of minor repairs couldn't cure. On the other hand, the air conditioner was powerful, the heater worked, and the brakes were almost new. I knew the real score—that eighty-five thousand miles was a fairy tale, and at a few hundred smackers I couldn't expect a Bentley. Back in his driveway we haggled a little. I worked the guy down to two-fifty, but he wouldn't go a penny lower. He signed over the certificate of ownership, and the beast was mine. . . .

This was my plan. A new job first, then a place to crash. I

spent all day on the phone, trying to line up interviews. Getting a pad was going to be tough without a steady source of income. If I couldn't come up with something, I'd have to settle for a flophouse or the big YMCA in Montfleur. I didn't fancy bunking with the fruits and mental cases, but when you had nothing, clean sheets were better than the street.

Livy was frantic for me to go. As soon as I agreed to vacate the premises, she was up to her old tricks. For three straight days and nights she failed to put in an appearance at the apartment on Roseland Avenue. When she finally did show, it was to exchange a load of dirty laundry for a few clean outfits. Dressed in jeans and sweater she looked damned fine. Her spirits were upbeat, the highest they'd been since our early days. There was an electric excitement in her limbs, born of the confidence and optimism of someone about to embark on a new adventure. Offhandedly I asked her what she'd been up to, but she was slippery. All she wanted to know was when I planned to split for good.

"As soon as I find somewhere to go. Don't worry, it won't be long now."

She ducked into the shower, locking the bathroom door. She stayed in there for an hour beneath the roar of water. When she emerged she was wrapped in a heavy towel like a nun in a habit. I followed her into the bedroom. She kept herself demurely covered.

"Max. Please. Leave. It wouldn't be *proper* for you to see me naked."

She was fucking somebody else, and that somebody else was Duke Johnston. She never, ever mentioned his name anymore—a dead giveaway.

I sat on the edge of the bed and looked out the window. The parts of me that weren't numb felt something like sadness and relief.

"Where have you been for the past three days?" I asked, mostly out of boredom.

"None of your business. I don't ask you where you go and what you do, do I?"

It was a familiar speech, one I recalled from a long time ago, when the guy on the receiving end was none other than Edward, poor, hapless Edward.

"Are you screwing Duke Johnston?"

She wheeled around to face me.

"*No.*"

"I don't believe you, Liv. And you don't have to lie to me. I'm just curious, if you want to know the truth."

"Believe whatever you want, Max."

"What happened to us, Liv? What the hell happened?"

She stopped fooling with her hair in the mirror and stared at me. The laser beams in her eyes were hard as marble.

I slid off the bed. She didn't move when I took three steps toward her and ripped the towel off her torso.

I was as possessed as a rabid wolf. I bit the nipple of her left tit, ran my hand roughly over the steel wool of her thatch until it parted. Inside she was as soaking wet as a rain forest.

"*The problem, baby, is that I've been too easy on you.*"

I sounded like a Satanic maniac, even to myself. I herded her like a barnyard animal to the bed. When I pushed her onto the mattress, she offered no resistance. I unzipped and made her suck on my cock. She did it like a starving animal. The object was to torture, so I made her keep it up until she began to moan. Then I pulled it away and made her beg for it.

"Why should I touch your pussy, Liv? Tell me. Duke Johnston's been fucking you, hasn't he, you goddamn whore! Talk— *he's been fucking you, hasn't he?*"

When she wouldn't, I mounted her and shoved it in with a desperate vengeance. All the madness and rage of the years we spent together seemed to have gathered in my member, transforming it into a blazing pistol.

We went at it like prehumans, instinctively and noisily contorting our torsos into positions we'd never tried before, even in all the million and one times we'd fucked. Head to feet, back to front, upside down and inside out, all of it, everything, until her cunt lips were baboon red and my dick was torn to shreds. It seemed to go on forever, like the slow-motion impact of a powerful narcotic—or a nuclear warhead.

"Christ—that was the best it's ever been," I said when it was over and we lay there panting like a pair of overheated dogs.

"Yes. . . ." she whispered. But she had to be somewhere in fifteen minutes.

That was to be the last time I would ever make love to Olivia Aphrodite, though I didn't know it at the time. You never know when something is ending when it's in the process. Maybe it's best that way—the mind can only take so much. It's only later that it all comes clear, like when the fog lifts from the shore and you can see the ocean. No, one last great fuck wasn't going to be enough to save us. They say a real love story never ends. But the truth is that given enough time, love will usually morph into its opposite—repulsion, hatred . . . indifference. What do you think the world's problem is? It's the exhaustion bred by familiarity and tedium, the transience of romance. You see it every single day in the dead eyes of the men and women on the street. And yet that's the way life itself has been built—everything is going to die. Even you and me. There's nothing that can be done about it. Call it God's joke on us. . . .

As the days wore on, Livy grew more impatient with the fact that I was still hanging around the apartment. She seemed incredibly antsy to execute some scheme that my presence prevented her from doing. I stepped up the pace of my search for honest work, but luck wasn't on my side. I checked out rooming houses, studios, basement apartments, sublets, but there was always some problem—the biggest being that I didn't have the jack for a security deposit.

That Saturday morning as I was on my way out, Livy threw herself in my path as I reached for the doorknob. With tears in her eyes she embraced me, squeezing with all her might. It was like she loved me all over again, even more than ever. Like I was the only thing she'd ever loved in her entire life. Like she was never going to see me again—or that I was going out to meet my death. Before I had the chance to ask what it was all about, she ran off and barricaded herself in the bedroom.

Looking back, I should have realized that it was a sign. A few hours later I returned to find all my earthly belongings, including the typewriter, on the front lawn. Furious, I ran upstairs and tried my key in the lock, but it didn't fit. I raised my fist to pummel the door like I had so many times before, but this time, instead of causing a scene, I turned around, went back down the stairs, picked my stuff off the grass and loaded it into the Ambassador.

Then I turned over the ignition and eased out of the parking lot. At the corner traffic light I contemplated whether to travel east or west.

I t was over. I was alive.

49.

Unless I wanted to end up in stir, I couldn't go near the apartment on Roseland Avenue. Along with the locks, Livy had the telephone number changed to a private listing, so I couldn't even talk to her if I wanted to.

I was consumed by fantasies of bloody violence. When you know for a fact that another man has taken your place in a woman's bed, you can't be blamed for what you think—or do. In my mind's eye I watched myself breaking down the door of 5C and blowing Duke Johnston away while he slept. Then I'd take Livy by force and make her do my bidding. She'd lick my balls. She'd kiss my asshole. She'd suck my cock dry. She'd fuck me until I was bored. I'd force her to watch me make love to other women. And when I'd had enough, I'd kill her, too.

But I did nothing of the sort. Like the broken husk I was, the best I could manage was having a dozen angry red roses sent by courier to Livy's doorstep. The gesture wasn't even acknowledged. Later, when I regained my wits, I felt humiliated, embarrassed. Man, what a sap I was. I pictured the two of them laughing at me, then tossing the bouquet into the trash.

After a couple of weeks on Bernie Monahan's sofa, I found a room in a boardinghouse in Montfleur. After all was said and done, I was back to square one. Life is that sort of illusion— you can think that you've traveled to the ends of the earth only to find yourself no farther than your own backyard. . . .

Earlier that same day I'd landed a job as a proofreader for a pulp consumer magazine that advertised everything from used washing machines to secondhand clarinets. The money wasn't going to make me rich, but it was enough to cover the rent and food.

When I stopped struggling to get back on my feet long enough to think about it, life really wasn't all that bad. Nevertheless, the one notion I still couldn't force out of my brain was the idea of Livy humping Duke Johnston. The weird thing was, *I didn't even really care.*

I was shuffling along Church Street in Montfleur one early summer evening when I spotted her behind the wheel of a long white Cadillac convertible. She was waiting on a traffic light. When she spotted me, she pulled into the curb.

She looked superfine—tan, sleek, healthy. She'd been poured into her tight clothes; there were bare patches of skin everywhere. She was puffing on a cigarette, something I'd never seen her do before. Well-buffed and well-fucked, she cut the perfect figure of a high-priced call girl.

I rested my elbows on the passenger's door. "Interesting wheels."

"Thanks. Duke wants me to drive in style."

"Of course. . . . Say, where does a janitor get the money for a Cadillac?"

She pretended not to hear the question. She ran her freshly manicured hands over her freshly waxed legs. Against my will, my mouth watered with desire.

"So, Liv, what's life like with Dukie?"

"Gosh, I don't know," she sighed, shaking her mane of hair and checking her makeup in the rearview mirror. "It's just about perfect—no thinking, no words, no books . . . *nothing but sex*."

Should I try and snuff her or fuck her? "Listen, why don't you come over and see my new crib," I suggested, leaning definitely toward the latter.

"No, thanks. I'm through with ratholes. Besides, *I can't sleep with two men at the same time*."

"Well, that's a new leaf, isn't it?"

"I don't have time for it, Max." She stepped on it and roared straight through the red light, nearly ripping off my arms in the process.

T he fan was blowing on my naked ass on a sweltering summer night when the telephone rang. It was her.

"I'm coming over tomorrow. I have something for you."

"What time?"

"Seven," she said and hung up.

When she arrived the next evening, she was lugging a fat manila envelope.

"Quite some palace you have here," she sniffed, taking in the sparse, threadbare furnishings. "I always knew you'd end up in a basement."

"I'm getting by," I said.

She handed over the package, which looked as if it had been shipped a few thousand miles. It was addressed to me. I tore it open and looked inside.

It was my coffee-stained, dog-eared manuscript of *The Old Cossack* as well as a white business envelope with my name typewritten on it.

I glanced at Livy, then opened it up.

JUNE 30, 1980

> *Dear Max Zajack:*
> *We regret to report that we have been unable to place*
> *THE OLD COSSACK despite our extensive efforts. It*
> *has been considered and rejected by McGraw-Hill Book*
> *Company; Pocket Books; Random House; Atlantic Monthly*
> *Press; Charles Scribner's Sons; the Viking Press; William*
> *Morrow and Co.; George Braziller; J. B. Lipincott; W. W.*
> *Norton and Co.; Fawcett Gold Medal Books; Harcourt*
> *Brace Jovanovich; Little, Brown and Co.; MacMillan*
> *Publishing Co.; Paul S. Eriksson; Crown Publishers;*
> *Ballantine Books; Dodd, Mead and Co.; Doubleday and*
> *Co.; G. P. Putnam's Sons; Stein and Day; Vanguard Press;*
> *Bantam Books; Coward, McCann & Geoghegan; Dell; and*
> *M. Evans and Co.*
> *All of the letters from the publishers were standard*
> *rejection slips.*
> *Your manuscript is being returned, enclosed, and you*
> *are released from your representation contract with us,*
> *freeing you to pursue other marketing avenues on all your*
> *literary work. I'm sorry our endeavors have not resulted in*
> *success, and I wish you much good fortune in the future.*
>
> *Sincerely,*
> *Henry Barr*

When I finished reading, I stole another glance at Livy. An omniscient, satisfied half smile danced on her face.

"Bad news, Max?"

I felt as if I'd been gutted. Before I could react, she was on her feet and out the door. Seconds later, I heard the wheels of the Cadillac peeling out of the gravel driveway outside the window.

When I got over the letter, I went up to the street and stood on the sidewalk. There was nobody around, which was always the way I liked it.

It was a spectacular night, the sky razor-blade blue and the dim lights of the stars and planets just beginning to show. Tomorrow . . . tomorrow was supposed to be more of the same good weather. I looked around for the moon, and there she was, pinned over the rooftops at the east end of the city like a cutout.

Man, it was almost like nothing at all had happened. Suddenly it hit me for the first time that I was going to make it. Really. I'd have my ups and downs, but I was going to make it. It was the sea change I'd been waiting for, the interior turning of the tide that always portends the shattering of an obsession. It's when you give up all hope that everything is finally right. I was going to get out of bed in the morning, and I was going to want to do it, even with a dead-end job waiting for me. Life was a juicy chunk of sweet fruit, and I had my teeth sunk in deep. I couldn't believe how much in love I was.

The music of a lone saxophone was drifting in from somewhere. A black-and-white alley cat on the prowl appeared from around the corner and sat on his haunches to check me out.

What are you up to, he growled.

Nothing. I was just thinking about Kafka's point of no return, and how we all get there sooner or later.

He nodded. I had the feeling he understood.

We didn't say any more to each other. I lit a cigarette, smoked it all the way down to the filter, ground it out with my heel. When I looked up, my pal was gone. Then I went back inside.

Epilogue

Olivia Aphrodite married Duke Johnston on the following Saint Valentine's Day. They set off on a cross-country honeymoon on the groom's Harley-Davidson. At the end of that year, a son was born.

The union was not destined to be a happy one. Within months, Johnston took off in the middle of the night, leaving Livy and her brat in their trailer home on the edge of an East Hanover swamp, and was never heard from again.

As for me . . . I moved around a lot, but once every few months she would track me down somehow and phone in the middle of the night; but there was nothing left for me to say to her. The anger from her betrayal had hardened into pure hatred.

From time to time I'd hear things from people who'd known us in those early days. That Livy had been ill and had had her gallbladder removed. That she'd done time in a psycho ward. That she'd done more time in another psycho ward. That Michael Goldfarb had come back into her life, and that she and her son by Duke Johnston had moved into his home when the jeweler's wife lay dying in the hospital of a malignant brain tumor. Later that she'd married Goldfarb after his wife kicked the bucket, and they'd merged their offspring into one big happy family. . . .

One day when I was living in Manhattan, a snapshot arrived anonymously in the mail from some Podunk town in Ohio. The picture was of the Goldfarb family in front of the mantel during the holiday season. None of the kids looked happy, especially Livy's son. Goldfarb, bearded like a proper rabbi, stared into the eye of the camera with gloomy defeat.

I could hardly recognize Livy, so thoroughly had her appearance changed. Her face was etched with deep lines and her black hair was streaked with iron. Her makeup was too heavy, her lipstick slightly askew. She was already a woman on the threshold of old age despite her youth.

Who did this to her?

For a long time, years, I heard nothing else. On the streets, even in foreign countries, I would think I'd spotted her, only to find myself mistaken when I moved closer.

Did I really want to see Olivia Aphrodite again? No, no, it wasn't that. A certain addiction, like heroin or cigarettes or alcohol, once overcome, will always remain a source of fascination— that's all. Maybe some little part of every love story never really ends.

I used to ask myself: What was all that insanity about? Why did I have to travel so far for nothing? Why does the thought of her, as I work over the keyboard on an autumn evening, leave me so empty, so curiously vacant? *Why do I not care if she's alive or dead?*

Long ago I gave up searching for answers. Now . . . I don't ask anymore.

Acknowledgments

Lorrie Foster, my lovely wife, who was there when nothing was happening except for my nonstop work. The work is still going on, and she's still there.

Dan Fante, who threw the doors open, and without whom this book would probably not be in your hands. You know everything you did. Thanks, pal.

Jack SaFranko, for being there.

John SaFranko, for inspiration and guitars.

Uwe Stender, agent extraordinaire. At the risk of increasing his volume of queries, this is the guy a writer really wants—he takes your call, and stays on the line.

Steve Hussy, Richard White, and Eric Vieljeux for taking the chance on me in far-flung places like England and France.

Tony O'Neill, for writing the review that put *Hating Olivia* on the map and for generously taking the book with him wherever he went.

Amy Baker and Amy Vreeland for their support and painstaking work, Carrie Kania, Gregory Henry, and everybody else at Harper Perennial.

Mary Dearborn, for writing endorsements whenever I asked, even if they led to nothing.

James Bacon, Kent Swanson, Mike Ferraro, James Ward, and Chris Byck for always listening to me yak.

Joe Ridgwell, Zsolt Alapi, Sal Difalco, and Ujjwal Dey for all the great ink.

Zosh (RIP) and Pete.

Lastly, and perhaps most importantly, all the people who tried to stop me along the way. You were messing with the wrong dude.

About the author

About the book

Insights,
Interviews
& More . . .

Read on

Meet Mark SaFranko

MARK SAFRANKO started writing at a young age. His novels *Hating Olivia* (2005, Murder Slim Press, United Kingdom), *Lounge Lizard* (2007), and story collection *Loners* (2008) have garnered rave reviews and become cult favorites in Europe. In 2009, *Hating Olivia* (under its French title, *Putain D'Olivia*) was published in France by 13e Note Editions and was selected by Virgin France as one of its Favorite Summer Reads. It was followed by *Lounge Lizard* (*Confessions D'Un Loser*) in 2010. His short stories have appeared in dozens of magazines and journals internationally, including the renowned *Ellery Queen's Mystery Magazine*. In 2005 he won the Frank O'Connor Award from *descant* literary journal for his short fiction. He was cited in Best American Mystery Stories 2000 and has been twice nominated for a Pushcart Prize. He is also a playwright, and his plays have been seen in many New York venues as well as in theaters in both Londonderry, Northern Ireland, and Cork, Ireland. In 1992 his one-act play, *The Bitch-Goddess*, was selected Best Play of the Village Gate One-Act Festival in New York. As an actor he has appeared both onstage and in several independent films as well as commercials. A songwriter and composer, his music is available through iTunes and many other online stores. If there is any time left in his day, he paints.

In his more mundane working life, SaFranko has held a multitude of jobs: political risk analyst, dating advice column ghostwriter, freight loader, teacher, landscaper's assistant, deliveryman, truck driver, clothes salesman, astrologer, short order cook, fast-food worker, bank clerk, proofreader, bar musician, government pensions clerk, brewery worker, reporter, telephone solicitor, stock clerk, and chauffeur, among others. His goal in life is to avoid further mundane work. ◡

© Nicolas Guerbe

2

On Writing, Discipline, and Perseverance

TRYING TO EXPLAIN where a book—in this case, *Hating Olivia*—comes from, is like trying to explain the mystery of a life. You can't do it because it's too complicated. But I'll try anyway.

From the beginning, all I wanted to do was create. What drove the urge is beside the point now, and the explanation for that, too, is complex. But coming from where I did—a working-class environment where earning the daily bread was the only important thing—I didn't have a clue where to start. Being an artist was something that other people did. How they did it, I didn't know.

One day I pulled a book called *Henry Miller On Writing* off a shelf in a Trenton, New Jersey, bookstore and the world was transformed. The author's straits were similar to mine. He desperately wanted an artistic life but didn't understand how to do it, yet he figured it out by trial and error. And he was there to tell the rest of us that it could be done. I damned near underlined every sentence of that book. And I was on my way.

But before I got to where I wanted to go, there were many, many stops along the way, mostly in the form of an endless number of jobs—bank clerk, deliveryman, reporter, and landscaper's assistant, to name a very few. I started writing, and all the while, no matter where I was and what my circumstances, I took notes and wrote. Novel after novel, song after song, story after story, play after play. It was a bona fide apprenticeship, with the writers I admired serving as mentors since I wasn't going the MFA route. And as Miller himself said (and I'm paraphrasing), "a writer must put down thousands of words before first signing his name."

Everything else—women, jobs, and, in many cases, at least in the beginning, my own well-being—took second place to my calling. It was my impression, and it hasn't changed much over the years, that the artist—the genuine article—cannot serve any god other than Art. Sure, you might have to work many a crummy gig to keep a roof over your head and food on the table, but even if you have to get up at three in the ▶

> **"From the beginning, all I wanted to do was create."**

3

On Writing, Discipline, and Perseverance (*continued*)

morning to get your real work in, then that's what you have to do. And it also means practicing your discipline every single day, day in and day out, year after year, no matter what.

Of course it's not always so easy. Life keeps butting in, sometimes more noisily and brutally than others. When that happens, even the thought of writing can be more than you can handle. Hell, you might not even be capable of getting out of bed. Nevertheless, you have to find a way.

That's the kind of period *Hating Olivia* covers. I was living with a woman who was beautiful but who really had her issues, as we say nowadays. (And, lest I present myself as blameless, so did I.) Every day was an adventure—and not a lighthearted one. There was sex, and fights, and lots of odd jobs, including, when things got really dicey, delivering newspapers and manning the night desk at a motel, among several others. There was deceit and treachery, booze and drugs. There were cops and shrinks and bill collectors. There were uncounted cigarettes and pawn shops and nightmares. There were many sleepless nights.

Through it all I somehow managed to bang out a couple of novels and a stack of songs. Don't ask how. I still don't know myself. Blame it on my youth.

With my first—and very bad—novel, I managed to land an agent. It was a miracle, the dumb luck of the neophyte, and after the agent cut me loose when he couldn't sell the book, I wouldn't be able to get another for damned near three decades. But that fortuitous event convinced me that I had something going for me, and so I kept on keeping on, come hell or high water, and there was lots of both hell and high water over the years. Years that would again and again test my resolve to make an artist of myself.

I always knew that the raw material of that stretch of time would be turned into a novel. About ten years afterward I tried to write it, but gave up after twenty-five pages. I was either still too close to the events or the voice wasn't right—probably both. A few years later I tried again. Still no go.

Fifteen years after the fact, I was sitting in my tenth-floor apartment in Hoboken looking at the lights of Canal Street across the river when I thought I'd take one last stab at the novel idea that by now was beginning to feel a bit like an albatross around my neck. By this time much had changed. I was married and a father. I'd had an on-and-off career as a journalist, I'd published scores of stories in journals, a couple of micropress novels, and my plays had been produced in theaters all over New York City. But something more important had changed—I'd finally acquired the requisite psychic distance from my earlier experiences. What had been painfully charged whenever I tried to deal with it in the past no longer was. What had happened way back then was just a series of ludicrous events now. And I no longer felt like I had to try to shoehorn into my book every second of my experience. I could merely lay down what happened and the reader could do the rest.

The character of Max Zajack had already been born, in an earlier, unpublished novel called *God Bless America*. By this time I had no illusions that getting Max into print would be easy. In fact, as soon as I put the finishing touches on *Hating Olivia*, I felt it would have virtually no chance of publication in America. The problem? The American appetite for books has not yet caught up with a certain type of literature: self-referential, "confessional," dark. And my countrymen especially don't like novels about struggling writers. It's part of the explanation for why writers from Patricia Highsmith and Jim Thompson to Henry Miller and Charles Bukowski always fared better in Europe than in the United States. To steer the book into print, if I wasn't going to try to publish it myself, I'd have to think out of the box for a change.

Nevertheless, I did contact a handful of American publishers with *Hating Olivia*. Just as I suspected, nobody was interested.

I retreated quickly to the idea of trying something I'd never tried before in order to get the book noticed. But what? Maybe I could solicit an endorsement from someone whose work was in the same ballpark as mine and, more important, who was still alive.

I was on my way home from somewhere—probably my job at an ad agency in Soho—when I stopped into the now-incinerated Border's bookstore at the World Trade Center. As usual, I perused some favorite names in the stacks: Miller, Bukowski, Dostoyevsky, Céline, among others. That day I spotted a new name: Dan Fante. Who the hell was he? I knew John Fante, of course, but had never heard of this guy. The title of the book was *Chump Change*. I opened it, read the first couple of lines, and bought it.

When I was through reading, I decided to write its author and introduce myself. It wasn't like me to ask for help, but I was at the end of my rope.

Much to my surprise, I heard back from him within a few days. "Send the manuscript out," he offered generously. "I've got some time on my hands. I'll read it and let you know what I think."

I mailed off the book and waited. I quickly got a blurb back that went something like this: "Put down your Grisham and Stephen King. *Hating Olivia* is the real deal. An addiction of the heart. I read it in one day. I recommend it one hundred percent."

Before I had the chance to repackage *Hating Olivia* and expose it again to the American publishing machine, Dan had an idea. Why not try his British publishers? He himself wasn't well known here, but he had a growing readership in Europe.

"Going European"—where my work might well find a more receptive audience—was always in the back of my mind. Through Dan I made the acquaintance of a small British house, Murder Slim Press, who at the time was only printing magazines. They offered to bring out *Hating Olivia* as their first novel. It was a flattering offer and I took it.

It was damned near ten years from the writing of *Hating Olivia* to its publication in England. The excellent reviews for the novel injected my writing career with a life it had never had before. It acquired a reputation. Then it began to travel all over the world. One day an email appeared in my box asking for permission to publish *Hating Olivia* in French.

Thousands of copies were printed in France, and thousands were sold. The book was selected by Virgin France as one of its Favorite Summer Reads of ▶

"Hopefully the torturous route to a worldwide audience for *Hating Olivia* will inspire another struggling writer on the road.**"**

2009. I got an all-expenses paid trip to Paris to read for booksellers and attend the Book Expo. All this for a novel that had been virtually shunned in the United States. I felt enveloped in a strange dream.

Other books have followed *Hating Olivia* in both the United Kingdom and France. In many ways, my European successes have justified my many years of work in obscurity. I might not be satisfied—I've written much more than has seen the light of day—but I can't say I'm not fulfilled as an author. And now, five years after the appearance of *Hating Olivia* in England and its long and twisted journey into print, Harper Perennial is bringing the book out in my native country.

Hopefully the torturous route to a worldwide audience for *Hating Olivia* will inspire another struggling writer on the road.

It can happen. It did for me. ◞

Seine Song

by Mark SaFranko

FOR SOME REASON, Dack Lambert felt uneasy.
Coming to Paris was his idea, but now that he
was here, he wasn't quite sure he wanted to be.

It was early spring. The reason for the jaunt,
he'd told his wife, was that he needed to see
Silverburg. It was part reunion, part business.
Silverburg had been living in Paris for a long
time now, decades, and he'd produced a couple
of Dack Lambert's first big features, including a
slick caper that had established him as a bona fide
movie star. The movie had been shot in Paris, and
it remained one of the key works in the Lambert
canon. He and Silverburg were talking about a new
project, a return to glory of sorts for both of them,
he explained to Mercedes, something he could
really believe in, sink his teeth into. These days
such things were hard to come by.

It had all been a lie. Yes, he was seeing
Silverburg, but they were talking about movies
and the future only incidentally. Silverburg had
nothing on his plate except for distant dreams,
for one thing, and for another, Dack Lambert
was only interested in coming to the City of Lights
for recreational sex. The simple fact was that it was
hard to get around anonymously in America, even
if you were a star well into middle age. Those
infernal paparazzi could slither out from under
their rocks at the damnedest times and screw
everything up. So his idea—a brilliant one if he
had to say so himself—had been to fly over to
Europe by himself, wander the streets and pick up
one or more of those delectable French girls and
enjoy himself—and her—in relative privacy.
Something like that. It was remarkable that more
guys in his position didn't think of it. Well, maybe
they did. He'd read somewhere that Joe DiMaggio
liked to visit Europe, where no one knew him, and
consort with prostitutes.

Nevertheless, now that he was here, there was
that strange uneasiness. . . .

Back at home things were tiresome, to say the
least. Mercedes was Dack Lambert's fourth wife,
twenty-five years his junior, and together they'd ▶

7

Read on

produced three children that he was bored with. Young as they were, they already regarded their father as nothing more than a bottomless piggybank. The uglier truth was that he was tired of his wife too. After all of his attempts at monogamy and matrimony, it still wasn't working. Dack Lambert needed something different on a consistent basis; this time he finally accepted it. He knew that his wife wasn't thrilled that he was traveling by himself—she might even have been suspicious of his motives when he left L.A., though he'd given her no reason for it in the years they'd been together—but as the undisputed economic power in the marriage (she was nothing but a middling real estate agent when they met, and, most important, not a celebrity), there wasn't much she could do about the decisions he made. And after all his earlier failures at wedlock, he'd made sure this time that his attorneys had drawn up the prenup heavily in his favor in the event Mercedes decided to do something stupid.

On the second night, after his jet lag had abated, Dack and Arthur Silverburg met for dinner at a small, unpretentious restaurant known for authentic home-style French cuisine around the corner from his hotel in the 6th.

"I'm out of the business," sniffed the producer with a mixture of self-pity and annoyance as he spread a napkin over his lap. With his thinning white hair and sagging, wrinkled face, he looked every one of his eighty years. It was a shock to see what age had done to the man—and would soon do to the movie star.

"Mm," grunted Dack. He knew all about it already; he knew more than the producer had ever given him credit for.

"Oh, I know my name will be attached to the two new pieces of garbage coming out later this year, but I'm through. The business nowadays is shit, you know? Kids running around blowing things up. I mean really, every thirty seconds something has to blow the fuck up. Get this. I sat there with a stopwatch recently and actually timed the explosions? Every thirty seconds! And the goddamn thing ends up winning an Oscar! They call that movie-making? In my book that's nothing but crap!"

Silverburg was getting all worked up, which amused Dack. It's just the fucking movies, he thought. He went on half-listening and digging at his cod-and-mashed-potato pie. It was a simple dish, but downright exquisite. He could never find anything like this back in the States.

The old guy rattled on, about the wonderful collaborations he'd had with Dack Lambert way back when, and how they didn't "make 'em like they used to anymore." But Silverburg was wrong. It was shit back then too, thought Dack. It had all been shit, only shit of a different color, but he didn't dispute the erstwhile executive. He didn't care enough.

"When you're here," Silverburg reminded him for the second or third time, "you really should go around and see Polanski. I think he's between projects right now. He gets lonely . . . I know, because I've run into him a few times. He tells everyone he loves Paris and all, but it's bullshit. Why the hell do you think he keeps fighting to get that child rape conviction overturned back in the States? He doesn't give a damn about clearing his name. He wants back into the action, even at his age. Though you'd think that young wife of his would be enough to keep him content, right . . . ?"

The men exchanged a leer.

A few minutes later Dack's brain was tired. He was weary of listening to the old man maunder. And he wasn't about to look up Polanski. He knew the exiled director would never use him in a movie, and he really didn't care whether or not he made another anytime soon. . . .

"I don't mean to interrupt, but I couldn't help overhearing your conversation. . . ."

The lady, petite and dressed in an understated outfit that reflected nothing short of perfect continental taste, was standing behind Dack's chair. She was older, not quite as old as Silverburg, but in her eyes was the world-weariness of someone who'd seen pretty much everything there was to see in life.

"For Christ's sake—Sylvia."

Of course she and Silverburg knew each other! They were in fact old acquaintances. Sylvia Rensick ran a prestigious PR firm on Madison Avenue, and her husband had once upon a time been the European editor in chief of a great, but now defunct American magazine.

"You know Dack, of course. . . ."

Of course she knew Dack. Didn't everyone?

"Oh my gosh—Dack Lambert! I'm one of your biggest fans. . . ."

As Dack had come to realize over the years, it was both true and it was hokum. So much existed only in the minds of these people. They projected their own fantasies onto him, fantasies he couldn't possibly live up to, and it provoked a reflexive aloofness in him when he was forced to deal with them. At the same time, he couldn't stop himself from glomming up the attention like a starving dog. In some hard-to-explain way he'd come to depend on the adulation to keep him alive.

Sylvia went on about a "boutique" division that she'd established that catered to established movie stars like himself, and how the next time he was in New York he just had to stop by and chat with her about it. If she was lucky, she giggled like a girl, maybe she could sign him.

And of course he said he would. He always said yes to everything, so long as it was scheduled for some indeterminate point in the future. It was a carryover from when he was a struggling actor all those years ago.

Eventually the two old friends said good night. Silverburg wanted to get together with Dack again before he left town, and they agreed to a loose plan, but Dack couldn't care less if he never saw the producer again.

He went out into the late March night and instead of heading straight back to his hotel, decided to walk. He felt a tad drunk from the two bottles of Alsatian pinot noir, a little disoriented in the dark, sinuous cul-de-sacs near the restaurant, and he immediately proceeded to get lost. In his pocket he carried a tourist map, but he preferred to rely on his own instincts. He found himself outside the Church of Saint Sulpice, where there was a great deal of activity, with bodies coming and going through the huge, ancient doors.

He decided to duck inside. It appeared to be the aftermath of a concert; musicians were packing their instruments away, and people were strolling ▶

around the great baroque house of worship ogling historical artifacts and gazing at the ceilings and stained glass.

Dack shuffled up and down the naves doing the same. It felt good to be out of the cold and damp. Since he was the furthest thing from religious, the mummery and flummery of the iconography meant little to him. And he was still plagued by that same sense of unease he'd experienced when the car had brought him in from Orly. Being in a church only exacerbated it. . . .

On the streets again. It was Paris itself, he decided now, that was making him feel so odd. Dead—that's how he felt. But alive too. With every step he took he experienced an ominous sensation of "eternity," though that didn't quite capture it either. It was something else . . . some mystical duality that was impossible to put into words. . . .

It was then that he first had the eerie feeling that he was being followed. He was on Rue Jacob, not far from the bistro where Sartre and Beauvoir held court once upon a time, when it struck him. Sure enough, the man doing the trailing was in a trench coat, not unlike the one the actor himself was wearing, and whenever Dack looked over his shoulder, he was there. Now that he got a decent look at the fellow, he realized that he may have first glimpsed him in the church.

Dack stared. The man wasn't young. Like himself, he had traveled over a certain hump in age. Could he possibly be a fan, someone who'd recognized him? Not likely . . . because why would a man of mature years want to stalk another old guy? It didn't figure.

At every corner Dack turned the man was there, trying not to be noticed. If Dack stopped to peer into a shop window, the man did the same a few steps away. No, there was no doubt about it now—he was being followed. But why?

By the time he reached his hotel, Dack was in a nervous state. What the fuck was going on? Heart thrumming against his chest, he jumped the three steps to the lobby, stopped abruptly and swung around, surveying the winding street up and down.

Nothing. One or two bodies straggling along in the darkness of the early morning, but they weren't his follower.

Maybe Dack Lambert was imagining things after all.

The next morning he was up and about early. Breakfast in the lobby was a croissant, a wedge of cheese, that strong, superb French coffee with steamed milk. He had no definite plan for the day except to take to the streets. He had to be out of doors, because that was the only way he could do what he'd come to Paris to do; it was all clear in his mind now, if it wasn't before.

This was what he envisioned: he would wander the streets until he made contact with a woman. It was just a matter of time. They were everywhere he looked, one more attractive than the next. She would recognize him for who he really was—they all did at some point—and a conversation would lead to a drink, and the drink to another, and then he would be able to blot out his existence for as long as he could manage. That's what a new woman could do for a man—expunge his very existence.

He was without a compass, without a direction, and so his movements were erratic; they were determined by nothing but the soft Parisian breezes. The Luxembourg Gardens. Rue de Rivoli. A landmark cemetery in Montparnasse. . . .

During Dack's perambulations, something strange happened. Whenever he encountered a mirror, whether a makeshift version formed by the glass in a shop front, or a real one in a café restroom, he was violently struck by his own image.

"Jesus H. Christ—when did I get so old?" he muttered to himself. He tried to shake it off and move on, reminding himself that only a few people on the face of the earth ever became movie stars, and that he still had something special, something few others had, no matter what his age.

In one of those encounters with his reflection he saw that man again. Over his shoulder. It was nothing but a glimpse lasting all of a millisecond, but Dack was certain it was him.

How had he found Dack again in this vast city? Was it possible his trail had been picked up straight out of the hotel?

His heart rate accelerated, the way it did yesterday, when he first registered the other's presence, but as soon as he began to look for the man, he didn't see him again.

Whenever he passed a cinema, and there were slews of them here, many more, it seemed, than back in America, with its marquees and billboards, he felt bitterness for the new wave of movie stars who'd replaced him. Pitt, Damon, Depp—he despised them all. Dack Lambert might still have something, but there was no question that like a world-class athlete who's lost a step on the field, he'd been superannuated. There was nothing he could do about it. Time wreaked its vengeance on everyone.

He was walking on the Boulevard Raspail when suddenly he remembered Natalie. She'd been a wardrobe assistant on his film *Desperation* back in the late seventies. At the time he'd been separated from his second wife, and he and Natalie had an uninhibited fling that lasted the duration of the shoot. Natalie was a sweet memory.

He stopped. Could this be the building? She'd lived right here, in a second- or third-floor flat, he was sure of it. God, it looked so familiar! He checked the names of the tenants, but no, of course not, Natalie Carrere was long gone. What was he thinking?

As he watched the hordes of Parisian schoolgirls flaunting their young bodies and their cigarettes, he caressed the memory of that long-ago interlude, one like so many others he'd enjoyed over the years, when on location he would pluck a girl out of the pool of extras, or from the crew, sometimes even from the crowd of onlookers, have a good time with her and when it was over never give her a second thought. And he could do it because he was a movie star, a superior being far beyond the pale of the ordinary human.

Suddenly he was afraid that everything was about to change—that it had already changed.

For a while Dack lost himself again. In Paris, there was always somewhere to lose yourself. The colorful little markets and shops. The bistros and clubs. ▶

Seine Song (continued)

There were always interesting characters on the sidewalks. He especially liked the man who sharpened his knives out of doors with a foot-operated instrument like in the old days. He was moved to dole out coins to the beggars he saw everywhere. This gesture somehow justified his existence, salved the guilt he felt from time to time as a result of his tremendous good fortune in life. Whenever he dropped a Euro into a filthy outstretched hand, he understood why there were so many "limousine liberals" in Hollywood. It was because they too were assaulted by remorse over the fact that they had so little natural endowment, except in some cases, good looks, and yet paradoxically they'd been given so much by way of worldly reward. Raising their voices in outraged indignation, paying court to America's enemies, tossing pennies to untouchables, was the least they could do to redress the balance.

After several hours of fruitless wandering, Dack began to question his strategy. Maybe he should just go to a sex club and get it over with; he'd read about such a place on the Rue Marcadet. Or maybe he should find himself a prostitute, but he didn't want to get ensnared in one of those café scams where he ended up paying all kinds of money for expensive booze and coming away with nothing, and he sure as hell didn't want to risk picking up some disease. . . .

He passed through the Parisian crowds like a ghost, which did nothing but increase his anomie. Feet aching, he'd made it all the way back to the neighborhood near his hotel when he found himself waiting for the change of a traffic signal on bustling Boulevard Saint-Germain. She was waiting too, in a beige London Fog and leather boots to her knees. Her hair was dyed ivory and it was cut short, almost like a man's. Yet she was very much a female, there was no mistaking that. Her nose was straight and perfect, her cheekbones high, her lashes long. He figured her for thirty-five, forty at the outside. Very attractive. Self-possessed. French. A little older than he might have liked, but he could certainly make do with her. . . .

Their eyes met. When hers lingered, Dack knew that he'd been recognized.

"Bonjour," he said. Whenever he spoke French he felt like a fraud, a philistine American.

She laughed, perhaps out of nervousness. "I know you, don't I?" she answered tentatively. Her English was the British-style, perfect, better than that of Dack's countrymen.

"Everyone says that," he answered with false modesty.

"But you really are, aren't you . . . ?"

The movie star felt a swell of his old power, and grateful suddenly for the cinemas that were as plentiful in the City of Light as the beggars, even if his face hadn't been seen on the silver screen in a couple of years.

And so he was forced to reluctantly admit it. Yes, he was indeed Dack Lambert.

She looked more than a little flustered now. "I have to confess to being a fan. . . ."

Yes, they all said that too, didn't they? And even if he was old enough to be her grandfather, he was still needy enough to suck up the flattery like a giant sponge.

And, just like that, they were having a conversation. From the corner of his eye, Dack could see that the traffic signal had turned from red to green twice but that neither he nor the woman were making a move to capitalize on it, which meant he'd already won half the battle.

The longer Dack took her in, the more he liked what he saw. Being alone as he was in the city, he suggested a drink. There was Danton's, conveniently, on the corner. It was late afternoon, and the singular radiance of Paris was taking on its classic melancholy hues.

They were shown to a small table near the window, where they could watch humanity in all of its incarnations pass by. As they waited for the waiter to bring their drinks, Dack exhaled: *Mon dieu*, it had been so easy. Just like the old days, when he could bed a woman with, literally, a nod of the head. Why, he hadn't lost a thing. . . .

Adriana—that was her name—worked in publishing, for a small company committed to bringing out the overlooked, politically engaged voices of the Third World. It was nothing in the scheme of things, but she'd had years of working for the big companies, and this was a refreshing change, because now she felt as if she was doing something that really mattered. Besides, a person had to do something, didn't she, even if this was France, where people knew better than in other places how to live. . . .

But she wanted to know all about him. When could she expect to see Dack Lambert in something new? Would he ever work here, in France, again? She could see him doing a movie with a man like Chabrol, who was still active and creative and vibrant in his old age, had he ever thought of that?

Yes, well, there were projects in the works, he assured her, and soon she'd be seeing him right around the corner at the local movie house.

He was growing a little anxious. It wasn't just that Adriana was socially conscious—always a bad sign—but that sense of psychic discomfort was stealing over him again, along with the spreading twilight of the city. He needed to get Adriana into bed, and as quickly as possible, before the moment slipped away.

Where did she live?

Across the Pont Neuf, but her office was here in the 6th.

He casually dropped that his hotel was only a couple of blocks away.

When the significance of this sank in, Adriana darted him an enigmatic look. What the hell was it supposed to mean?

As he had since the beginning, he felt out of his depth, as if in some way the night, if he let it too close, could devour him. And there was that accursed man who'd been dogging him. He feared being drawn into a vortex, losing his equilibrium. The only thing that could save him was getting inside this woman's body.

Adriana began talking about her husband.

"He has lots of tattoos. And he writes music like Bruce Springsteen."

"Ah," said Dack, not knowing what else to say. But he wasn't tempted to extend the thread of the conversation. Why would he want to talk about some ▶

nobody loser when he, the great Dack Lambert, an icon of the modern silver screen, was sitting right here?

Then he reminded himself that this was France, for Christ's sake, and marital ties meant nothing, nothing whatsoever. No doubt Adriana was just being open and honest and stating the obvious.

"But things are complicated sometimes," she went on.

Yes, he exulted, *this is where we want to go.* He was all for "complications" if they benefited him. And Dack Lambert was certainly someone who knew all about complicated lives.

She'd just been in court the other day, she went on, providing support for her husband as he tried to win custody of his daughter from his ex-wife. And yet when she went home just last night after a long day's work, he was passed out and hadn't heard her when she'd rung the buzzer and banged on the door trying to gain access to their apartment. Nic had his issues with substances and alcohol, and the emotional strain of a legal battle made everything more nerve-wracking.

Yes, thought Dack again—exactly where he wanted to go. Adriana needs a distraction, an outlet. She's unhappy, too. Like me.

"But none of that matters. The important thing is that there's passion between us," she continued, tilting her lovely head. Realizing that Adriana was truly beautiful made Dack's craving that much more insistent.

The word "passion" disturbed him. Not in itself—it was the fact that she used it in connection to this Neanderthal of hers. He actually felt a little jealous.

"You are married too, no?" she asked. As if she read the celebrity rags like everyone else.

How could he dodge it, really? This was precisely where his fame was a trap, a trap he could never completely escape but only attempt to negotiate.

"Well, yes . . . but like you, it's not easy."

Her head twitched. "How, 'not easy'?"

Damn it, he didn't actually want to explain any of this! To be forced to do it smacked much too much of a sleazy extramarital affair. And now here he was, in the position of having to do just that. It was as if this Adriana had subtly turned the tables on him, that she was now in control of what was going to happen.

"You love her still, your wife?"

"Well, you know. . . . My wife is a very fine woman. . . ."

"Of course—she's your wife."

No, this wasn't where he wanted to go. It was the wrong direction altogether. And so it was now or never, before his chance slipped away.

"Will you come to my hotel . . . ?"

Adriana blinked. "Why?"

There was a kind of challenge, something Dack was unused to, in Adriana's question. He laughed, a little uneasily.

"Well, why do you think?"

Her eyes turned out the window. It was dark now. Perhaps she was looking at her reflection.

"No, I don't think so. Life is tangled enough, isn't it?"

"But this isn't at all tangled. This is just. . . . This is easy, simple—*facile*."

How in hell had this happened? Christ, he hadn't seen it coming.

He wasn't about to beg. He'd never begged for anything in his life, except for mercy from his ex-wives, but that was something very different. Every divorced man could relate to that weakness.

Adriana peered at him across the tiny table.

"You're just sad, that's all," she whispered.

Dack was at a loss for how she meant the word, whether that she thought he was in a negative emotional state, or that his life was a disaster, and he didn't understand how she could grasp any of this about him so quickly.

"You're a sad man," she repeated. "I could tell the moment I saw you. You're lonely, being here by yourself. Why don't you just go back home to your family?"

"Because—"

The waiter reappeared. He and Adriana began to discuss something in French. The words tumbled out so rapidly that he couldn't make out the meaning of any of them. Just this morning Dack had been thinking that he could care less if he never heard American English again, but now he loathed the sound of a foreign tongue.

When Dack and Adriana exited the bistro, they headed wordlessly in opposite directions, without so much as a farewell. He halted on the sidewalk, undecided about what to do with himself. Then he stepped across the narrow Rue Odeon and into another place, where he went straight for the bar.

He knocked back a bourbon. His mood had soured—he didn't want anyone recognizing him now.

But when he looked up and into the dim recesses of the bistro, there was that man again, his back half-turned, flitting from one table to another. Whether or not he wanted it, Dack had been seen, and recognized.

Three drinks later and back at the hotel, he placed a call to Los Angeles, where, by some miracle, it was still morning, and got Anna on the phone.

"Where's Mommy," he slurred when he heard her little voice.

"Having a beauty treatment," said the child. "Jimi's watching us. . . ."

Not even noon yet, and his wife was already frittering her time away— or . . . or something else. Maybe there was someone else. It wouldn't have surprised him if Mercedes was cheating on him out of revenge for this trip, but he didn't care.

He went on chatting with the little girl, which, combined with the alcohol, had the effect of making him want to weep. He said hello to his other kids. They each asked the same question: "Daddy, when are you coming home . . . ?"

He wanted to be rid of them, but they still loved him. Nothing in life made sense.

After hanging up, he looked out the open window, which gave onto a view of the sumptuous, glimmering Eiffel Tower. From the street five stories below he heard the incessant churn of life and, donning his coat, decided to go out again.

The man who'd been following him these past few days was nowhere to be ▶ seen. Dack wended his way through the bustling streets to the river, crossed Quai

Seine Song *(continued)*

Malaquais, and started over the Pont des Arts. There were all sorts of bodies milling about on the span: lovers, pickpockets, scammers working con games. None of them concerned or interested Dack.

At the apex of the bridge he leaned over the parapet and peered into the black waters of the antediluvian river. He could feel the presence of the dead, from centuries past, all around him. He would soon be one of them. A long boat full of noisy tourists was passing beneath him. As soon as it was all the way through the arch, he was going to jump.

From somewhere in the distance came the wheezy strains of an out-of-tune accordion. If Dack Lambert was confused before, he was no longer. He realized now that this was what he'd come for. This is what his journey had been about. His life was beyond empty . . . it was nothing, a void. And he was tired, too tired to fight the strange urge beating at the insides of his brain.

The vessel seemed to take forever to emerge from the mouth of the bridge. When it finally passed, Dack didn't move. Instead, he remained transfixed by the colorless depths below.

From the shadows shambled a cripple in a white shroud holding out a half-crushed cup for alms. When he spotted Dack with his leg up, he smiled and shook the cup, producing a sound like a tambourine.

Dack let his leg drop and felt around in his trousers pockets. No coins.

He shook his head. The apparition frightened him—it was his pursuer again. Shaken to the core, he dashed across the busy boulevard, dodging the flow of vehicles, and kept running, running, until he was swallowed up altogether in the bowels of the city. ❧

Don't miss the next book by your favorite author. Sign up now for AuthorTracker by visiting www.AuthorTracker.com.